DUTCH COURAGE

DUTCH COURAGE

MARTIN PARSONS

Matador
Unit E2 Airfield Business Park,
Harrison Road, Market Harborough,
Leicestershire. LE16 7UL
Tel: 0116 2792299
Email: books@troubador.co.uk
Web: www.troubador.co.uk/matador
Twitter: @matadorbooks

ISBN 978 1803134 888

British Library Cataloguing in Publication Data.
A catalogue record for this book is available from the British Library.

Printed and bound by CPI Group (UK) Ltd, Croydon, CR0 4YY
Typeset in 11pt Minion Pro by Troubador Publishing Ltd, Leicester, UK

Matador is an imprint of Troubador Publishing Ltd

MIX
Paper from responsible sources
FSC® C013604

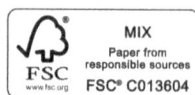

ONE

JAKOB'S WAR

Amsterdam, Holland. May 15, 1940

Jakob Jansen's Food Shop on the Prinsengracht Canal. Jakob, a forty-seven-year-old shopkeeper, average height, slim build, wearing a white shirt and black tie. His wife, Rini, forty-six years old, average height, plump build with short, dark hair. And assistant shopkeeper Angelina, a stunning twenty-six-year-old brunette, tall and slim, wearing a red blouse and a tight black skirt. They were all standing around the counter listening intently to the wireless.

'And so we pray, now that our royal family are no longer with us, and our country officially surrenders to the might of the German blitzkrieg. We put up a good fight but to no avail. The Germans have now taken every major airfield. Rotterdam and the Hague lie in ruins. It's been five days now since the initial attack...' Jakob switched off the wireless. Rini looked from Jakob to Angelina, noticing their concerned expressions. 'I'll go and put the kettle on' she said, and she made her way to the kitchen, exiting through the back of the shop. Angelina turned to Jakob, who leaned back and peered through the doorway to the back, making sure his wife was out of sight, then turned back to Angelina. She leaned into his shoulder while he put his arms around her.

'Does this mean this has to be the end of us?' she asked him, her voice muffled in his shoulder.

'Not at all,' he reassured her. 'Just because the Germans have overrun us, doesn't mean my mind is taken off you.'

'But won't it complicate things?' she asked, still in each other's arms.

'Well, you know what they say, one problem can overshadow another.' He gave her a reassuring smile as they broke apart to gaze into each other's eyes. They began to move in for kiss when they heard men's voices coming from the kitchen. Jakob and Angelina paused and frowned at each other before making their way out to the kitchen themselves.

Standing by the back door in the kitchen were two very determined-looking men. The taller man carried a suitcase and a typewriter, his blonde hair swept back in a side parting. The other man, also carrying a suitcase, was very young yet intelligent-looking, with dark wavy hair.

'Otto, what are you two doing coming through the back, and what's with the suitcases?' asked Jakob looking confused.

'Jakob, it's time we put our plan into action,' replied Otto, brandishing his typewriter.

'What, you mean down in the cellar?' asked Jakob.

'Precisely.' Otto smiled as he made his way past Jakob and Angelina. 'We need to operate from the last place the

Germans will think of looking; oh, and this is Anton by the way, don't worry, he's one of us,' Otto explained, as everyone followed him out to the short hallway between the kitchen and the shop, while Anton managed a brief handshake with Jakob. Otto put his suitcase down and then just looked at Jakob as if waiting for him to do something. Jakob, realising this, bent down to roll the long red carpet back, revealing the door to the cellar.

Opening the cellar door with a slight creak, Otto was the first to climb down the steps, followed by Anton and then Jakob.

'Angelina, roll the carpet back over when I've closed the door, I won't be long,' Jakob told her; she nodded and complied.

The cellar was huge, with a small electric lamp emitting a dull light on a wooden table, and food stacked up everywhere, but all was tidy.

Anton and Otto unpacked their equipment. They each used two ordinary wooden tables as their own desks.

'As you know, Jakob,' Otto explained, 'as I am second in command in the Dutch resistance, second only to Walraven Van Hall, and Anton here is a forger and a spy, we would like to thank you personally for letting us use your cellar at this critical time.'

'Oh, anything I can do to help really—'

'Let me shake you by the hand, Mr Jansen,' Anton cut in.

'Please, call me Jakob.'

'So, you two have known each other for some time then?' asked Anton as he consulted the contents of his suitcase.

'Yeah, we went to school together,' Otto explained. 'When we left school, Jakob here took over this shop from his father, while I went straight into studying radar and telecommunications, perfect for a future Dutch resistance fighter, even if we are supposed to be neutral, but you can bet your lives that won't last,' he said gravely.

'Well in that case, let's hope we can put all our talent to good use then,' smiled Anton.

'So, you're a spy and a forger?' Jakob asked Anton, genuinely intrigued and somewhat excited about the prospect.

'Yeah, that's right, well, it'll only be a matter of time before the Germans will want us all to have ration books and identification cards, I can create as many as you like and in very little time. Plus, it comes in very handy being a spy, I can masquerade as almost anybody with the correct identification.'

Jakob didn't quite know what to feel, but he was experiencing both excitement and dread for whatever the future may have in store for the Netherlands.

'Right, well, I'll leave you two to it then,' Jakob replied as he began to ascend the steps. 'If you need me just knock on the door,' he added.

He then knocked on the door himself and waited for it to be opened from above. Once Jakob was out of the cellar, his wife Rini laid the red carpet back over the cellar door.

'I hope you know what you're doing,' she said to Jakob rather unexpectedly sternly, while handing him his cup of tea and walking off.

Jakob remained by the cellar door and replied quietly to himself, 'So do I.'

At that precise moment, Jakob heard the jingle of his shop door opening. He walked out to the shop behind the counter and saw that two German officers had entered. As they were contemplating the bottled water on a top shelf, Jakob could see that one of them was a General; he looked a giant of a man, at least six foot four inches with a stocky build, close-cropped blonde hair and glasses. The other was a captain, average height and build with dark hair.

Jakob watched as the General specifically reached for the bottle of water on the top shelf on the extreme right. All too soon for Jakob's liking, they walked up to the counter and the General placed the bottle of water on the counter.

'Good morning, proprietor,' he spoke in his strong German accent. 'I am General Klaus Schneider, and this is Captain Fritz Muller, and I wish to purchase this bottle of water.'

Jakob thought the General had a cocky way about him, not to mention an evil stare through his thick glasses, which unnerved Jakob.

'Right,' Jakob replied, trying to concentrate, 'that'll be six Duit please.'

'Come now,' replied the General, 'is that any way to treat a conquering hero?' And picking up his bottle, he placed half the amount asked for on the counter, before turning around and laughing with the Captain as they left.

Otto came in from the back, where the cellar was, and stood beside Jakob; both of them just stared at the door that the two German officers just left through.

'That was General Klaus Schneider,' Otto explained. 'A ruthless, merciless man, he got transferred here from the Polish campaign. He has a deep hatred for Jews and will slaughter them as soon as look at them.'

'But I thought all Germans hated the Jews?' Jakob queried.

'Not like this man,' Otto explained. 'Six months ago in Poland, a Jewish boy of eleven collapsed through exhaustion. Schneider beat him with his belt to stand back up and continue working, but the poor boy was too weak to stand. The General continued to beat his lifeless body, and because he didn't stand, Schneider ordered the shooting of fifty slave labourers right before Christmas. The only man more powerful here in Holland is Syess-Inquart, the Reich Commissioner, who absolutely adores General Klaus Schneider.'

Jakob was listening to Otto intently when all of a sudden, BANG! BANG! BANG! A volley of shots rang out in the street followed by screams. Otto and Jakob rushed to the door and peered through the blinds. They saw the back end of a military truck opened up, with General Schneider standing by. There were two men lying dead on the ground; two German Privates picked them both up one at a time and mercilessly chucked them into the back of the truck. The General closed the back of the truck up, then turned and made direct eye contact with both Jakob and Otto through the blinds. They jumped back out of sight while the General got in the truck and drove away.

Rini and Angelina came in from the back with expressions of bewilderment.

'Don't tell me that was gunshots we heard?' Rini asked, her expression not changing as they made their way cautiously to where Jakob and Otto were standing.

Jakob hesitated at first and looked to Otto.

'I have to get back down into the cellar,' Otto said as he patted Jakob on the shoulder before leaving for the cellar.

Jakob couldn't find a tactful way of saying it, 'Two Jews were just killed and their bodies were taken away by the Germans,' he blurted out, unable to believe his own words.

Rini, unable to hide her shocked expression, slowly lowered her head and turned to leave for the kitchen, while clutching her stomach.

'Oh Jakob,' Angelina whispered as she reached up to hold his face in her hands. Jakob tried to speak but the words didn't come. His eyes began to fill with tears as his face contorted into a plea for help. Angelina sharply pulled his head to her shoulder where he finally let it all out, holding her tight and trying in vain to muffle his cries on her shoulder.

Seconds later, the little bell rang as the shop door opened behind Jakob, who quickly let go of Angelina and dried his eyes on his cuff.

'Hello Jakob,' said the customer.

'Ah Peter, nice to see you,' Jakob replied, avoiding eye contact with his friend.

'Angelina, could you see to Peter please? I'm just popping out for a moment,' Jakob informed her as he exited the shop.

Angelina made her way behind the counter, her long dark hair swaying at her lower back as she walked.

Peter leaned on the counter, his ageing face eyeing Angelina.

'You don't want to go out there, love, the place is covered with Germans.'

Angelina just stared at the front door with a concerned look, clearly thinking about Jakob.

Jakob stood with his back to the shop door, his head tilted up to the sky, his face basking in the sun.

Jakob Jansen's Food Shop was on a long stretch of road, containing several bridges connecting to the street on the other side, under which ran a canal, host to several fishing boats. The streets were just as busy as ever, full of shoppers and cyclists, the difference now of course were the pockets of Germans scattered around.

Jakob crossed the road and continued on down the pavement; the canal with the fishing boats was on his left-hand side. The sun glistened beautifully on the water; everything seemed so peaceful that Jakob found it a struggle to believe that the earlier incident ever took place.

He eventually came upon a group of German soldiers standing in a huddle, talking and laughing with each other. Jakob noted their smart uniforms and polished boots, but what stood out to him most of all were their menacing MP40s slung over their shoulders. They suddenly stopped talking and turned to look at Jakob, who stopped in his tracks and stared right back. Jakob had never felt so tense; time appeared to stand still.

'Jakob! Jakob! wait for me!' called a voice behind him. Jakob turned to see Anton running up to him. 'Jakob, come with me, come on.' Anton took the paralysed Jakob by the arm and pulled him on and walked him down the street. Jakob looked over his shoulder to see the Germans had resumed their conversation.

'There are a few things you need to know about the Germans,' Anton gasped as he and Jakob marched down the street. 'Rule number one, never make eye contact; eye contact is an invitation for conversation, something we

Dutch are best avoiding if we can help it, and rule number two, if you do happen to make eye contact, make it brief and show no fear on your face. Don't give them a reason to become suspicious.'

They continued on past the canal and found a bench to sit on to catch their breaths.

'Look at them,' Anton scoffed, as he leaned forward, elbows resting on his knees. 'Brainwashed sheep who believe they're better than anyone else, and they're trying to turn us the same way against the Jews.'

'You don't think it'll work, do you?' Jakob asked, concerned.

'Well, there might be one or two bastards around here willing to collaborate for money,' Anton answered as he lit a cigarette.

This reply didn't do much for Jakob's nerves.

'No don't worry,' Anton replied seeing Jakob's expression then blowing out a fog of smoke, 'we'll be safe, it's the poor Jews who'll suffer.'

'It's not right,' Jakob replied, looking around at everyone and shaking his head.

'Well, I know that, but do you want to explain that to these brainwashed zombies?'

'I have a good mind to,' Jakob replied as he looked up and surveyed the streets.

'Yeah well, just as long as you don't do it while I'm around,' smiled Anton.

'Have you heard of General Klaus Schneider?' asked Jakob, thinking about what Otto had just told him.

'Of course I have, he's a merciless bastard who enjoys killing innocent people; he's famous for it,' Anton explained.

'He shot two Jewish men just across from the shop, I saw as they loaded the bodies in the back of the truck, Otto saw it too... I suppose you and Otto are used to that sort of thing?'

'Not as much as you might think, but we'd better start getting used to it, all of us,' Anton said as he got to his feet and stomped out his cigarette. 'Come on then, let's get back, shall we?' Jakob stood and strolled back to the shop with Anton.

TWO

POISON IN A BOTTLE

Otto was working by lamplight at his desk in the cellar. He was contemplating the contents of his hands, each containing a little white pill. He opened the bottle of water in front of him and dropped both pills inside.

'Goodbye, General Schneider,' he said as he screwed on the lid and watched the pills fizz to the bottom.

Otto got up, climbed the steps and knocked on the door.

Moments later, Otto put the same bottle of water on the top shelf on the extreme right, the exact same place the General had taken his bottle from. He then walked round behind the counter and waited for Angelina to finish serving the elderly lady buying a loaf of bread.

'Angelina, make sure nobody picks up the bottle on the top right, it's reserved for the General,' he told her.

'Oh right, OK,' she replied with a confused expression. 'Goodbye, Mrs Geering,' she called to the elderly lady as she left the shop.

Otto made his way back down into the cellar, while Rini pulled the red carpet over the cellar door, and then went into the shop to relieve Angelina.

'You can go on your break now, Angelina, I'll take over,' she told her.

Angelina nodded and went out back to the kitchen.

A new customer arrived, a Dutch police officer. A shifty-looking character, average height and build, with strawberry-blonde hair poking out under the rim of his hat. He picked up the very bottle that Otto had just placed there.

'Just this,' he said rather sternly as he put the bottle on the counter.

'Six Duit,' Rini replied just as sternly.

He put the money down on the counter with a smug face and turned to leave. Rini watched him exit and shook her head in disgust.

•

General Klaus Schneider's office

A random young German officer was busy hanging up pictures on the wall. One was a large portrait of Adolf Hitler proudly sporting a swastika, his piercing blue eyes penetrating anyone who dared to look.

The General was busy doing written work at his desk when there was a knock at the door directly in front of him.

'Come in,' the General called.

Captain Fritz Muller entered the office.

'General, there is a man outside to see you, he's a police officer.'

'OK, send him in,' the General replied, still focusing on his paperwork.

'You may enter!' the Captain called.

The policeman entered the room rather proudly and saluted the General, 'Heil Hitler!'

This caused the General to look up in surprise. 'Well, I am impressed,' the General replied, leaning back in his chair to study the policeman. 'And how may I help you?'

'Well, General, my name is Officer Baker, and I'm a big admirer of yours, and I just wanted to tell you that, if you ever need any assistance at all with any uncooperative civilians, especially the Jews,' he added with menace, 'well, I am more than willing to help. I also have a little something here for you,' he revealed the bottle of water. 'I hear through the grapevine that you love this kind of bottled water, so here you are.' He placed the bottle on the General's desk.

General Schneider leaned forward, cupped his hands together on his desk and looked up at Officer Baker.

'So, you're volunteering to be an informer, is that what you're saying?'

'I'm ready and willing, sir,' Baker replied, coming off as incredibly crawly.

The General picked up the bottle of water and looked at it with a sly smile. 'I'll bear that in mind then, Officer Baker.'

'Thank you, General, Heil Hitler!' Baker raised his right hand enthusiastically.

'Yes of course, Heil Hitler,' the General replied with a smirk.

Officer Baker turned and left the office in a soldier-like fashion.

•

Jakob and Rini were in mid conversation behind the counter, waiting for the next customer.

'Well, I don't know what this war is going to bring to our front door, Rini,' said Jakob gravely.

'Well, we'll be all right, we're not Jewish,' Rini replied in what Jakob considered a harsh tone. He looked at her, disgusted.

'How can you say that?' he raised his voice. 'What about our friends, the children? Anton knows all about these Germans, they're brainwashed sheep who think that if you're not of Aryan race, you're not worth one Guilder.'

'OK, OK,' Rini replied. 'I just think we'll be fairly treated, even the Jews if they keep a low profile.'

'They shouldn't have to keep a low profile!' Jakob snapped as he stormed out the back.

Jakob went through to the kitchen where Angelina was sitting at the table drinking a mug of tea.

'Jakob, where did you go?' she asked.

'Just out for a walk,' he replied as he walked round and stood behind her, his hands massaging her shoulders. 'How are you anyway?' he asked her as he moved her beautiful long hair away from her neck and bent down to kiss it. He could smell the scent of her perfume. She closed her eyes and dropped her head back with a sigh, as he continued kissing her neck. She looked up at him and, as they made eye contact, they locked lips. Continuing to kiss, she slowly stood up out of her chair. She wrapped her arms around his neck, while he placed his hands on her sides, slowly running his hands down either side of her slim, curvy body, past her tiny waist, and down to her hips, feeling everything through her short, tight skirt.

•

Meanwhile, down in the cellar, Otto and Anton were in mid conversation.

'So then, right,' Otto continued, 'I put the two cyanide capsules in the bottle of water, which is at this very moment sitting on the top shelf on the far-right side; the General always goes for that one.'

'I don't think I'm ever going to leave my drink lying around you again,' Anton joked.

'Wait a minute,' Anton just had a thought, 'I've got a German uniform and German papers, I could give the bottle to him myself, save anyone else picking it up.'

'All right then, top shelf, right-hand side,' Otto reminded him.

Anton got out his suitcase from beside his mattress on the floor; he looked like a big kid at Christmas.

•

The General tidied the papers on his desk. He then picked up the bottle of water in front of him, leaned back in his chair, unscrewed the lid and proceeded to take a sip. He immediately spat it out, spraying the wall to his side. He lifted the bottle to his nose and sniffed, and then eyed the bottle with suspicion. He put the bottle down, picked up his telephone receiver and began to dial.

'Hans? General Klaus Schneider here, I want you to bring all your testing equipment to my office right away, there's a suspicious odour coming from my bottle of water, thank you.' He put the phone down and leaned back in his chair, studying the bottle through narrowed eyes.

•

Anton left the shop dressed as an ordinary yet sinister-looking German Private, carrying with him the bottle of water he'd picked from the top shelf on the far right.

•

Hans, the gentleman the General had just been on the telephone to, was in the General's office. He very much resembled a scientist in his long white coat and white bushy hair. He extracted some of the water from the bottle, using a syringe, and released it into a glass containing some clear liquid. To the General's surprise, the clear liquid in the glass slowly began to turn a pale shade of blue. The General watched with anticipation as Hans lifted the pale blue liquid up to eye level to study it.

'Well?' asked the General impatiently.

'Cyanide poison,' Hans replied, completely devoid of any emotion.

'Cyanide?' The General couldn't hide his disbelief so easily.

'Yes,' Hans replied in his monotone voice. 'Who did you say gave this to you?'

'A Dutch police officer, said he was a collaborator.'

'Judging by this it's pretty clear whose side he is on,' Hans said matter-of-factly.

Then there was a knock at the door.

'Come in!' called the General a little louder than he intended.

Captain Fritz Muller entered the office.

'General, there is a member of the sentry outside who wishes to see you.'

'Oh, all right, send him in,' the General replied reluctantly.

'OK, you may enter!' the Captain called as he left the office.

Anton marched into the office with confidence and raised his right hand in salute.

'Heil Hitler!'

'Heil Hitler,' the General and Hans replied simultaneously.

'General, let me start off by saying I am a huge admirer of yours, ever since your fortunate conquest of Rotterdam. I also hear that this is your favourite type of water, so I brought some for you.' Anton placed the bottle down on the desk like a schoolboy proudly showing the teacher his work.

'Did you indeed?' the General replied as he took the bottle and slid it directly across the desk to Hans.

'Test it,' he told him.

Anton's face dropped; he felt as if a lead weight had just dropped into the pit of his stomach.

'Well, I really must get going, Herr General—'

'Stop right there,' the General boomed. Anton and the General watched in silence as Hans repeated the process of testing the bottled water for cyanide using the syringe. Beads of sweat began to form under Anton's helmet as his mind was racing with all sorts of scenarios and explanations. Hans brought the clear liquid up to eye level to examine it. Anton chanced some brief eye contact with the General, who stared right back, stone-faced. Anton's eyes quickly shot back to Hans. The atmosphere was tense and could be cut with a knife.

'Well?' encouraged the General.

'All clear,' Hans declared, putting the glass back on the desk.

'Good,' the General replied smiling at Anton. Anton felt the world just levitate off his shoulders, but tried his best to keep his composure.

'Sorry about that, young man, but you can't be too careful; only a few minutes ago I had a gentleman standing where you're standing now offering me the exact same brand of water; turned out it contained cyanide poison.'

Anton tried not to show too much concern, after all, he was supposed to know nothing of any poison.

'Who was this man, Herr General?' he asked in what he hoped was a casual yet slightly concerned tone.

The General just looked into Anton's eyes for a few seconds before getting to his feet and walking over to him. 'May I see your papers?' the General held out his hand.

Anton was a little taken aback by this odd change in behaviour, but he put his hand inside his breast pocket nonetheless and revealed his identity papers. The General examined them carefully. His eyes rose to meet Anton's, then back to the identity papers, while Anton tried to keep his composure once more.

'All seems sufficient,' he said handing them back. 'His name was Officer Baker,' the General continued as if asking for the identity papers never took place, as he sat back behind his desk. He rested his chin on his cupped hands and studied Anton once again with his penetrating gaze.

'So, you're a big admirer of mine?'

'Oh yes, Herr General, very much so.'

'You may leave now, thank you, Hans.'

'Very good, sir,' Hans replied as he gathered up his equipment and exited through the door now being held open by Anton.

'Since learning of this, for want of a better term, assassination attempt, I've been devising a plan in my head, and here it is,' the General explained. 'I want you to find this Officer Baker, I'll give you his description in a moment, and I want you to lure him down the alleyway between the butcher's and the florist's tomorrow at noon, where I shall be waiting with a firing squad, do you understand?'

Anton hesitated for a moment, trying to process what he'd just heard.

'Yes, Herr General,' he responded with his chin up.

'If you can pull this off, young man, there may be a reward in it for you, say 500 Guilder?'

Anton couldn't believe his ears; he'd never heard of such money before.

'Yes, Herr General,' he repeated.

'Good, Heil Hitler,' the General smirked.

'Heil Hitler,' Anton replied and then turned around to leave the office.

As soon as he closed the door behind him, he collapsed into the chair outside the door and removed his helmet, took a deep breath and did a big sigh. What had he just agreed to?

•

Back at the shop in the kitchen, Jakob and Angelina were reclothing themselves, Jakob buttoning up his shirt, while Angelina sat in the light of the kitchen window, elegantly brushing her hair.

'Well, that was different,' she said calmly, still slowly brushing but not looking at Jakob.

'Didn't you like it?' he asked, now tucking his shirt inside his trousers.

'Oh yeah, I meant doing it in the kitchen while your wife is working on the till,' she replied with a naughty, playful smile, which was returned by Jakob.

'Well, it made it more exciting, and besides, she couldn't have gotten in anyway, not with that there,' said Jakob referring to the chair propped up against the kitchen door.

Angelina put her brush down, stood up and made her way over to where Jakob was standing.

'I love you, Jakob Jansen,' she said as they stood face to face, unable to break eye contact.

'And I love you,' he replied with a most sincere expression as he scooped her up in his arms.

•

Otto was sitting in his chair down in the dimly lit cellar, his feet outstretched up on a cardboard box and eating a banana, as Anton stepped dreamily down the steps.

'So, how'd it go? Did he take the bait? Otto asked, grinning through a mouthful of banana.

Anton reached the bottom of the steps and looked at Otto as if he'd seen a ghost. Otto uncrossed his legs and got up out of his chair.

'Anton, what's the matter? Come and sit down.' He pulled up another chair for Anton who sat down at once. Otto pulled his chair closer and sat down to listen to what Anton had to say.

'Tomorrow, a man's fate will be in my hands,' he began.

Otto was confused.

'You know that bottle you set up?'

'Yeah… well what about it?' Otto asked eagerly.

'Well, it was bought earlier by a police officer, he gave it to General Schneider. The General found out it was poisoned.'

'What, how?!' gasped Otto.

'There was some sort of doctor in the General's office, his name was Hans, he tested the water with some kind of special equipment,' Anton explained, still ghost-faced.

'My God! I don't believe it. I could have sworn cyanide was undetectable.' Otto was puzzled.

'Apparently not, and that's not all, the General has asked me to get hold of this police officer, and he wants me to lure him down the alleyway between the butcher's and the florist's tomorrow at noon, where he will be waiting with a firing squad,' explained Anton.

Otto stood up from his seat and began to pace, his eyes narrowed in concentration.

'But there's one tiny problem,' Anton added as Otto paused to look at him. 'The General never gave me his description, he said he would, but he didn't, he just ended the conversation and I got out of there as quickly as I could without thinking.'

Otto thought hard.

'Did he give you the police officer's name?' he asked as he continued to pace.

'Oh er… Officer Baker.'

Otto abruptly stopped pacing and stared eagle-eyed at Anton.

'Baker?!' exclaimed Otto as he quickly sat back in his seat and faced Anton. 'Anton, you've got to go through with it.'

'What?! Otto, listen, I'm not going to lure an innocent man down an alley—'

'Listen to me,' Otto interrupted. 'Officer Baker is a Dutch Nazi, a collaborator, he needs to be gotten rid of. Don't you see, Anton? This is like a gift from God, it wasn't the way I planned things, but it could still work. You see, I was hoping to get rid of Schneider, but getting rid of Officer Baker is good enough. Get rid of him, Anton, and you could be saving the lives of countless innocent civilians.'

Anton sat motionless for a few seconds while his mind took all of this in. He was about to do something terrible, yes, but in the long run he'd be saving countless more lives.

'So, he's a collaborator then?' Anton wanted reassurance.

'Yes Anton, he's on their side. He must've brought the bottle from Rini when it was the start of her shift, planning on giving it to the General as some sort of peace offering, but it's clearly backfired. This is why you must go through with it, Anton. Tomorrow at noon, Holland will have one less Nazi to worry about.'

THREE

A WANTED MAN

Anton was dressed in his German uniform facing the front door of the shop, staring out onto the street, Jakob and Otto fussing either side of him.

'Now, if what you two told me yesterday is anything to go by, I wish you the best of luck,' Jakob said, dusting off Anton's shoulders.

'Now remember,' Otto added while placing Anton's helmet on his head, 'Officer Baker will be doing his rounds out by the German headquarters about now. You've got less than ten minutes to change the course of history, do you understand?'

Anton turned to look at Otto with a blank expression.

'You really know how to cheer me up, don't you?' he drawled lazily.

'Oh Anton, don't be like that, if you're successful in this, after the war you'll be a hero,' Otto replied encouragingly.

Anton's face changed to sincerity as he turned to face them both,

'All right, now listen to me,' he told them matter-of-factly, his hands on their shoulders. 'If I don't make it—'

'Oh of course you'll make it,' Jakob cut in reassuringly.

'No listen, if I'm not successful, and something happens to me, I want you to both promise me that you'll keep on fighting, that you won't give up hope. I want you to remember what I died for, and to not let my death be a weight upon your shoulders, but to let it be an inspiration, something to use as weapon, do you understand me?'

Anton noticed both Otto's and Jakob's eyes begin to sparkle in the afternoon sunlight emitting through the window.

'Death to all collaborators,' nodded Jakob.

'And Nazi scum,' Otto added.

Anton turned around, and without another word he opened the door and exited the shop.

It was a very busy day in Amsterdam. Sentries marching along, Dutch citizens on their bicycles, even the canal was carpeted with fishing boats.

Anton walked confidently over the bridge leading to the German headquarters, his boots echoing as he crossed, and right on time, just as Otto said, there was Officer Baker. Anton recognised the description that Otto had given him earlier in the day, right down to the strawberry-blonde hair poking out from under the hat. Anton took a deep breath and made his way casually over to him.

'Officer Baker?' Anton called out authoritatively.

Baker swung round and surveyed Anton, a mere Private addressing him.

'Yes, what of it?'

'Can you follow me please, sir, my superior would like

to have a word with you,' Anton told him and turned to walk in the direction of the alleyway.

'What is this all about?' Baker queried as he reluctantly followed him.

'General Schneider has a proposition for you, we're going to meet him in the butcher's,' Anton improvised.

'General Schneider wants to see me? Oh, this is an honour,' Baker replied excitedly as he attempted to keep up with Anton.

Anton eventually led him to the completely abandoned alleyway between the butcher's and the florist's.

'Why are we going down here?' Baker asked as he was about to go into the butcher's, but before Anton could answer him, they both received a surprise. The General came around the corner pointing his Luger at them both, and he was alone; there was no firing squad. Just as stunned as each other, both Baker and Anton put their hands in the air.

'Did you think I was stupid?' the General snarled at Anton. 'Passing yourself off as a German. I saw your papers, and guess what, nobody had heard of you.'

Anton didn't know what to say to this. What could he say? He had been caught red-handed.

'And you,' the gun switched to Baker. 'A fine water indeed, pretending to be a Nazi sympathiser while secretly plotting an assassination attempt.'

'I'm afraid you've lost me, Herr General,' Baker pleaded, his hands still raised.

All of a sudden, an air-raid siren filled the air. All three of them got distracted and looked up at the skies. Before they knew it, the silhouettes of planes swept the skies. Anton and

Baker, hands still raised, looked back at Schneider who was still brandishing his Luger. They just stared at each other while the civilians in the main street ran in panic.

'Well, what a predicament you two are in,' the General sneered. 'Death by bullets or bombs? Make your choice.'

But before either of them had time to make a decision, they were all distracted again, this time by a flurry of leaflets floating down from the sky, masses of them littering the entire area for miles around. It seemed there was no threat, it appeared that the RAF were simply dropping propaganda leaflets. Realising this, both Baker and Anton decided to use this distracting opportunity and ran.

Bang! The General's gun fired; Baker collapsed into a heap on the pavement.

Bang! This time he fired at Anton and caught him in the left thigh, but miraculously, Anton managed to keep limping around the corner.

Schneider ran past Baker's lifeless body to the entrance of the alleyway, and pointed his gun round the corner where Anton had limped off too… but he was gone.

•

The leaflets were lying in clusters all over Amsterdam. They were floating in the water, they had covered the boats, even the roofs of the buildings, and they were lining the roads.

'Do not touch the leaflets!' the Germans were shouting while proudly brandishing their MP40s through the streets.

'Leave the leaflets where they are; if you pick any up, we will be forced to shoot!'

Jakob, Otto, Rini and Angelina were among those out

in the street, observing the peculiar scene as they stood outside the shop.

Otto, very craftily, removed the chewing gum from his mouth, lifted his left foot to his right knee, placed the chewing gum on the bottom of his shoe, put his foot down on a leaflet, and casually turned around and walked back inside the shop with the leaflet attached. The others followed him inside.

'Very clever, Otto,' Jakob grinned as he closed the door behind them.

'It worked, didn't it?' smiled Otto as he took the leaflet and studied it.

'So, what does it say?' asked Angelina with anticipation.

'Over here,' Otto replied and led them all behind the counter out of view of any passing German.

'Jakob, would you like to do the honours?' he asked, handing the leaflet to Jakob, who willingly took it.

'To our fellow Europeans,' Jakob began. 'We urge you all to keep calm and carry on. It is only a matter of time before the British crush the Nazi war machine. It's going to take time but we will win, so just bear with us and hang in there.'

CRASH! Suddenly it sounded as though the back door had flown open and heavy breathing could be heard. They all dashed into the kitchen to find Anton a bloody mess on the floor holding his leg, and a trail of blood leading in from outside.

'Oh my God!' Jakob called and crouched down next to him.

'I've been shot in the leg,' Anton gasped.

'Angelina, get me a bowl of hot water, Otto, give me your belt, Rini get me a sponge and some tweezers,' Jakob ordered. They all dashed off to collect exactly what he'd asked for.

Otto gave Jakob his belt who then wrapped it tightly around Anton's thigh.

'Bowl of hot water straight from the kettle,' Angelina said as she placed it on the floor beside them.

'Sponge and tweezers,' Rini said, also placing them on the floor, and then left the kitchen for the shop with Angelina.

'Right, I'm going to have to clean this up, Anton, so bear with me.' Jakob dunked the sponge into the hot water, while Otto got a mop to clean up the blood on the floor and the back doorstep.

Jakob began by tearing the trousers around the wound as carefully as possible. Anton cringed and gritted his teeth. Dabbing the sponge around the wound, he slowly wiped it clean. He put the sponge back in the water which turned red in an instant. Jakob then took out the tweezers he'd already placed in the hot water, and looked deadly seriously at Anton, who was still breathing rapidly with his face contorted with pain.

'Are you ready, Anton?'

Anton nodded while gritting his teeth once again.

Jakob proceeded to gently poke the tweezers through the bloody hole in his thigh.

'AHHHHHHHHHHH!!' Anton yelled out in pain. Otto dropped the mop, swung the back door shut, got down behind Anton and threw his hand over his mouth to muffle the screams.

'Keep the noise down, Anton, for God's sake!' he called out over his cries.

Jakob, trying to concentrate and keep a steady hand, pinched the tweezers together.

'Have you got it?' Otto asked, now holding both hands over Anton's mouth.

Jakob slowly pulled the blood-covered tweezers back out and took a look; he looked up at Otto and shook his head. Otto looked concerned while struggling to hold Anton still.

Jakob looked at Anton in the eye; he looked like a deer in headlights. Jakob decided to make a second and daring attempt, and once again proceeded to penetrate the wound.

'Ahhhhhhhhh!' Anton's cries were partially hidden under Otto's hands.

Jakob squeezed the tweezers together, and as gently as he could he began the descent back out of the wound. As Jakob was halfway out, he felt the tweezers' grip give way. Jakob rolled his eyes and shook his head; Otto looked on hopelessly as he held on to Anton, whose face was saturated in sweat.

'Wait a minute,' Jakob said with a glimmer of hope. 'I can see it; it's protruding from the wound. If I can just get a firm grip on the edge, I can give it a good fast pull.'

'All right, Anton,' said Otto reassuringly, 'this is it, one last hard tug and it's all over.' Anton nodded ferociously.

Without another word, Jakob put the tweezers up to the protruding silver bullet, gently clasped the round tip, squeezed as hard as he could and gave one hard pull.

Anton didn't scream, in fact he looked relieved as Jakob held up the bullet for them all to see. Otto released Anton, grabbed an empty cup off the kitchen unit and held it out to Jakob, who dropped the bullet in with a clang.

•

General Klaus Schneider and Captain Fritz Muller, were walking alongside the canal. The General was holding a thick pile of papers in his hands.

'Here,' he said to the Captain as he thrust several of these sheets of paper into his hand. 'I want one of these posters put up in every shop window this side, I'll do the other side.'

'Yes, General.' The Captain took the posters and went into the next shop he came to.

•

Jakob was busy piling tins of custard on a shelf, when he heard the jingle of the little bell as the front door opened. He looked round to see the General enter carrying the A4-sized posters. Jakob watched from behind the shelf as the General strolled over to Angelina at the counter, who was leaning on the counter and writing something in her notepad.

Her attention was brought back to the present moment by the General's towering stature in her peripheral vision; she stood up straight at once.

'So,' he began as he placed the posters on the counter face down. 'Tell me, what's a pretty thing like you doing in a decrepit old hovel like this?'

Angelina was taken aback. The fact that he called her pretty had just been drastically overshadowed by the fact that he just offended her place of work, and not just that, but her lover's business.

'Ah… it's my break-time… Jakob would you mind?' she

smiled an awkward smile at the General, before grabbing her notepad and retreating out the back to the hallway leading to the kitchen. The General watched Angelina leave with hungry eyes. Jakob made his way over to the other side of the counter.

'Your daughter, I presume?' the General said casually.

'No, she's just my employee,' Jakob corrected him, dislike etched on his face.

'And you haven't even had a go at her?' he smirked.

Jakob just stared back at the General, unblinking.

'Is she available?'

'No.' Jakob felt a little anger begin to develop in the pit of his stomach.

The General then looked deadly serious and leaned his six-foot-four frame over the counter and whispered, 'You're having an affair, aren't you?'

Any anger that had been building inside of him had just been doused by a cold hose. Jakob saw his own face drop in his reflection in the General's glasses. How could the General possibly have found out about his affair with his twenty-six-year-old shopkeeper?

'Pahahahahaha!' The General suddenly burst out laughing, and Jakob realised he'd been having him on. A wave of relief came over him.

'What is it that you want, General?'

'I just want one of these posters put up in your window, if you wouldn't mind doing the honours? I'll just leave this one here with you,' he said as he picked back up all but one of the posters, still lying face down on the counter. He marched to the door, turned round and raised his right hand, 'Heil Hitler!' he called.

Jakob cleared his throat, and reluctantly replied with much less enthusiasm.

'Heil Hitler.'

The General turned and left. Jakob breathed a sigh of relief, but his peace of mind didn't last long, as he turned the poster over to see Anton's face staring up at him on the front, with writing underneath.

WANTED alive.

Reward for information: 500 Guilders.

Reward for capture: 1000 Guilders.

'Oh my God!' Jakob put a hand to his mouth while reading the poster. He darted into the hallway and called to Angelina as he pulled the red carpet back to reveal the cellar door. 'Angelina, can you mind the shop for me? This is urgent.'

She came rushing out of the kitchen, her long dark hair billowing out behind her.

'What's the matter?' she asked, seeing the alarming state Jakob was in.

'There's no time now, I'll tell you later, I promise,' he replied as he clambered down the steps as quickly as he could. Angelina pulled the red carpet back over.

Anton was lying on a mattress on the dusty concrete floor resting his injured leg, while Otto was sitting at his desk reading a newspaper in the dim cellar light.

'Otto! Anton!' Jakob called as he made his way over to them. 'You've got to see this.' He held up the poster for them both to see. Otto dropped his newspaper in a crumpled heap and slowly rose to his feet, as he stared in disbelief at the poster.

Anton heaved himself up straight as he struggled to see through the dim light.

'Is that me?' His face was reminiscent of a deer in headlights once again.

'I'm sorry to say, Anton, yes, it is,' Jakob said gravely.

'My God,' Otto whispered as, open-mouthed, he took the poster from Jakob.

'Where did you get this from?' Otto asked, his eyes still focused on the poster.

'The General just gave it to me, he wants me to put it up in the shop window, can you believe that?'

'Then you must do so.' Otto ordered, taking his eyes off the poster for the first time to look at Jakob, who looked flabbergasted.

'What?!' chorused Jakob and Anton.

'Listen to me,' Otto explained. 'If General Schneider suspects any funny business, he'll be round here to search this place high and low, and he will not stop until he's found what he's looking for… you, Anton. Jakob, you have to put this in the window right away.' He handed the poster back to Jakob.

'And Anton,' Otto continued. 'I'm getting you out of here.'

Jakob climbed the stairs and exited through the cellar door.

'What do you mean?' Anton asked, his brow furrowed.

Otto reached under his desk, pulled out a radio and headphones and placed them on the desk.

'You'll see,' was Otto's reply as he fiddled with the radio.

Anton struggled to his feet and hobbled on over to Otto, then dropped into the nearest chair.

Otto picked up the receiver and fiddled with the frequency button, causing a lot of static and interference.

Anton got very confused when he heard a voice at the other end giving a series of numbers.

'Eighteen, five, one, four, twenty-five,' called the voice. Otto replied with even more series of numbers, with the word 'gap' between some of them.

'Nineteen, five, fourteen, four, 'gap', sixteen, twelve, one, fourteen, five, 'gap', twenty, fifteen, 'gap', six, nine, five, twelve, four, 'gap', twenty, twenty-three, fifteen, 'gap', thirteen, nine, twelve, five, nineteen, 'gap', twenty-three, five, nineteen, twenty, 'gap', fifteen, six, 'gap', one, thirteen, nineteen, twenty, five, eighteen, four, one, thirteen, 'gap', thirteen, nine, four, fourteen, nine, seven, eight, twenty, stop.'

'Four, fifteen, fourteen, five,' came the reply, and Otto turned off the radio.

Anton looked utterly bewildered.

'What the hell was that all about? Are you pulling my leg or what?'

'Now would I pull your leg in that condition?' Otto smirked.

Anton smiled and shook his head.

'And anyway, the code is constantly changing; the Germans aren't stupid, this one will probably be broken any day now, but they won't break it before midnight, could take them days, weeks or even months, but they will break it, and when they do, we have other codes in place.'

'Come on then, what did all those numbers mean?'

'It's code, I can't say any more than that.'

'But we're on the same side,' Anton pleaded.

'And what would happen if you were ever caught by the Gestapo? They torture people for information like that.'

'Well, yeah I know that, but… yeah all right.' Anton could see his point.

'All you need to know is that I'm having a plane sent over from England, it's going to land in a field two miles west of Amsterdam, and it's going to take you to England.'

'England?!' Anton replied incredulously.

'Yes Anton, England, I mean, can you think of a better place to go into hiding when you're being hunted by Klaus Schneider?'

Anton thought about this for a while and then his face slowly broke into a smile.

'And you can tell all that by a number code?' Anton asked with the biggest grin.

'I'm second in command of the Dutch Resistance, Anton, I have to know what these codes mean.'

Anton was still smiling like a little boy winding up his father.

'If you're second in command of the Dutch Resistance, where are all the others?'

'Underground, corner shops, the post office, we're everywhere, but underground mainly. You see this newspaper?' Otto held up the newspaper he was reading. 'This was printed by the underground press, you won't find any Nazi propaganda in this; on the contrary, I've just read an article on Hitler having only one ball…'

After a few seconds' silence, they both erupted with laughter.

•

The clock on the wall above the shop counter read 11:30pm. The shop took on a different atmosphere at this time of night, especially in wartime.

Jakob, Otto and Anton were all standing at the counter, Anton still in his German Private's uniform.

'Now remember the plan,' Otto whispered, with only the street light outside lighting up his face. 'Jakob and I are ordinary Dutchmen and Nazi sympathisers; you, Anton, are a German soldier who's had too much to drink, hence why we are helping you walk as you lean on us.'

'Got it,' Anton nodded.

Anton put each arm around the shoulders of Otto and Jakob, as they helped him over to the front door.

'Wait a minute,' Anton stopped and turned his head to Otto. 'You said we'd have to walk two miles to that field the plane is going to land in.'

'So?'

'So, I don't know if I'm going to make it.'

'Of course you will, we're here, aren't we?' replied Otto encouragingly.

Anton thought about this for a second.

'Yeah, all right,' he agreed. Otto proceeded to reach for the door handle when Anton spoke again.

'Wait a minute.'

'What is it now?!' Otto replied, getting frustrated now.

'Well, shouldn't we go by the back door?'

'No, we don't want to arouse suspicion should anyone see a German soldier leaving by the back door this late at night; now let's get going.'

The cool night air hit their faces as they stepped outside. It was a cloudy night, not a star in sight, but the street lights reflected beautifully on the water. The only sounds in the distance were dogs barking, German soldiers laughing, and the slight trickle of water coming from the canal.

With Anton in between Jakob and Otto, his arms wrapped around their necks, they began their two-mile walk.

'How are you bearing up so far, Anton?' Otto asked him as they just passed the butcher's, all shut up for the night.

'So far so good,' he replied.

They came upon a noisy bar, full of Germans and Dutch alike. Three drunk soldiers were swaying arm in arm. They were walking mindlessly backwards away from the building, singing at the tops of their voices, when they suddenly bumped into Jakob, Otto and Anton.

'OH! Excuse me,' said one of the soldiers, his eyes glazed over.

'That's quite all right,' Otto replied, trying to avoid eye contact and continue moving.

'What's wrong with him?' one of the other soldiers asked to their horror.

Otto and Jakob had no choice but to stop.

'Oh, we're taking him back to his quarters, can't handle his liquor,' Otto smirked, hoping to befriend the soldier. Anton tried his best to appear drunk.

'Ha-ha-ha, you Dutch and your sense of humour,' the soldiers laughed and let them go.

'That was a close one,' Anton whispered once they were out of earshot.

'My heart was in my mouth,' Jakob added.

•

They eventually made it to the countryside, two miles west of Amsterdam. It was absolutely pitch black, and all that could be heard was the rustling of leaves on the trees, and the hoot of a distant owl.

'Are we there yet?' Anton said breathlessly.

'We must be by now, let me just get my torch.' Otto got his torch out from inside his jacket pocket while Anton held onto Jakob. Otto shone the torch on the road ahead. It illuminated enough of the road to see a gate entrance to a field on the left.

'How are we supposed to find the plane?' Jakob asked, looking around into the pitch darkness, his breath visible in the torchlight.

'No it's all right, I don't think the plane has arrived yet,' Otto answered.

Suddenly, all eyes were scanning the sky, as they all heard the unmistakable sound of a plane in the distance.

'I'll shine my torch up so he can follow it,' Otto suggested, as he let go of Anton again, who leaned on the iron gate with a loud clang. Otto shone the torchlight up to the sky. Its attempts at reaching even the tops of the trees was pathetic, but at least the pilot would be able to see the light.

The sound of the engine grew louder as their necks began to ache looking upwards. And there it was, the silhouette of a large plane swooped across the sky above them.

'It's going away,' Jakob said, confused.

'No, it's just going to turn around to land,' Otto corrected him.

Sure enough, the plane was on its way back, this time much larger and lower to the ground.

The wheels touched ground and the plane eventually came to a halt.

They looked on in awe at the beautiful beast in front of them. A two-seater Supermarine Spitfire, looking both graceful and intimidating in the dim torchlight.

'How in God's name did a Spitfire manage to fly across the North Sea, over occupied territory, land in a field outside Amsterdam, and not even have the air-raid siren go off?' Jakob asked, completely dumbfounded.

'Two reasons,' Otto began. 'Firstly, there was only one, much easier to miss than if it were a whole squadron, and secondly, I purposely chose the next moonless night, in addition to the cloud making him almost impossible to spot.'

Jakob stood open-mouthed at the ingenuity of Otto.

'When you two have quite finished rabbiting, I've got a plane to catch here,' Anton reminded them.

'Right, come on then, let's get you over this gate. I'll go first, Jakob, you help him over from that side.'

Working together, and with great difficulty given Anton's injured leg, they managed to get him safely on the other side of the gate, which clanged loudly in the night.

'Otto of the Dutch Resistance, I presume?' came a voice from the cockpit. As they approached the plane, they saw the head of a young man poking out smiling at them.

'That's correct,' Otto replied.

'Good heavens, you've bagged a Jerry,' the pilot exclaimed.

'What? I'm not a Jerry, I'm—'

'No, it's all right, he doesn't really think you're a Jerry, Anton, this is how we know we can trust him, by him saying the password,' Otto explained.

'Oh… yeah… well… I thought it sounded a bit rehearsed,' Anton replied, smirking at Otto.

'Right, well, when you're ready,' said the young pilot, jabbing his thumb to the seat behind him.

With great difficulty, once again, Jakob and Otto heaved Anton up into the back seat.

After sounds of heaving and painful screaming, Anton was finally sitting more or less comfortably behind the pilot, who switched the engine on the moment he was in.

'You take care of yourself, Anton,' Otto called out over the sound of the engine.

'And keep in touch,' Jakob called.

'It's been a good few days,' Anton waved.

'It's certainly been an interesting seventy-two hours,' Otto waved back.

'TTFN!' called the pilot, and the plane began to move off. It sped off across the field, slowly picking up momentum before the wheels left the ground and then it was airborne. Jakob and Otto watched as the plane vanished into the night.

Anton felt himself being pressed back into his seat as the plane picked up speed and soared through the night sky. As he looked down, he could see the lights of Amsterdam getting smaller and smaller.

'Are you all right there, mate?' the plot shouted back to him.

'Yeah, just never flown before,' Anton replied, holding on tight.

'Oh well, there's nothing to worry about, mate, just enjoy the view.'

Anton was looking down at the view, but he wasn't

exactly enjoying it; the thought of being hundreds of feet off the ground made him feel very uncomfortable indeed.

'So how long you been a spy?' the pilot asked, making conversation.

'Only since the end of March. I knew Hitler wouldn't let Holland stay neutral, so I decided to make myself useful, first in Poland then Holland.'

'Then England,' the pilot chuckled, trying to make light of Anton's situation.

All of a sudden, an unexpected flash of light swept past the plane.

'What was that?!' Anton called to the pilot.

'Oh no, I don't believe it!' the pilot shouted. Another flash of light fell across them. Anton, rather begrudgingly, looked down, and saw that the lights they saw were coming from the searchlights on the ground. Suddenly, the eerie sound of the air-raid siren filled the air, and if that wasn't frightening enough, next they heard the unmistakable sounds of anti-aircraft guns.

'Oh my God, oh my God, oh my God,' Anton repeated quietly to himself, squeezing his eyes shut tight.

'Hold on, my man!' the pilot called out, as he began to frantically steer the plane in any direction that he saw fit.

Anton screwed up his face with his hands over his ears, for the sound of the artillery connecting with the plane was horrifically loud. Like being inside a large tin can and having a group of people outside throw big stones at it.

'I'm afraid I've got some bad news!' the pilot shouted out as he struggled to handle the plane. 'We're not going to make it to England!'

'What?!' Anton replied, horrified, although the next statement was even worse.

'We're going to have to ditch in the North Sea!'

Anton tried his hardest not to think about the noise of the air-raid siren and the anti-aircraft guns, but it wasn't easy.

'You mean ditch by parachute?!' he asked.

'If we make it that far, yes!' came the reply, but he didn't sound too hopeful, as he continued his feeble attempts at avoiding the artillery.

Anton looked out at the wing on his right-hand side; it was completely riddled with small holes, and chips of paintwork missing, caused by near misses. Anton suddenly felt all the blood rushing to his head; he looked up and saw the distant lights of Amsterdam, and realised they were flying upside down. His natural reaction, then, was to look down out of the window, where he saw the pitch-black abyss that was the sky.

His stomach then somersaulted as the plane rolled the right way up, and thankfully it seemed the pilot was managing to create some distance, as the sounds of ripping metal were petering out, and the sounds of the air-raid siren and anti-aircraft gun were fading away.

•

Jakob and Otto managed to get back to the shop OK.

'First thing in the morning I'm going to have to get on the radio, and find out if Anton got to England OK,' Otto whispered as they entered the shop. Jakob closed the door behind them, then walked over to the counter to switch on the light.

'So you think that air raid was to do with Anton then?' Jakob asked, as Otto walked over to stand with him.

'I hope to God I'm wrong, Jakob, but there were no other planes around. I really hope they make it.'

'I'm sure they will, one way or another.' Jakob replied reassuringly.

•

An hour later, and Anton and the pilot were in a rubber dinghy in the middle of the North Sea. Apart from the sound of the black icy water there was a deafening silence, with nothing but the pilot's torch for light.

'It's so quiet,' Anton blurted out to break the eerie silence, his injured leg stretched out in front of him.

'Yeah, too quiet,' the pilot replied, his torchlight skimming the surface of the dark water.

'So where are we?' asked Anton, beginning to shiver.

'We're in the middle of the North Sea, old chap, but the problem is we're closer to Holland than we are England, and the current is taking us inland.'

'So what do we do now?'

'Now we wait.'

'For what?'

'The inevitable.'

Anton waited to hear what that was, but the answer never came.

'So,' Anton prompted him, 'what's the inevitable?'

'Well, put it this way, there's no way we're going to England now, my guess is you'll go back to Amsterdam, and I'll go to a Prisoner of War camp.'

Anton looked at the pilot with disbelief.

'Do you mean to say that this has all been for nothing? Are you telling me that I'm going back to the shop, and you came all this way just to become a POW?' Anton asked incredulously.

The pilot was staring over Anton's shoulder when he replied, 'Not necessarily.'

'What?' Anton looked over his shoulder to see what the pilot was looking at. He saw something large and metallic surfacing the water.

'What the hell is that?'

'Looks like a submarine to me,' the pilot replied, 'and if I'm not much mistaken, that's a British submarine.'

Anton looked back at the pilot with an excited expression.

'Looks like we'll be heading back to dear old Blighty after all.' The pilot broke into a smile.

Anton looked out across the sea to the distant lights of Holland.

'Goodbye Holland, till the end of the war,' he said in a low voice.

FOUR

I SPY A SPY

June 14, 1940

Jakob, Rini and Angelina were gathered around the counter listening to the wireless.

'It is with great regret that we inform you, that the Germans have now marched into Paris. The German Blitzkrieg has been as destructive as ever, and now that the British are back home after the evacuation of Dunkirk, these are indeed dark days for mainland Europe—'

Jakob switched off the wireless while Angelina began to quietly weep. Burying her face in her hands, she turned around and walked into the hallway.

'Angelina!' Jakob called after her.

'I'll go,' Rini replied, stopping Jakob and going after Angelina herself.

Jakob would've given anything to be in her place, just to grab an extra five minutes with Angelina.

•

Meanwhile, down in the cellar, Otto was in mid conversation to London over the wireless, a candle on the desk as his only source of light.

'Now listen, there is to be a nineteen, sixteen, twenty-five sent to you,' said the voice over the radio in a very posh British accent. 'He's to stay upstairs, do you understand?'

'I'm not so sure that's a good idea,' replied Otto.

'Orders are orders I'm afraid.'

Otto put his fingers through his hair as he sighed. 'Very well then, when can we expect him?'

'Some time tonight, if all goes to plan our end,' came the reply.

'Right, we'll expect him tonight then, over and out?'

'Over and out.'

Otto switched off the radio.

•

Jakob was in mid conversation with an elderly man who'd just brought a pint of milk.

'It's just unbelievable, I mean when is it all going to end?' Jakob said to him, leaning on the counter.

'My bet is an invasion of England next, you mark my words,' said the old man.

'I hope not, a very good friend of mine went to England last month, if the Boche invade England, he'll have to move on to America next,' explained Jakob.

'Yeah, that's another thing, where are all the Yanks? They

helped out last time, didn't they? I mean I know they were late, but better late than never,' said the old man matter-of-factly.

'What're you talking about, we weren't involved in the last war?' Jakob replied puzzled.

'I know we weren't, but England was, weren't they, and the Yanks helped them out.'

'Oh I see what you mean. So you don't see the Americans lending their services this time then?'

'Well, who knows what could happen, but if you ask me, after what happened at Dunkirk, the British could do with a helping hand,' the old man nodded to Jakob and turned to leave the shop.

No sooner had the bell rung when the old man exited, than it rang again as the General entered the shop. He removed his hat and casually walked up to the counter.

'Good afternoon, General,' Jakob smiled pleasantly.

'Mr Jansen,' the General replied, 'heard the good news, have you?' he said as he placed his hat on the counter.

Jakob thought for a moment, 'You mean the fall of France?'

'You make it sound like a terrible thing, Mr Jansen, no it's not "the fall of France", it's another triumph for Germany, don't look at these things so negatively, that's the trouble with you Dutch,' he said, as he wandered away from the counter to grab one of his favourite bottles of water. 'You always fail to see the positive side,' he said as he came back to place the money on the counter.

'Thank you,' Jakob said, picking up the money and placing it in the till; he noticed the General hadn't left.

'I need a quiet word with you, Mr Jansen, while we're

alone.' The General leaned a little closer to Jakob, who was feeling nervous.

'You are to have a spy stay here at your shop, it's orders from Berlin.'

Jakob was stunned, he couldn't find the words. How did Berlin know about his little shop? And why would they choose his shop to be the live-in quarters of a German spy?

'What? But why? How?' Jakob stuttered.

'Yes, I'm afraid I don't beat about the bush, the spy will be arriving later tonight. I shall accompany them here, so I will see you tonight. Goodbye for now, Mr Jansen.' The General turned on his heel and left, clutching his bottle of water, leaving Jakob staring after him open-mouthed.

Seconds later Otto came in from the back while Jakob was in deep thought.

'Jakob, I've got something important to tell you, now it's not agreeable with me but orders are orders. We are apparently to have a spy come to stay at the shop with us, he'll have to stay upstairs out of sight of course but… Jakob are you all right?'

'What? Oh, yes, yes I'm fine,' Jakob replied, still thinking.

'Did you hear what I said about the spy?'

'Oh yes, yes I already know about that.'

'Really? Oh, I see, right, well I just thought I'd let you know,' Otto replied, frowning but also assuming Jakob must've overheard the radio.

'Well, I've got to pop out for a moment, I'll see you later, Jakob.'

'Yes, see you later,' Jakob replied, still distracted as Otto exited the shop.

Angelina, however, did manage to pull Jakob from his deep thoughts, when she came in from the back and just stood there with her arms folded.

'What is it?' Jakob asked innocently.

'You were supposed to come after me,' she told him sternly, 'instead of that, I had your wife come after me, and she ended up telling me about all her plans with you when the war was over.'

'Oh baby, I'm sorry, I did attempt to go after you, but then she jumped in,' Jakob replied helplessly.

'How long do you think we can keep our affair a secret?' Angelina asked him as she began to straighten his tie.

'I don't know, baby, as long as it takes,' he replied, brushing her hair aside from her face.

'It's so hard going around wanting to tell everyone I'm with you and I can't,' she explained. 'And it's even harder creeping around this place in secret. You don't love your wife any more, and we know she doesn't love you any more, Jakob, so why don't you just tell her?' Angelina asked as they stood with barely an inch between them.

'You know I can't do that, especially in wartime, it just wouldn't be right.'

'She doesn't deserve you, Jakob.'

'Oh no? Who does deserve me then?' he asked as he took her by her tiny waist.

'You're looking at her,' she whispered as they leaned in closer and kissed, her arms wrapped around his neck, his hands stroking her long dark hair down her back.

•

17:25. A man entered the shop wearing a long beige raincoat and a dark brown hat; he was quite tall and very slim, and he carried a suitcase. He strolled casually over to the counter; his dark blonde hair and blue eyes could be seen just beneath his hat.

Jakob was too busy looking through a notepad on the counter to notice him right away.

'Mr Jansen?'

Jakob looked up from the notebook. 'Yes?' he replied cautiously.

The stranger held out his hand. 'My name is Gary.'

Jakob absent-mindedly shook his hand.

'I believe you have a room for me upstairs?'

'Oh, you're the spy?' Jakob asked in a surprised tone.

'Yes.' Gary removed his hat to reveal a surprisingly friendly and trustworthy face.

Otto entered from the back.

'Otto,' Jakob whispered, 'it's him, it's the spy, he's arrived.' He pointed at Gary.

'It's Gary,' he smiled extending his hand.

'Pleasure, Gary, I'm Otto of the Dutch Resistance,' he replied shaking his hand.

'So you're English then?' Jakob asked, a little confused.

'Of course he is.' Otto rolled his eyes. 'OK, let's show you to your room shall we?' Otto smiled and assisted Gary through to the back.

Jakob was still confused, but he just shook it off and continued to look through the notepad.

The bell chimed again as the door opened. Jakob looked up and did a double take; he saw the General accompanying the most stunningly beautiful blonde woman he'd ever laid eyes on. She was tall and slim, with long curly locks and sparkling blue eyes. Jakob watched as she came over to the counter; he noticed her perfectly shaped silk stocking-covered legs, teasingly hidden from above the knee upwards by a luxurious black fur coat. The General appeared to be carrying her suitcase.

'Mr Jansen,' the General smiled with confidence, 'may I introduce the beautiful Eva, all the way from Berlin. I trust you have a room ready for her?'

Jakob was speechless as he struggled to find the words.

'Is this the spy you were talking about, Herr General?' Jakob asked as casually as he could.

'Yes, she is to stay here above your shop, and you are not to reveal to anyone her true identity; as far as anyone else is concerned she is simply a lodger, only you, me and the Captain know who she really is.'

Whether it was the General's intention or not, this made Jakob feel quite important; perhaps it was to encourage Jakob to keep the secret.

'Right then, madam,' Jakob said as he went round to collect the suitcase from the General, 'please follow me,' and he led the beautiful Eva round to the back. The General said goodnight to her and left the shop.

They made it halfway along the red carpet which was covering the cellar door when Jakob turned to his right and pulled back a long red certain revealing the stairs. Jakob led her up the stairs; they met Otto and Gary on the landing in deep discussion. They stopped talking and both turned and stared in awe at the incredible sight that approached them.

'Ah, uh, Otto and Gary, this is Eva, a lodger. Eva, this

is Gary, also a lodger, and this is Otto, he's a friend of the family,' Jakob explained, his nerves getting the better of him.

'Hello Otto,' she said as she held out a gloved hand. Otto shook it politely and smiled.

'And Gary,' she said with a more seductive tone. She held out her hand and Gary shook it gently; they stared into each other's eyes for what seemed to an awkward Jakob like eternity.

'Yes, well, how would you like to see your room?' Jakob said clapping his hands together and rubbing them.

'Certainly,' she smiled.

'It's just in here—'

'Wait a minute, Jakob, that's supposed to be—'

'Trust me, Otto, trust me,' Jakob cut him off with a look in his eyes that Otto found difficult to decipher, but knew enough to stay quiet. Gary, however, looked a little put out.

The room was basic but clean and tidy. There was a single bed with white sheets, with the foot of the bed directly opposite the door, a window behind the headboard, a small white chest of drawers to the left, and a beautiful picture of Amsterdam on the wall to the right. Jakob placed the suitcase down on the bed.

'Well, I hope everything is to your satisfaction, madam?' asked Jakob.

Eva gazed around the room. Jakob was preparing himself for a negative comment, when she turned to face him and said, 'It's lovely,' with the smile of an angel, revealing the most perfectly aligned white teeth, framed by plump, protruding red lips.

Jakob smiled back and breathed a sigh of relief. 'Well I'll

let you unpack,' he said as he left the room and closed the door behind him.

Otto and Gary were just standing there waiting for Jakob to explain.

'Gary, I'm sorry, I'm afraid you'll have to stay in the room opposite, it's not quite as nice, but you see, I had a little problem.'

'Jakob, what are you talking about?' Otto asked.

'That woman in there,' Jakob whispered, 'she's no lodger.'

'So who is she then?' Gary asked, genuinely intrigued.

'She's from Berlin,' Jakob hesitated, 'she's a German spy.'

'No!' Gary gasped.

'Oh my God,' Otto clasped a hand over his own mouth.

Suddenly the bedroom door opened and they all recovered their composure instantly.

'Excuse me, Mr Jansen?'

'Oh please, call me Jakob,' he smiled curtly.

She held out her hand and passed Jakob a wad of notes.

'For my room,' she smiled.

'Oh, I can't accept all this.'

'No please,' she closed his hand over the money, 'I insist. Well, I must be off to bed. Goodnight Jakob, Otto, Gary.' She closed her door not taking her eyes off Gary.

'Are you absolutely certain she's German?' Otto asked, smiling.

'Positive,' Jakob replied, stuffing the money in his pocket.

'Well, I've got to say it, she is gorgeous,' Gary blurted out, still staring at the spot where her eyes left his.

'Hey, let's not have any of that sort of talk, Gary,' Otto warned in jest, 'remember, you're British, she's German, so that is a big no-no.'

'Well, I suppose I'd better be off to bed too,' Gary smiled, 'thanks again for the room, goodnight.'

'Goodnight Gary,' Jakob and Otto replied in unison, as Gary made his way into the bedroom opposite to Eva's.

•

June 15, 1940

Jakob was flicking through his notepad on the counter when Gary came in from the back.

'Morning, Jakob,' Gary said brightly as he put his hat on and lowered one side purposely over one eye.

'Gary, how are you this morning? Sleep well?' Jakob noticed he was wearing the same smart brown suit as yesterday, yet his trousers looked as though they'd just this minute been pressed.

'Very well, thanks.'

'No need to ask what you were dreaming about of course,' Jakob chuckled.

Gary smiled and looked at the floor, shaking his head slightly abashed.

'So, what are your plans today, young Gary?' Jakob asked casually as he jotted something down in the notepad.

'Well, actually I thought I'd go and…' Gary paused; his gaze was fixed on the floor between two aisles.

'What is it?' Jakob queried, trying to see what he'd spotted.

Gary walked slowly forward and stopped by the front door. He bent down and picked up what Jakob recognised as an ordinary Guilder note, which Gary seemed to be studying for some time.

'What's the matter, Gary?'

'Jakob, I think this Guilder note is fake.'

'It's what?' Jakob said in surprise.

'What's a forged note doing in your shop?' Gary's eyes were now on Jakob. Jakob couldn't help but wonder for a second if Gary was implying that he'd had something to do with it.

'Well, I have no idea, Gary, but how can you tell it's fake?'

'Well, you see this bit here?' Gary walked over to show Jakob. 'It looks a bit creamy-coloured, doesn't it? Whereas on a genuine one it's white.'

'My God, well in that case, Gary, would you mind checking the till for me? I can't be seen handling forged banknotes.' Jakob opened the till and stepped aside, his brow furrowed over concerned eyes.

Gary checked the contents with the air of an expert in this field.

'No these are all fine, Jakob.'

'Oh thank goodness for that.'

'What about that money Eva gave you last night?'

Jakob's sigh of relief for his till money was short-lived, as he plunged his hand into his pocket and handed the wad of notes over to Gary to inspect.

Gary held them up to the sunlight beaming through the window, each in turn, examining them closely.

'These are all fine too,' he handed the money back to Jakob, who immediately stuffed it back into his pocket with a satisfied grin.

Gary then strolled over to the door.

'Is everything all right?' Jakob called after him.

'Someone is passing around forged notes, it's my job to find out who,' Gary replied and left without another word.

•

Rini and Angelina were having toast for breakfast at the kitchen table.

'So you haven't actually met them yet then?' Rini asked through a mouthful of toast.

'Not yet, no,' Angelina replied, eating a little more politely.

'Well apparently, Gary knows Eva is a German spy, but she thinks Gary is just a Dutch lodger; she's also met Otto,' Rini informed her.

'Yes, but she thinks Otto is a friend who lives nearby, she has no idea about the cellar under the red carpet.' Angelina added.

•

The next moment, Eva came into the shop from the back.

'Eva,' Jakob welcomed her, but he was taken aback by her beauty. She was standing there by the entrance to the hall in black high-heeled shoes, silk stockings, and a tight satin red dress coming down to just above the knee. She had perfectly proportioned facial features, her long blonde curls cascaded down her bare shoulders, and she emitted the most beautifully scented aroma of perfume.

'Jakob,' she smiled at him, once again revealing that Hollywood smile.

'Have you had breakfast yet?' he enquired.

'Well not yet,' she replied a little sheepishly. Jakob had a hard time believing he was talking to a spy who worked for the Third Reich.

'Well please, go into the kitchen and join my wife and assistant, help yourself,' Jakob insisted.

'Thank you,' she replied with a nod and a smile, as she turned to enter the hallway leading to the kitchen, her heels knocking loudly on the parts of the wooden floor that the red carpet did not cover.

•

Gary was sitting alone at a table for two by the window in a cosy little cafe. It was very busy, Dutch men, women and children filled every table. The whole place seemed to be made out of mahogany, the chairs, the tables, even the beams crossing the ceiling.

Gary took out a cigar and a box of matches from inside his beige overcoat. Lighting the cigar, he leaned back in his seat and blew out the smoke; his eyes narrowed and focused on a tall German officer.

His attention was fixed on General Klaus Schneider, who was the centre of attention at a table on the other side of the room, his companions being Captain Fritz Muller, and two ordinary Privates. Gary couldn't hear their discussion, due to the many conversations going on in the room, but he could hear the roar of laughter that was coming from their table.

He noticed the General handing the Captain some notes, the Captain then stood up and made his way over to the till to pay for the drinks, presumably.

Gary picked up his matches, stuffed them back inside his overcoat, stood up and made his way over to the till. Standing behind the Captain, he took a good but inconspicuous look at the money as the Captain handed it over; it appeared genuine. Gary was racking his brains as he was called up next.

•

Eva was now sitting at the kitchen table with Rini and Angelina.

'Right, I'm off to do my shift behind the till, see you both later,' Rini said as she got up from the table and went out to the hallway.

'It was nice talking with you.' Eva smiled.

'Likewise.' Rini looked over her shoulder and raised her eyebrows to Angelina.

'I get the feeling she doesn't really love Jakob,' Eva said while taking a sip of her cup of tea.

Angelina almost choked on her tea as she turned to Eva with surprise.

'Well, I know that, but I thought I was the only one who knew; you pick up on people very well, Eva,' Angelina praised her sincerely.

'Thank you, it has been mentioned,' she smiled back.

'So how did you come to work here?' Eva asked politely.

'Oh, well I already knew Jakob so…' Angelina stopped, she wondered if she'd already said too much. 'Well,' she continued, 'Jakob was a friend of my father's, so he sort of gave me the job as a favour, I suppose,' she lied, rather convincingly she hoped.

'I see,' Eva replied taking a last sip of her tea. 'Well, I must get going, I have an appointment.' Eva put her cup down on the saucer and stood up out of her chair. 'I'll see you later,' she looked back at Angelina, but accidentally bumped into Jakob who had just entered the kitchen.

'Oh! Eva, I'm so sorry,' Jakob responded apologetically; he noticed his hands on her beautiful, slender bare shoulders and removed them at once.

'It's quite all right,' Eva replied and continued on past.

'You can put your tongue away now, Jakob,' said Angelina, rolling her eyes.

'What do you mean?' he asked sitting down in front of her, and immediately started buttering some bread.

'Nothing,' she replied dismissively.

'Is everything all right, my love?' Jakob stopped buttering now and focused on Angelina.

'I'm fine, it's just that…' she hesitated, 'this Eva is a very intelligent woman, Jakob, watch what you say when you're around her.'

Jakob smiled and continued to butter his bread.

'I'm serious; she's already picked up on the fact that Rini isn't in love with you, and may very well have, for all I know, picked up on the fact that I am.'

'Stop worrying, just mind what you say, and everything will be fine,' Jakob reassured her as he took a bite of bread.

•

Gary arrived back at the shop, and with a polite nod to Rini at the counter, made his way upstairs to his room. As he put his key up to the lock, Eva came out of her room;

she noticed Gary and walked up behind him.

'Oh Gary, you dropped this,' she said. She bent down and picked up a Guilder note off the floor. Gary turned around to greet Eva, when he immediately realised she was holding a fake Guilder note.

'Thank you,' he smiled, taking the note, and not giving away what he knew.

'Would you care to join me in my room for a drink at all?' she asked unexpectedly.

Gary felt he should decline, but he couldn't resist getting to know this attractive Fraulein.

'Of course,' he smiled as Eva turned and led the way. He caught the sudden waft of her shampoo as she turned and flicked her hair. Gary watched with pleasure as her slender figure glided to the bedroom door.

'Please sit down,' she said, gesturing to the bottom of the bed. Gary removed his hat and sat down. Eva picked up one of the two small glasses off the chest of drawers next to a bottle of wine.

'Wine?' she asked.

'Please,' he smiled.

She poured him his glass and handed it to him, then poured her own and sat down on the bed beside him. She crossed her silk-stockinged legs, and raised her red satin dress up her thighs.

'So you are Dutch?' she asked casually.

'Well,' Gary hesitated, his brain on overdrive, 'I was born in England, hence my name, but I did grow up in Holland. You?' he returned the question.

'I have grown up in Holland also, I have a Dutch father and German mother, but I was born in Germany.'

'Germany?' Gary tried to sound surprised and impressed at the same time. 'Very nice.'

'Have you been?' she asked, taking a sip of wine and observing him over her glass.

'Yes, once or twice. I remember staying at a hotel in Berlin back in '36,' Gary flat out lied.

'Berlin,' she smiled, staring into space, 'you can't beat Berlin.'

'Is that where you're from, is it?' Gary asked, knowing full well she was.

'Yes, that's where I've lived for most of my life, I do miss Berlin,' she said thoughtfully.

'It's a shame, this war, isn't it?' Gary explained. 'Dragging people miles away from home.'

Eva smiled. 'And you, Gary, do you miss England?'

'Yeah, yes I do,' he sighed, looking at the now-empty glass in his hands. He leaned across Eva to put the glass on the chest of drawers, but she didn't move for him; instead, she just looked at him dead in the eye with a seductive expression on her perfect face. Gary managed to return his glass, but when he sat back again, he didn't sit back quite as far as he had been. She then returned her glass and turned back to face Gary; she also leaned in a little closer.

'Sometimes, I wish this war had never started in the first place,' she said.

'Me too,' Gary replied in a dazed state, absorbed into her ocean-blue eyes.

'Gary, forgive me for asking, but are you currently involved with anyone?' As she said it, her eyes shot down to Gary's legs and rose slowly up to lock onto his eyes.

'No, I'm not, are you?' Gary couldn't hide the hopeful tone in his voice.

'No,' she replied simply and smiled.

Gary smiled back, but it was soon wiped off.

'Gary, did you recognise anything different about the banknote I gave you?' she blurted out.

He was taken aback. 'What? What do you mean?'

'Oh come off it, Gary, you're not that good an actor, you know, don't you?' she said with a naughty smile.

'Is it you who's been passing forged notes?' Gary whispered, leaning in a little closer still.

To Gary's surprise, she nodded. 'Gary, I'm not a lodger.'

Although he knew this, it was still a shock to hear her admit it.

'I know, you're a German spy,' he replied calmly.

'How did you find out?' she asked as if she was asking him to pass the salt.

'I just knew.' Gary didn't know why, but he felt an unusual air of honesty, and he couldn't help but give in to his feelings. 'Eva, I'm not a lodger either,' he confessed.

'I know, you're a British spy,' she said casually, and to Gary's surprise gave a little smile, and leaned in a little closer.

'How did you know?'

'I have many talents,' she whispered, and before they knew where they were, they'd locked lips in a passionate embrace. Gary ran one hand through her soft, long locks, while the other he placed on her firm, smooth exposed thigh, slowly sliding it up and around to a very sexy and prominent hip bone. They broke apart briefly, for Gary just had to ask, 'Why did you tell me that?'

'Because I like you, of course,' she smiled, her hand still

on the back of his head. 'And why did you tell me about you?' she asked.

'Because you tugged on my heartstrings the moment I first laid eyes on you,' he said simply, still caressing her hip and her tiny waist. 'You know by rights I should shoot you,' Gary jested.

'You could never,' she winked and pecked his lips.

'But why the forged notes, Eva?' he asked as if it was painful to say.

'I don't spend them, Gary, the General gave them to me, I have a whole suitcase full, but I never touch them, I knew right away he'd given me forgeries.' She leaned forwards and fetched the suitcase from under her bed. She put it on the bed and opened it up to reveal a smart black briefcase inside, laid on top of her clothes. Eva entered the combination and opened it up, and revealed a stash of Guilder notes, piles of them laid out in neat rows.

'Jesus! There must be thousands here,' said Gary amazed.

'Hundreds of thousands actually,' she corrected him.

'You have to get rid of this,' Gary told her urgently.

'Gary, have you forgotten whose side I'm on? I am committed to the Fuhrer and the Fatherland,' Eva told him quite sternly.

'But Eva, you're on the wrong side,' Gary replied, trying to make her see reason.

'How do you know you're not on the wrong side?' she raised her voice slightly.

'Eva, listen to me,' he told her calmly, as he took hold of her hands and held them gently. 'Hitler, your Fuhrer, he's a very clever man who, over time, has managed to brainwash an entire nation. He has hated Jews all his life just because he had a couple of bad experiences with them. He has been a very patient man, slowly bringing in laws, each one more hostile and racist than the previous. He has been manipulating people into his way of thinking. He did good things at first, yes, but that was just to gain people's trust, and on top of all that, he is a compulsive liar. He said he had no quarrels with Denmark, what happened? He had no quarrels with the Netherlands, what happened? And he was never a gift from God, or even a great man, it was just a question of perfect timing, being in the right place at the right time. Join me, Eva, join the Allies, you'd be absolutely amazing. Just think of it, the General thinks you're spying for the Germans but you're spying for the Allies instead, you'd be the greatest double agent ever,' Gary pleaded with her.

Eva listened to everything he had to say without interruption, and she looked as though she were in deep thought.

'I need time to think about this,' she replied simply, but Gary wasn't convinced.

'Please Eva, I don't want to see you get hurt, and I don't want to see such a beautiful woman have her head turned by a controlling monster. We could survive the war together,' he told her poetically.

Eva studied Gary's eyes for a brief moment, then nodded slowly.

'I'm going out, there's something I have to do,' she said abruptly as she stood up quickly.

'What are you going to do?' he asked.

'I'm getting rid of this,' she replied, closing the briefcase.

'Well, could I come with you?' Gary asked looking up at her like a puppy at feeding time.

'I'd like that,' she smiled down at him.

•

The sun was still beating down on Amsterdam, when Gary, holding the briefcase, and Eva, were walking alongside the canal, Gary struggling to keep up with her.

'We should slow down a bit, we don't want to draw attention,' he told her in hushed tones. She slowed down to walk beside him, putting her arm through his, and laying her head on his shoulder as they strolled alongside the canal in a casual manner.

They eventually reached a relatively secluded area of the canal with fewer people, and the pavement was now replaced by a grassy bank.

'This looks like a good spot,' said Gary as he took a good look around to make sure nobody was looking. He went to step forward when Eva stopped him.

'Wait, I have an idea,' she said, 'the briefcase isn't heavy enough to sink, let's put a couple of these bricks in it to weigh it down,' she suggested, gesturing subtly to some discarded bricks on the bank left by builders.

Gary got down on one knee and placed two of the bricks inside the briefcase, while Eva stayed standing keeping watch.

'It won't close!' Gary whispered urgently.

Eva didn't reply right away, she was watching two people chatting on the other side of the water, but they were not paying her or Gary any attention. She then waited for an elderly gentleman to pass behind her, to whom she gave a friendly smile, and he lifted his hat in return before she replied to Gary.

'It doesn't matter if it closes properly or not, as long as the bricks are inside, they'll sink the briefcase to the bottom along with the money, which are in their own little compartments anyway,' she replied in a low voice but still staring straight ahead across the water.

Gary placed the open briefcase containing the bricks into the water; to his surprise, the moment he let go it shot beneath the surface, leaving behind subtle ripples on the surface.

Gary stood up immediately, his eyes darting about the area; Eva too was observing. It appeared that nobody had seen them make thousands of forged Guilders sink to the bottom of the Prinsengracht canal.

•

Otto was down in the basement talking on the radio, Jakob was standing idly.

'There's an old friend here who wishes to speak to you,' said the voice crackling over the radio, 'I'll put him on.'

'Hello? Is that O?' asked the familiar voice.

'A? Is that you?' Otto asked with excitement.

'Of course it's me.'

'It's Anton,' Otto whispered to Jakob, who clearly already knew this as he was nodding and smiling.

'It's good to hear your voice,' Jakob called.

'It's good to hear the two of you as well, but listen, I can't talk for long, I have something very important to tell you.' Anton left a pause before passing his message. 'Very soon, the boss will be paying a visit next door, should he pass you on the way, do what you can. I'll keep in touch, goodbye for now, my friends.'

'Take care A,' Otto replied and switched off the radio.

'So what does all that mean?' asked Jakob.

'OK, let me think. He said something about the boss visiting our next door neighbour…' Otto was thinking, rubbing his chin.

'And should he pass our way we are to do what we can?' Jakob prompted him.

'Ah yes, so what that roughly translates into is…' Otto cut off and looked as though he'd seen a ghost; the only source of light coming from the candle on the desk emphasised his shocked expression.

'Otto, what is it? What does it mean?

Otto took his time, he looked up at Jakob and spoke slowly.

'"The boss" means Hitler.'

Jakob was now the one who looked like he'd seen a ghost.

Otto continued. 'Our "next door neighbour" means France.'

'And what about "if he should pass our way we must do what we can"?' asked Jakob, still looking worried.

'Assassination!' Otto said gravely.

They just looked at each other, their staggered faces contorted by the candlelight.

•

Gary and Eva were sitting rather cosily on a bench overlooking the canal, and watching the world go by, including cyclists passing by, and ordinary people going about their business. The sun sparkled beautifully on the surface of the water, and the birds were chirping in the trees.

'You did the right thing, you know,' Gary reassured her.

'I know,' she smiled at him and crossed one leg over the other, which didn't go unnoticed by Gary. He looked down at her crossed, perfectly shaped thighs, the stockings thinning out at her small knee as it protruded. Slowly his eyes travelled up to her tiny waist, her smooth, firm cleavage poking out the top of her red satin dress, her dominant collarbone, her swan-like neck, her prominent jawline, her long flowing blonde hair, her ocean-blue eyes. He was captivated.

'I really like you, Eva,' he blurted out, but not without thinking.

Eva just stared at him, examining him as if she were seeing inside his soul. Gary began to wonder if he'd said the wrong thing, he could feel himself being X-rayed by those stunning blue eyes.

'I like you too,' she finally replied, and most sincerely.

'Phew, you had me panicking there,' Gary laughed, a little embarrassed.

She gave him a naughty one-sided smile and leaned in for a kiss, which he gladly returned.

'You do realise that it would actually be in our favour to show ourselves off as a couple,' he told her. 'I mean, nobody would think we're anyone special if they just saw a normal everyday couple.'

'True,' Eva nodded and then paused for thought. 'Too bad Jakob and Angelina can't do the same thing,' she replied as an afterthought.

'What?' Gary said, half surprised, half laughing.

'Oh I know I shouldn't say anything, but as it's you,' Eva turned slightly to face Gary. 'I was talking with Angelina earlier, and she didn't say anything in so many words, but I could just pick up on the fact that they are very fond of each other.'

'Wow, I didn't see that one coming,' said Gary in shock.

'I feel sorry for Jakob though,' said Eva looking out across the water.

'Why?'

'Because his wife doesn't love him, and I don't think he loves her any more either; they've drifted apart without actually drifting apart, if you see what I mean.'

'Yeah I know what you mean, still living together,' Gary clarified.

'Well, well, well, Eva! How is everything going?'

Eva looked up and squinted in the sunlight to see General Klaus Schneider standing in front of them, hands clasped behind his back.

'Oh General, I'm well, thank you,' she smiled pleasantly.

'Enjoying the sunshine I see,' he smiled as he turned to look at the sun briefly before looking back at Eva.

'Yes, it's lovely, isn't it? Oh General, may I introduce Gary Isaac, he's an old school friend.'

'Hello Gary,' the General reached out and shook him by the hand.

'Pleased to meet you, General.' Gary nodded curtly.

'Very unusual name, Gary,' the General smiled.

'Oh, well I was born in England, but I grew up in Holland,' Gary improvised.

'Oh, I see, yes well, you can't beat Holland,' the General

replied looking around, 'well there's always Germany of course,' he laughed, as Gary and Eva joined in politely.

'Right, well, enjoy the rest of your day, see you soon Eva,' the General smiled and continued on strolling along, hands still clasped behind his back.

'If my sources are correct,' Gary said, talking more to himself as he watched the General walking away, 'that's the bastard who shot Anton.'

'Oh, the spy who was here over a month ago,' Eva added.

Gary looked at her surprised.

'I have my sources too,' she smiled.

Gary smiled momentarily but then he had a thought.

'Eva, you don't think he's going to check up on me, do you?'

'No of course not, I spy for him, he trusts me,' she winked at Gary, who, looking relieved up to a point, put his arm around Eva and they leaned back comfortably on the bench and enjoyed the view.

FIVE

HITLER'S COMING

June 23, 1940. Belgium

Jakob, Gary and Otto were out in the middle of the Belgian countryside, accompanied by three unknown members of the Belgian Resistance, the summer sun beating down on them as they assembled their new sniper rifles. The subtle breeze was very welcome; the birds chirped in the trees without a care in the world, unaware of the seriousness of the situation below them. The road on the other side of the hedgerow was the focus of attention.

'So, let's run through the situation,' Otto called out to everyone as they gathered round, brandishing their sniper rifles.

'In approximately fifteen minutes, Hitler, yes, *the* Adolf Hitler, is going to be driven and escorted down this very road. There could be as many with him as there are of us. They are trained marksmen; you will take your positions and brace yourselves.'

Everyone was listening intently; this could mean the end of the war in Europe if everything went according to plan.

'I will be aiming at the primary target from behind that tree,' Otto continued, pointing to the only tree in the field behind them. 'Gary, you're aiming at the driver's head.'

Gary nodded, tightening the grip on his rifle.

'Jakob, now I know you have no previous shooting experience, but I've shown you all I can, so just remember what I said.'

Jakob nodded, looking nervous.

'And finally, to you three gentleman, members of the Belgian Resistance. May I say, on behalf of the Dutch Resistance, and the British,' he acknowledged Gary, 'it is an absolute honour to be working with you on this day, a day that could go down in history. Gentlemen, this could be known as the day when the Belgians, the Dutch and the British joined forces to assassinate Adolf Hitler. Who knows, in years to come this could be known as the nine-month war,' a chorus of laughter echoed around the field.

Another Belgian Resistance member came running over to them from the other end of the field.

'There's an armoured car approaching!' he called out as he bustled over towards them.

'Right, into position everyone!' Otto ordered, who ran directly to his spot behind the tree. He lay flat on his front and aimed through the long grass, through the hedgerow and out to the road. It was a tense moment; everyone was in position, ready and waiting. Suddenly, the sound of a car could be heard, the sound of the engine grew a little louder until they all saw a dark grey armoured car come into view.

Everyone concentrated intently through their lenses. But all of a sudden Otto called out, 'Don't shoot, hold your fire, it's not him.'

They all lowered their guns.

'And a good thing too,' said Gary.

'What?' Otto frowned.

'It was an armoured car, Otto. What use are our guns going to be against an armoured car?' Gary explained.

'Well, I'll be honest, I never expected an armoured car, I only expected him to be surrounded by security,' Otto admitted.

'Well, I thought the same,' Gary replied, 'but if Hitler is in an armoured car, which he probably will be, then there's nothing we can do.'

Otto was in deep thought.

'Well, that's not entirely true,' Otto explained, 'all we have to do is aim at the tyres.' A murmur of agreement broke out.

'That's a damn good idea,' said Jakob, looking eager now.

Gary nodded, and they were all in agreement.

'OK, everyone, back into position,' Otto called out, and they did nothing but wait silently.

An hour had passed and no sign of Hitler.

'It's no good,' said Gary disappointed, 'he's obviously not coming down this road.'

'He has to!' Otto demanded. 'He just has to.'

'Is it possible your contacts could have been… wrong?' Jakob asked carefully.

'Well, I suppose it's possible,' Otto had to admit. 'Oh, we were so close! That could've been the end, do you realise that?' Otto raised his voice in frustration.

Everyone nodded in disappointment.

They all carried their rifles and made their way out to the road. They walked along the roadside for just a short distance, when they came upon a military truck pulled over on the side of the road.

The driver's side window was wound down, with an elbow sticking out resting on the door.

'OK Peter,' said Otto as he walked up to the man in the driver's seat, 'no luck, it's time to go.'

Peter was a member of the Dutch Resistance dressed as an ordinary German soldier. He nodded to Otto with shock and disappointment written all over his face.

Otto, Gary and Jakob said their goodbyes to the three Belgian Resistance members and climbed into the back of the truck. They lay on the floor and pulled multiple large green blankets over themselves, covering themselves completely. Peter, the driver, then got out of the truck, a stout, balding middle-aged man, and made his way round to the back. He climbed into the back to cover the men under the blankets in a mountain of hay; he closed the latch up behind him as he made his way back to the driver's seat again and drove away into the Belgian countryside.

They hadn't quite made it back to the Dutch border when they all felt a sudden jolt and the truck ground to a halt. Peter climbed out and looked around for a reason for the sudden jolt, when he noticed the back tyre was as flat as a pancake. He looked back up the road and saw a large jagged-edged rock in the road. No sooner had he spotted the rock than he heard the thunderous sound of Nazi jackboots stamping on the road. He turned his head and a lead weight dropped into the pit of his stomach: three German soldiers were running towards him from the road ahead. Peter was frantically thinking of a convincing story in his head, but nothing sprang to mind for why he was a German soldier, carrying three men in civvies in the back of his truck.

'Heil Hitler!' called the soldier at the front as they approached.

'Heil Hitler,' Peter replied raising his right hand but not feeling the confidence.

'What seems to be the trouble here?' he asked Peter. Peter could see this particular German had spent a lot of time outside in the Belgian sun, his blue eyes and blonde hair were remarkably enhanced against his heavily tanned skin.

'I've gone and got myself a puncture,' Peter pointed at the flattened tyre.

'Oh don't worry, we'll soon sort that. Gerhart, get the spare tyre out the back,' he told one of the soldiers behind him. 'Von Dannikan, you start taking that one off.'

Peter's heart had jumped into his mouth, as he watched one of the soldiers going round the back where everyone was hiding. The other climbed in the front, and re-emerged holding tools with which to lift the truck and unbolt the wheel. Peter began to take a step backwards, while reaching inside his jacket for his pistol. He had hold of the pistol when, to his relief, the other soldier returned from the back with the spare tyre, Peter took his hand back out of his jacket.

'So where are you heading to?' the German who appeared to take charge asked him.

'Oh, I've just dropped off some ammunition and I'm on my way back to HQ,' Peter invented, his nerves on tenterhooks the whole time.

'Oh I see, well it's easily done in a place like this, not like our own German autobahns, eh?' he elbowed Peter and chuckled. Peter forced a laugh.

'Right, that's all done,' called the soldier who had collected the spare wheel. 'Do you want this put in the back?' he asked Peter, referring to the old wheel.

'No, no I'll have it in the front with me,' Peter replied and took hold of the wheel. 'And thank you very much, gentleman,' he smiled pleasantly.

'No problem,' they replied, 'pleasure,' and they marched on the way they were going.

Peter dumped the wheel on the front seat, then went round the back to check all was OK.

'Is everyone all right?' he peered in the back. There was a sudden movement as Jakob revealed himself from under the hay.

'That was too close for comfort,' he breathed a sigh of relief, 'let's just get home.'

Peter nodded and closed the back up before continuing on the road.

•

It was now dark but they'd finally arrived back in beautiful Amsterdam. Peter could make out the familiar architecture, the tall, slim buildings all lined in rows, the artistic bridges overarching the spotless waters of the canals. They were home.

They pulled up outside Jakob Jansen's Food Shop. Otto, Gary and Jakob climbed down from the back of the truck, where they had a good stretch and shook off all the hay.

Otto went round the front to talk to Peter, while Gary and Jakob made their way down the alley to the side of the shop to go through the back door.

'Thank you for today, Peter,' Otto told him as they shook hands.

'Not a problem. I'd best get this truck back to where it belongs before it's missed,' Peter told him. 'I'll see you soon.' Peter then drove away into the night.

Otto joined Gary and Jakob round the back, and they entered through the back door into the kitchen.

'Where is everyone?' Jakob asked as he switched on the light. The kitchen was exactly as they'd left it, but no sign of life, except for a small crackling noise that seemed to be coming from the shop.

They all made their way slowly and quietly out to the hall, which separated the kitchen from the shop; it also contained the entrance to the cellar, which was concealed under a long red carpet, and behind the long red curtain was the entrance to the stairs leading to the top floor.

As they neared the shop, Jakob realised that someone was tuning into the wireless. They wandered through to the shop to see Angelina and Eva, both leaning on the counter attempting to tune the wireless.

'Jakob!' Angelina called when she spotted him and went straight over and put her arms around him. 'How are you?' she asked.

'All the better for seeing you,' he whispered in her ear, his hands spreadeagled on her back.

Gary and Eva simply smiled at each other; as she slowly walked round to greet him, they mimicked Jakob and Angelina.

'I'm glad you're OK,' Eva told Gary.

Otto gave an intentional cough so that they would give him their attention; they pulled apart and looked at him.

'I'm afraid we have some bad news,' he began. 'The assassination never took place.'

'What?' Angelina looked puzzled.

'Hitler never showed up,' Otto explained.

Suddenly, as if the wireless had more success at tuning itself, an English voice spoke up. 'Well, he didn't stay long, only a few short hours, but earlier this morning, Hitler visited Paris.'

'Wait, what?' Now Otto was confused.

'Shhhhh,' Eva told him as they listened intently.

The Englishman's voice continued. 'He toured about the place, most notably visiting the Eiffel Tower. We can now only assume that he's gone back to his headquarters, currently in Belgium, which is also where—'

Eva unexpectedly switched off the wireless. 'He does a lot of this,' she sighed.

'What are you talking about?' Gary asked, joining her at the counter.

'He'll make sure that the public know he's going to be somewhere, and he'll end up going somewhere else, or he'll take a completely different route. Or he'll make sure that everybody knows he's going to do a speech on a certain date, but a select few know that actually he'll do the speech a day early. It's tactics he uses to avoid assassination attempts, looks like it worked again.' A mixture of shock and disappointment was felt in the room.

SIX

THE GESTAPO ARE COMING

August 15, 1940

Amsterdam was overshadowed by a dark-grey thundery sky. The rain was pouring down hard on Gary as he walked quickly alongside the canal, head down; the rain was falling so hard, he struggled to see in front of him. He continued on with his hat pulled down over his squinting eyes, hands stuffed deep in the pockets of his raincoat.

A little further along, something caught his eye. Looking down towards the bank of the canal he saw a pair of black boots lying on their side, poking out from the side of a boat, which was beached on the bank. He climbed down the nearest stone steps and walked over to the boat. As he continued around the boat, he realised that these boots were attached to the dead body of a German soldier.

'Oh my God,' he whispered in shock, as he stared in disbelief at the soaking wet dead body. Gary got down on one knee and noticed that there was bruising around the neck and throat, and he appeared to have a look of horror instilled on his face, indicating that his last few moments of life were not pleasant. All of a sudden Gary noticed a shadow appear over the body; he quickly turned around to face a man in a black coat and hat, pointing a Luger at him which was being held in a black gloved hand.

'On your feet,' the man told him in a harsh yet calm tone.

Gary slowly rose to his feet with his hands in the air, his heart now pounding in his chest.

'Could you come with me please, sir?' he told Gary. He had a sinister way about him, his expression was hard, his robotic manner was unnerving. He beckoned Gary to walk in front of him, his Luger remaining fixed on Gary.

Gary had been escorted to the Gestapo headquarters, a large building on Euterpestraat 99. The sinister-looking man in the black coat and hat opened the entrance door for Gary, who had no alternative but to enter.

The interior was very posh, thought Gary. There were many corridors all lit dimly, the walls were decorated with works of art in elaborate gold frames. The floors were carpeted in the deepest red.

The sinister stranger escorted Gary along one such corridor, and the man stopped Gary when they came to one particular door, upon which was inscribed the name 'Engelbert Schultz'. The man opened the door and nodded his head at Gary, indicating him to enter.

It was just like any other office, only it was dark and gloomy, lit only by the small lamp standing on the desk, next to which was a nameplate which also read, 'Engelbert Schultz'.

'Sit down there,' the stranger told him, indicating the black leather chair on one side of the desk, while he went round to sit on the other side.

'So,' Engelbert Schultz began in his sinister tone as he placed his Luger on the desk in front of him. 'I caught you in the act, didn't I?'

'What do you mean?' Gary asked defensively, sitting up straight. He could now see the small craters on the man's lower face lit up by the lamp, while his eyes remained in the shadow of his hat.

'The soldier dead on the bank of the canal is a Private Schleirkamp, and you killed him,' replied Schultz.

'I did nothing of the sort, I found him and so I went over to check for a pulse.' Gary told a half-truth, in truth he was merely curious, and knew it was pointless checking for a pulse on a man who was clearly long gone.

'Do you have any evidence to verify your story?' Schultz replied with a tiny curl of his lip.

•

Jakob came dashing into the shop soaked from head to foot, looking alarmed about something. Flashes of lighting were flickering through the windows, as the thunder rumbled overhead. Rini was behind the counter of a currently empty shop.

Jakob dashed over to her and, trying to catch his breath, leaned on the counter, rainwater dripping down his face.

'Rini, I've just seen Gary get taken away at gunpoint!'

'What?' Rini started, but before she could ask him to clarify, he'd dashed off through to the hall.

'I have to let the others know!' he called back to her.

Eva and Angelina were chatting and laughing over a cup of tea in the kitchen, when Jakob came bursting in.

'Eva!' he called.

'Jakob, what is it, what's the matter?' she asked, seeing the horrified look on his face.

'It's Gary, I just saw him moments ago, he was down by the canal when he was taken hostage by a man with a gun.'

'What?!' Eva sprang to her feet, looking glamorous even in a crisis. 'What did this man look like?' she asked as calmly as she could, knowing she was best keeping a cool head if she had any hopes of helping Gary.

'Er, he was all in black, black hat, black coat, even black gloves, and he—'

'Gestapo,' Eva said with confidence. 'I know exactly where their headquarters is,' she said, as she walked out to the hallway to take her black fur coat off the hanger.

'Do you need any help?' Jakob asked frantically, still dripping rainwater all over the kitchen floor.

Eva, noticing the state of Jakob, asked, 'Where's Otto?'

'He's not here, something about resistance work?' Jakob replied, unsure.

'Then I must go alone, don't worry,' she added hastily reading Jakob's concerned expression, 'I have a plan.' And with that she walked out through to the shop.

Jakob turned to Angelina, who had by now stood up from the table, and made her way over to the sink, which she was now standing in front of, facing Jakob. Her hands were behind her as she leaned back on the sink, one knee bent slightly, causing the opposing hip to rise, her head tilted and looking at Jakob with hungry eyes.

'Have you got a spare couple of minutes?' she asked him in a seductive voice, shaking her long brown hair behind her back, revealing a very sexy collarbone out of her partially unbuttoned red satin blouse.

Jakob had suddenly forgotten what he was so worried about. She beckoned him over with a wiggle of her index finger.

He walked over to her and planted his hands on her hips, which were protruding out of her tight black satin skirt. She reached up to put her arms around his neck, and they locked lips in a passionate embrace.

Suddenly, the romantic atmosphere was shattered by the sound of the air-raid siren. Jakob and Angelina moaned and tutted as they broke apart.

•

Eva was getting soaked in the downpour as she picked up the pace, her fur coat resembling a dog who'd taken a swim, her hair sticking to her face. The sound of her high heels marching along the pavement was drowned out by the combination of rain, the air-raid siren, and panic-stricken people, who were dashing about all over the place trying to find shelter from the possible raid. Eva, on the other hand, was calm and focused.

As the rain was beginning to lift, Eva finally made it to the headquarters of the Gestapo. She knocked on the entrance door with confidence, and a moment later, a rather elderly man answered the door; he reminded Eva of a butler.

'Yes, madam?' he asked pleasantly.

'My name is Eva Van Houten, sent here by General Klaus Schneider, he wants me to question the prisoner known as Gary,' she told him with an air of authority.

'Madam, I don't know if you've noticed, but there's an air raid on, come inside for goodness' sake, you look absolutely drenched,' he moved aside as Eva stepped in.

Once inside, they heard the drone of planes going overhead.

'This way, madam, please, it'll lead you straight to the shelter,' said the old man kindly, as he guided her along a corridor. They walked quickly along the corridors, taking left and right turns. Eva knew she had to get to the shelter, but she kept her eyes peeled for any sign of Gary on the way. Maybe he was down in the shelter, she thought, but no, what was she thinking? Of course they wouldn't allow that, not unless they thought he had vital information to give them, and how could they possibly know he's a spy? Eva's brain was doing overtime.

The planes kept coming, there was no mistaking their engines for the thunder.

'Down these steps, miss.' the old man told her. 'The shelter is just down here.'

Out of nowhere there was an almighty blast, and Eva felt herself being propelled backwards through the air before she felt her back slam against something hard. Eva, now in tremendous pain, felt a strong breeze on her face. As she squinted around, she realised that an entire wall next to where they'd been standing had been blown away; the street was clearly visible from indoors. Although the street could now be seen from where she lay on the red-carpeted corridor floor, Eva couldn't hear a thing. She looked up and what she saw through her dusty eyelashes almost appeared to take place in slow motion, as her brain tried to make sense of this unexpected surprise. She saw a small, frightened boy kneeling on the pavement, calling for his mother, tears streaming down his face. Eva then noticed he had blood on his hands, and upon further inspection, noticed the blood was from his dead mother lying beside him. Eva, hard as she tried, was struggling to keep her eyes open; she felt cold, weak and tired, she just wanted to go to sleep.

•

After what felt like a well-deserved sleep, Eva opened her eyes, but the scenery had changed. She had just been looking around at rubble, piles of bricks and debris, now she was seeing a large white room full of beds and other injured people. It didn't take her long to realise she was now in hospital. Covered from head to foot in dust, she felt the need for a bath more than she did treatment.

Her face soon broke into a smile, when she rolled her head to her left and saw a pleasant familiar face looking back at her, although he was also covered in dust.

'How are you, sweetheart?' said Gary, sincere concern on his face, as he leaned forward in his chair beside her bed.

'I think I'm OK,' she replied, her voice a little hoarse from lack of use. 'How did you know I was here?' she asked him.

'When I managed to make it to my feet after the blast, I used the telephone, which was surprisingly still connected, to call Otto. That's when I saw them loading a woman into the ambulance; when I noticed it was you, I was stunned. Why were you there, Eva?'

'When Jakob came home during the storm, he told me he'd seen you get taken away at gunpoint, by a man dressed all in black. I knew exactly where to go.'

Gary reached out and held her hand.

'I didn't think we were ever going to have a proper air raid in Amsterdam, or indeed anywhere in Holland?' she said, a little confused.

'Yes, it's a little strange, but I overheard the authorities talking about it, apparently, for some reason they want it hushed up, it was only one bomb, so apparently it's not going to be talked about in any newspaper or on the wireless or anywhere,' Gary explained.

'So that's one air raid that won't make the history books then,' Eva rolled her eyes. 'So where is the Gestapo officer now?' she asked.

'At this very moment he is in the hands of Otto and the Dutch Resistance,' Gary replied, looking pleased with himself.

•

The Gestapo officer, Engelbert Schultz, felt strangely restricted as he awoke in a darkened room. Three unfamiliar men were staring at him. He suddenly realised that he was sitting in a chair with his hands tied behind his back; he struggled to free himself but to no avail.

'It's no use, Schultz,' said Otto calmly. 'Now, you are going to tell us why you planned to frame that gentleman for the death of the German soldier?'

'Ha! Never,' Schultz replied rebelliously. Now he was no longer wearing his hat, the craters and scars could be seen clearly all over his face.

'Well, it's your choice,' Otto replied as he pulled out a gun from his inside pocket, and pointed it at Schultz's head, who suddenly began to look anxious.

'Who are you people?' Schultz demanded angrily.

'Dutch Resistance,' Otto replied simply, 'and if we don't get the answers we're looking for, we can get quite nasty about it, so you are going to tell us who killed the German soldier, and why you tried to frame an innocent Dutch civilian?'

Schultz looked around at the three Resistance members, his brain on overdrive.

'You won't get away with this,' he cracked a sinister smile.

'Oh I think you'll find we will, you see, if you don't start talking I will shoot you.'

'The other Germans will come looking for me, then you'll be in for it,' Schultz replied with a smirk.

'Nope, wrong again, my slippery friend, you see as far as the rest of the town is concerned, you were killed two hours ago in an air raid, so if I were you I'd start talking,' Otto ordered.

Schultz, looking around and realising there was no alternative, reluctantly complied.

'That German soldier you speak of down by the canal, he wasn't even German, he was Dutch, a Dutch collaborator who spied for us. His codename was Private Schleirkamp. He messed up a secret mission really badly; I spoke with him, we had words which led to a fight; before I knew it, he was dead. Luckily nobody saw me, so I waited around a corner, and waited there for somebody to discover him. And along came this man, I thought I'd hit the jackpot, then that damn air raid ruined everything. Those damned Allies!' he cursed. 'And what do the Dutch Resistance propose to do about it?' he smirked.

'Shoot you,' replied another Resistance member, raising his gun.

'But… but I've just told you everything, at great personal risk,' he pleaded, attempting in vain to wriggle himself free.

'With innocent Dutch, Jews, Poles, French, British, and God knows who else being slaughtered every day, who in their right mind is going to miss a single German?' Otto replied coldly.

BANG!!! A single shot rang out, and the Gestapo officer slumped in his chair. But it was not Otto's gun that had fired. Otto looked behind him at one of his fellow Resistance members holding a smoking gun. Otto looked at him with a 'How could you do that?' sort of a look, and as he looked back at Schultz, he couldn't help but feel a twinge of guilt building in his stomach.

'Hey, come on, Otto,' said the man who'd shot him, 'you know very well, if it wasn't him it would've been us eventually, you know he would've sought revenge. Not to mention the fact that he was trying to frame this Gary for a murder he didn't commit.'

Otto nodded. 'Yes I suppose you're right, bloody war!' he cursed. 'I never wanted to be a monster like them.'

'Well, now a true monster has been slain,' the man replied consolingly.

SEVEN

REVENGE

August 17, 1940

Jakob, Otto and Gary were down in the dark, candlelit cellar, listening to a German radio station on the wireless. Jakob was sitting on a stack of tins, Otto and Gary were in chairs leaning towards the wireless on the desk.

'... and as he makes himself comfortable in the city of Amsterdam, he warns the Dutch public that there will be trouble if the killer of his brother, and fellow Gestapo officer, Engelbert Schultz, does not come forward. As the police found no body, he is adamant that somebody took and killed his brother, probably for information, and probably, he says, the Dutch Resistance. So if you're listening, come forward, your life may be spared.' Jakob stood up and switched off the wireless.

'I thought you said nobody would find out?' asked Jakob, looking concerned.

'How was I supposed to know he had a brother?' Otto replied defensively.

'This is your mess, Otto, I don't want any trouble brought to my door,' Jakob told him.

'Well, we did agree to these kinds of situations, before the Germans even marched into Holland, we all agreed we'd use your cellar under your shop as a base.'

'Yes, well, more fool me,' Jakob replied heatedly.

'Hold on,' Gary cut in, 'I think I may have a plan.'

Jakob and Otto looked at each other.

'Go on,' Otto prompted him.

'What if Eva goes to see the Gestapo at their new headquarters, and tells his brother that he was shot by a British agent called Anton; this way they will find out that Anton has gone to England, which means there's nothing they can do about it, and will hopefully say no more about it?'

Otto and Jakob looked impressed.

'This could work,' Otto replied enthusiastically, leaning forward in his seat. 'Where is Eva now?'

'She's in the kitchen, I'll go and tell her the plan,' Gary said as he got up and made for the stairs.

'If she can pull this off, she will make me a very happy man!' Otto called after him.

'I'm gonna be the one she'll make happy, when she says "yes"!' Gary called back.

'Oooooooo,' Jakob and Otto teased.

•

Eva was sitting at the kitchen table with Angelina, chatting away and sipping on their tea. Eva looked surprisingly radiant considering her ordeal less than forty-eight hours previously. Her red lips glistened as she smiled, in turn creating the sweetest dimples. Her wavy blonde hair shimmered with health with each turn of her head.

'Eva,' Gary called as he made his way into the kitchen, 'we have a situation and we need your help,' he told her seriously. Eva was listening intently.

•

Eva was walking along the streets of Amsterdam in the brilliant sunshine, her long, black high-heeled boots echoing as she strutted along, the motion of her hips in her tight black dress resembling a cat-walk model. Her long blonde locks hung up high, revealing her elegant, sun-kissed neck.

She finally approached the new Gestapo headquarters, a modern multistorey building, and she knocked on the door. A middle-aged, good-looking man answered the door, average height and build, wearing a smart black suit, and his hair greased back with a side parting. He looked at Eva like an eagle would look at its prey.

'Hello, my name is Eva, I work for German intelligence.' She held out her dainty black-lace-gloved hand. He took her hand and raised it to his lips. He kissed it gently while maintaining eye contact.

'The pleasure is all mine,' he replied smoothly, 'and I'm Officer Schultz, but you can call me Dolph,' he finally released her hand.

'I know who you are, Mr Schultz. May I come in to speak with you?' Eva replied bluntly.

He stood aside, giving her barely enough room to step past. He watched her pass with hungry eyes and breathed in her seductive perfume. He closed the front door, then rested his hand on the small of her back to gesture her into his office. It was a small room but the sunlight beaming through the window was most inviting.

'Please, take a seat,' he gestured to the black leather chair on one side of the desk.

'Cigarette?' He offered an open packet to her.

'Thank you.' She took one and put it to her soft red lips. He walked back round the desk and pulled a lighter from his trouser pocket. She leaned in and he lit it for her; there was constant eye contact throughout.

Schultz went back and sat on the other side of his desk. He leaned back comfortably in his chair and watched her intently as she put the cigarette to her rose-coloured lips, crossed her smooth, pale bare legs in her short, tight black dress, removed the cigarette and blew out a cloud of smoke.

'So, tell me Eva, what is the nature of your visit?' he asked, surveying her through narrowed eyes.

'I know who killed your brother,' she blurted out.

His whole face changed in an instant. He leaned forward on his desk. 'I'm all ears,' he told her.

'His name is Anton, he's a Dutch Spy. He attempted to assassinate the General by cyanide poisoning back in May of this year. The General put up posters all around the city with a reward for his capture, but to no avail. The last we heard, he escaped to live in England.' She drew another breath of her cigarette.

'Anton,' he mumbled to himself.

Eva could already see a plan formulating in his mind.

'Here's what I want you to do,' he told her. 'I want you to go to England…' Eva held her breath, 'and I want you to find this Anton, and charm him, worm your way into his confidence, and persuade him to come back with you, not here to Amsterdam, of course, he wouldn't be that stupid, but at least to Holland.'

Eva detected a trait of psychopathy in this Gestapo officer.

'I'm sorry to disappoint you, Mr Schultz, but I work for General Klaus Schneider, and the Gestapo have no jurisdiction over the German army,' she said confidently, but any confidence she felt by using the General's name had just abandoned her.

Schultz did not look happy with her disobedient response. He stood up out of his chair and made his way around to her side of the desk. He took her cigarette out of her hand and stubbed it out in the ashtray on the desk. He then leaned over her, placing each of his hands on the arms of her chair. He stood nose to nose with her, his legs either side of hers, her legs still crossed. While he had the pleasure of the scent of her hair, she had the pleasure of his rotten breath.

'If you don't obey me, Eva, I will make life very difficult for you, do you understand me?' he told her in a low and deadly voice. She reluctantly nodded while keeping her composure.

'Good,' he smiled, then stood up straight, and made his way back to his seat.

Eva also got to her feet. 'Good day, Mr Schultz,' she said coldly and showed herself out.

Schultz picked up the cigarette he'd just stubbed out and studied it closely; he noticed the faded red lipstick on the end. 'Eva,' he whispered to himself with a sadistic grin.

•

When Eva arrived back at the shop, she noticed Jakob in her peripheral vision at the till.

'Eva, how did it go?' he asked

But to his surprise she just continued on to the hallway, shaking her head. There were unmistakably tears in her eyes. She continued through to the kitchen.

'Oh Gary,' she cried and flung her arms around him the moment he turned to face her.

'Eva! What's the matter, sweetheart? I've never seen you like this before,' Gary asked as Otto and Angelina looked on with concern from the table. Eva pulled away and dabbed her eyes with a single finger, careful not to smudge her make-up.

'He said to me that he wants me to go to England—'

'What?' they all replied in unison.

'And he wants me to bring Anton back.'

Otto stood up from his seat in shock.

'And if I don't, he says he's going to make life difficult for me,' she said, her eyes welling up again.

'OK, come and sit down.' Gary pulled out a chair for her, Otto kindly handed her a tissue as she sat down, and Angelina came over and put her arm around her.

'This is just going to take a bit of working out, that's all,' said Gary as he paced the kitchen floor deep in thought. 'So, he wants you to go to England, and bring Anton back?'

Eva nodded, though Gary didn't see her; he was hyper focused.

After a brief pause, Gary clicked his fingers. 'I've got

it!' he exclaimed as he knelt down in front of Eva, her eyes still red from crying. 'Here's what we do: lie low for a couple of days, then go back to the Gestapo officer, tell him that during your absence you'd been to England, and while you were there, you learned that Anton was killed in an air raid.'

'Do you think that'll work?' she asked, sniffling.

'It's certainly worth a try,' Otto encouraged. 'Do as Gary says, lie low, and in a couple of days we'll put this plan into action.'

•

August 19, 1940

Once again, Eva was knocking on the door of the new Gestapo headquarters, and just like last time, it was Schultz who answered the door.

'Eva,' he said with a smile, 'how nice to see you back so soon.' He stood aside to admit her. 'So how was England?'

'Awful weather,' she replied blankly. Schultz didn't say anything, he just guided her to his office.

'So,' said Schultz, as they both sat down at his desk, 'where is this Anton?'

'Dead,' she replied bluntly. Schultz was taken aback.

'Dead?' He was genuinely surprised.

'He was killed working at a factory during an air raid, he was fixing the roof when it was hit with an incendiary bomb,' she explained.

'Wow, just like that, eh?' his eyebrows raised. 'Where did you learn this?' he asked sceptically.

'In England, of course.'

'Yes, but who informed you?'

Eva thought for a moment, 'The authorities,' she invented. 'With false identification papers, I passed myself off as a reporter, and they gave me all the necessary details, they told me where he was working, what he was doing, how it all happened, everything.'

'Well, I suppose that concludes our business,' he replied, looking a little disappointed.

Eva went to stand up when Schultz added, 'Oh, there is just one more thing.'

Eva stayed where she was, held in suspense.

'Are you currently involved with anyone?' he asked in an almost business-like manner.

This took Eva by surprise, but her reply was honest, 'Yes I am.'

'Oh, fine, well I should have guessed, a beautiful woman like you,' his smile was beginning to sicken her. 'So, who is he? A soldier? A fighting man?' he asked as he began to light a cigar.

'He's a Dutchman,' Eva replied.

'A Dutchmen?' he raised his eyebrows as he released a cloud of smoke. 'And are you happy?'

'Yes,' she replied simply.

'Well then, that's all that matters.' He smiled and stood up. 'Thank you, Eva, let me get the door.' He opened the door, and as she passed he added, 'He's a very lucky man.'

Eva smiled awkwardly and walked out.

•

Back at the shop, the General was being served by Angelina.

'So Angelina, tell me, are you currently involved with anyone?' he asked with a smirk.

'Yes,' she replied simply, not looking very impressed.

'That's a shame,' he replied, picking up his favourite brand of bottled water from the counter, 'do I know him?'

'No, he's just an ordinary Dutchman,' said Angelina looking bored.

'Lucky man,' he smiled and started towards the shop door. As he opened it, Eva came inside.

'Eva! How are you?' he asked, smiling at her.

'General! I'm fine thank you,' she smiled, attending her hair.

'Good, you're looking particularly lovely today.'

Angelina rolled her eyes at this; Eva spotted her but didn't give her away.

'Well, things are going well for me,' she told him.

'Good, good. Eva, I've been thinking, you should come to my quarters and join me for a drink some time.' The General looked hopeful.

Eva was caught off guard. 'Oh, well, if I can find some time in my busy schedule then sure,' she nodded with a smile.

'Excellent, I'll be seeing you,' he nodded to her and exited the shop.

Eva breathed a sigh of relief while rolling her eyes and walking over to Angelina.

'What is it with some men? They just can't help themselves, can they?' Angelina said as Eva came over.

'Oh tell me about it,' she replied as she rested her elbows on the counter.

'So how did it go?' Angelina asked.

'We're in the clear, it's all sorted, life can finally go back to normal,' said Eva.

Angelina breathed a sigh of relief.

'I'll go in the kitchen and get some glasses,' Eva said as she walked around the counter and out the back, 'I think this is cause for celebration.'

'Make mine a double,' Angelina called after her.

EIGHT

BIRTHDAY WITH A BANG

September 3, 1940

Gary rubbed his tired eyes as he made his way downstairs in his cream-coloured dressing gown. He thought he heard several people say 'Shhh' as he neared the kitchen.

'Happy birthday!' they all cheered as he entered, suddenly forming a childish grin on his face. Eva was the first to say good morning, as she planted a kiss on his lips and handed him his present.

'Happy birthday darling,' she smiled.

Gary began to unwrap the little red package with a permanent smile etched on his face. He found himself confronted with a small black velvet box. Opening it, he was blinded by a shimmering gold wrist chain.

'Oh Eva, this must've cost you a fortune,' he said in a high voice of surprise as he took it out and admired it.

'Well I can promise you the notes were not forged,' Eva smiled, causing the room to erupt with laughter.

'Turn it over,' she told him, and as he did so, he saw three words expertly engraved on one side: 'I love you, Eva.'

'Oh Eva, I love you too.' They pecked each other's lips again.

'Here, hold out your arm,' she told him, and she put it around his wrist; it was a perfect fit.

'Happy birthday, Gary, this is from myself and Rini.' Jakob came over smiling, handing Gary a large, rectangular brown package, which Gary took, half smiling half frowning. He unwrapped the brown packaging to reveal a large book entitled, *How to Cook The Dutch Way.*

Gary's grin broadened as he came to a realisation. 'This is because I burned those sausages the other night, isn't it?'

'Yeah,' Jakob agreed chuckling along with the others.

'Thanks, Jakob, Rini,' he nodded to her.

'This one is from me,' Otto handed Gary a small box; it wasn't wrapped but was similar to the little black box Eva had handed him. Gary put the book down on the table and took the box from Otto. Opening it up, his face dropped, but not in a disappointed way, more of an 'I don't deserve this' sort of a way. He pulled out a long piece of purple ribbon; hanging from the ribbon in front of everyone's eyes was a large gold medal in the shape of a cross. Gary stared at it open-mouthed.

'It's the medal for bravery in the Dutch Resistance,' Otto explained.

'But… but I haven't done anything brave,' Gary replied in awe, still examining the medal.

'Haven't done anything brave?' Otto said incredulously. 'You come over here willingly into Nazi-occupied territory? Get taken hostage by a Gestapo officer? Survive being bombed by the RAF in a raid very few people will ever know about… and then there's what's happening tonight,' Otto added delicately.

'Tonight?' Gary asked distracted.

'Yes, you see, today also happens to be the birthday of General Klaus Schneider, he's holding a gathering tonight in the Great Hall at his headquarters, and I will need you two gentlemen to help me with a little job.' Otto eyed both Gary and Jakob.

'Well, thank you for this, Otto, you can now consider me ready and willing,' Gary replied, to Otto's delight.

'Well, I'd better open shop,' Rini said and made her way out to the hallway.

'What is that lovely smell?' Gary asked, now distracted from the medal as he stepped out of Rini's way.

'Oh, that's my present to you,' said Angelina, 'I'm making you a birthday cake,' she smiled.

'Oh, that's really sweet of you, I look forward to making a start on that, it smells delicious.'

'Well, you won't have long to wait, I've been working on it over an hour,' she explained while opening the oven and examining her work.

'Eva,' Rini called from the kitchen doorway, 'it's the General, he wants to see you.'

Eva felt a mixture of intrigue and confusion as she made her way out to the shop.

'Eva!' the General smiled, his six-foot-four-inch frame unmissable among the aisles.

'General Schneider, happy birthday,' she smiled back as she made her way over to him. He lowered his head subtly as she kissed his cheek.

'Thank you, now listen, Eva, tonight I'm having a little gathering in the Great Hall at my headquarters, just a few friends and colleagues. I would be most honoured if you would be my companion for the evening?'

Eva automatically thought about what Otto had just said, about them having a job to do at the General's headquarters; she hesitated for a moment before accepting.

'Of course, General, it would be my pleasure,' she smiled.

'Excellent, I will meet you at the door at eight o'clock tonight,' he smiled.

She smiled back as he left the shop with a tinkle of the bell.

Eva's smile soon left her face as she turned round and marched back out to the kitchen.

Before she could say anything to them, Otto beat her to it.

'It's OK, Eva, we heard the whole thing, now here's the plan for tonight, gather round everyone,' and they huddled around the kitchen table, except for Angelina, who was attending to Gary's birthday cake.

•

Eva was walking up to the doors of the General's headquarters. The lights from the inside shone brightly in the darkness of the night and the therapeutic sound of classical music travelled on the warm evening air. The General saw Eva through one of the large windows, making her way towards the building. He sprang up from his seat and opened the main doors to admit her inside. He stared in awe as he watched this goddess of a woman making her way across the road towards him. She glided along in a long red figure-hugging satin dress, a long split all up the side, revealing her long, slim, pale bare legs. She wore a stunning large necklace that covered almost all of her bare chest; her long golden locks were tied up high, with loose curls hanging down by her ears, and her piercing blue eyes were beautifully enhanced by a black frame of eyeliner.

'Good evening, General.' She smiled at him as she entered.

'Eva, you look absolutely enchanting, shall we?' he offered her his arm, which she took, and they made their way inside the hall.

The Great Hall was filled with guests, lots of uniforms, bow ties, and evening gowns everywhere Eva glanced. There were couples dancing in the centre, chairs and tables around the outside, mostly occupied, a small orchestra in one corner, and a large drinks bar in the other. The ceiling was at least thirty foot high, and the upstairs could be seen from downstairs. Eva looked up and saw a select few people upstairs overlooking the railing to those downstairs, and the wide, elaborate stairs rose from the very centre of the hall, adorned by two twenty-foot-high scarlet Swastika flags either side.

Meanwhile, around the other side of the building, Jakob, Gary and Otto were now dressed as fire fighters, sitting in a fire engine which was reversed down a dark narrow street, facing the back end of the German headquarters.

'OK, Jakob, you know what to do,' Otto said in a low voice. Jakob nodded, opened the door and climbed down from the fire engine. Gary and Otto watched as Jakob, barely visible in the pitch darkness other than his white hat, jogged to the end of the narrow road, and peered around the corner. He saw that the coast was clear, all the civilians were indoors, and all the Germans were at the party. He beckoned Otto and Gary over.

They too climbed down from the fire engine, and they unhinged the long ladder from the side, trying to make as little noise as possible. Carrying it together, one at either end, they jogged over to meet Jakob at the back of the headquarters, and the three of them steadily lined the ladder up outside one particular window, and luckily, being a muggy night, all the windows were open.

'Are you sure this is the right window?' Jakob double-checked.

'Just trust me, now keep watch, we are on limited time, remember,' Otto told him as Otto began to ascend the ladder, followed closely by Gary. Jakob footed the ladder and kept his eyes peeled.

Once inside, Otto found himself in a darkened bedroom, with just enough light from the street light to make out a bed to his right, a wardrobe to his left, and the bedroom door straight ahead. Gary climbed in behind him.

'Have you got the string?' Otto whispered.

'Yeah,' Gary pulled a long piece of string from his pocket, while Otto, with great care, pulled from his pocket a grenade. Gary looked at it with apprehension.

'Right, now tie one end of the string to the door handle,' Otto instructed. While Gary did this, Otto attempted to lift the wardrobe. 'Could you give me a hand when you've done that?'

'One second,' Gary replied as he finished tying a knot.

Gary assisted Otto to lift the wardrobe just enough for Otto to place the grenade underneath it to hold it in place, while the wardrobe leaned back on the wall. Gary then tied the other end of the same piece of string as carefully as he could, to the little hook on the grenade.

'For God's sake, be careful,' Otto exclaimed.

'What do you think I'm being?' retorted Gary, beads of sweat appearing on his forehead. Once done, he stood up slowly to admire his handiwork with Otto, whose narrowed eyes were following the piece of string from the door handle to the grenade.

'That'll do it, now let's get out of here.' Otto began to climb back through the window, followed by Gary.

•

Eva and the General were walking arm in arm, greeting various people they passed.

'Colonel!' the General called, reaching his hand out to a short, plump, balding middle-aged man.

'Ah, and a happy birthday to you, General,' said the Colonel shaking his hand, but his eyes kept darting to Eva, and her revealing dress.

'Thank you, and may I introduce a very close friend of mine, Eva Van Houten.'

Eva smiled and offered her hand. 'It's a pleasure to meet you, Colonel.'

He took her red-nail-varnished hand and put it to his lips.

'The pleasure is all mine,' he smiled.

'Help yourself to another,' the General referred to his

almost empty glass, 'and enjoy the rest of the evening,' the Colonel smiled at them as they continued on to greet more guests.

•

Jakob, Otto and Gary were back in the fire engine, all looking up at the centre window with apprehension.

'Just a matter of time now,' explained Otto.

'Do you think I've earned that medal yet?' Gary asked, smiling.

'You've more than earned it,' Otto told him seriously.

Rain began to lightly touch the windscreen, slowly at first, and then faster and faster, until it was almost impossible to see the window that they were keeping an eye on.

'Well, at least this'll help put any flames out,' Jakob joked, raising his voice above the pounding rain.

'Whoever opens that door,' Otto paused, 'well there's going to be a big explosion.'

'Well, I just hope and pray it's not Eva who opens the door; I mean, what if she goes to his bedroom with him?' said Gary concerned.

'Gary, I've already told you, Eva already knows about it, so she's going to be very careful not to go near that room. The only ones who'll go near it are the General himself, or whoever he asks to go in there. I just hope it's the General himself.' The rain continued to lash the windows of the fire engine. The street light was the only source of light they had to just about make out the General's bedroom window.

•

Eva and the General were sitting at a table full of the General's friends and acquaintances. The General broke away from them and leaned over to Eva, who was sitting very quietly.

'Are you OK? You're very quiet,' he asked, leaning close.

'Oh yes, I'm fine, honestly,' she smiled and raised her glass to her lips.

The General smiled at her, his eyes glazed due to the drink.

'You know, I can't express how gorgeous you're looking tonight,' he said.

Eva smiled and looked at the floor looking bashful.

The General's eyes swept over her like a searchlight across the sky. He began at her tiny, pale narrow feet in her black, open-toed high heels, his eyes then focused on her long crossed legs, teasingly exposed by the open slit in her dress. He then continued on up to where her red satin gown revealed a very smooth-looking and very full cleavage, above which her elaborate necklace was hung around a long, kissable neck. He then met her eyes, her sensual deep blue eyes.

Without another word, and to Eva's complete surprise, the General's lips were on her neck. She didn't know which way to turn, she just froze, she knew that if she showed the slightest sign of disinterest, she could be in trouble. He was slow and deliberate; her bare chest began to rise and fall a little more clearly as she tried to control her breathing. The scent of her perfume behind her ear was enticing him more. Suddenly, to her relief, he stopped. He turned to say something to Captain Fritz Muller, but Eva couldn't make out what, all she saw was the Captain look past the General at her and smile before nodding and standing up.

The General turned back to Eva. 'I've just told the Captain to go and check my room is in order; when he comes back, I'll show you upstairs.'

He leaned in again and planted his lips on her soft warm neck, this time, putting his rather large hand on her long slim thigh. Her thigh was cold but his hand was hot. He started at her little knee, and slid his hand up slowly, inch by inch, until Eva abruptly got to her feet, this time taking the General by surprise.

'Sorry,' she replied smiling, 'I just realised, I need another drink,' she showed him her empty glass.

'Oh of course, here,' he replied, and he took out several Guilder notes from the inside pocket of his field-grey uniform.

'Thank you,' she replied, taking them, and as she made her way over to the bar, she could just feel the General's eyes upon her back.

The Captain reached the top of the elegant stairs with the golden bannisters, centred between the two Swastika flags, and made his way along the corridor, the one visible from downstairs. He appeared to be looking for a particular door. When he had passed several, he stopped at one particular door and opened it. It was the bathroom; he entered.

Eva was waiting at the bar for her drink. She knew what was coming; whoever opened that door was going to get blown away. She felt her heart beating in her chest as she tried to keep her composure. She glanced around the room nervously and caught the General's eye; he nodded and raised his glass to her.

The Captain exited the bathroom, the sound of the chain audible for a second with the opening and closing of the door. He continued on down another corridor passing several doors. Once again, he was looking for a particular door.

The barman placed Eva's drink down on the bar in front of her with a smile, as she passed him the money and waited for her change.

The Captain stopped outside the next door he came to, he put his hand on the handle and he turned it... BOOM!!!

•

Jakob, Otto and Gary witnessed the explosion from the safety of the fire engine. The glass from the bedroom window flew across the street, as the room momentarily lit up.

•

Eva threw her hands over her ears and ducked down by the bar; the sound of the explosion was immense and thick black smoke came billowing into the hall from upstairs.

The whole atmosphere in the Great Hall changed drastically, the therapeutic classical music was instantly replaced by screams of panic.

Eva watched many of the guests running for the exit, while a select few soldiers began running up the stairs, with their Lugers and MP40s at the ready.

'*I demand to know what's going on!*' the General yelled after the soldiers.

While the General was distracted, Eva took a chance and made for the exit with everyone else.

•

'My stomach wasn't half doing turns when I tied the string to that grenade,' said Gary, perched in the front seat between Jakob and Otto. 'I thought I was going to bring up my birthday cake Angelina had made me, delicious though it was,' he added.

'Well, there's no fire,' said Jakob as they all peered through the windscreen to the top window, which was now windowless.

The street light revealed black scorch marks around the outside of the window frame.

'This fire engine wasn't just in case there was a fire, this was our cover story in case we were spotted with the ladder,' Otto explained.

'Well, there's no reason to stay, so let's get this fire engine back to the depot, and go home,' said Jakob.

Otto started up the engine, which sounded strangely loud in the dead of night, and slowly pulled away.

•

Eva managed to make it back to the shop unscathed. She opened the front door, which now said 'Closed', but as they were expecting her back soon it was left unlocked.

She looked very out of place now, dressed up like a goddess in the middle of a local food shop.

She made her way through the dark aisles, out through the back and into the kitchen where Angelina and Rini were sitting. They both turned in their seats to see Eva come through, Rini looking at her with slightly jealous eyes, Angelina looking at her with admiration.

How did it go?' asked Angelina enthusiastically.

'Oh, what an eventful evening.' Eva pulled up a chair beside Angelina. 'So I'm sitting there at the party, and from out of nowhere the General tries it on.'

Both Rini's and Angelina's jaws drop.

'He's kissing my neck, he's touching my leg, and next minute there's an almighty explosion from upstairs, I then knew that our boys had planted the grenade successfully.'

'So the General is still alive?' Angelina exclaimed.

'The General is yes, but the Captain wasn't so lucky.'

'The Captain? said Rini, shocked.

'The General sent him upstairs to check his room, he must've opened the door and that was it,' Eva explained.

Angelina put her hands to her mouth.

'Well at least that's the Captain gotten rid of,' said Rini quite heartlessly.

'So where are Jakob and everyone now?' Angelina asked.

'Right about now, they should be taking the fire engine back to the depot,' explained Eva.

•

September 4, 1940

The General was fast asleep in his chair behind his desk, still in uniform, his huge feet upon the desk, and a blanket pulled over him. A gleam of early morning sunshine streaked across his chest from the tiny gap in the curtains.

He was awoken by a knock at the door. He slowly opened his sleep-deprived eyes, and took a few seconds to realise where he was, and what major event last night led to his present situation.

There was a second knock.

'Come in,' he called, not sounding at all like himself. He dumped the blanket on the floor beside him, and took his feet off the desk, just in time to see a shifty-looking man dressed in black enter.

'General Schneider,' he said robotically as he approached the General's desk. 'I am Herr Schultz of the Gestapo,' he offered his black leather-gloved hand. The General got to his feet and shook his hand.

'Good morning, Herr Schultz.'

'I have taken a good look around the scene, I can quite confidently say that this was the work of the Dutch Resistance,' Schultz told him with a subtle smirk. 'You should count your lucky stars, General, that explosion was meant for you.'

The General had already figured this out, but there was still something he couldn't understand.

'But how could they possibly have known that was my room?' he asked.

'That wouldn't have taken much figuring out with the right information; leave it to us, General, I'll be in touch.' Schultz turned to leave, he got to the door, turned back and raised his gloved hand. 'Heil Hitler.'

'Heil Hitler,' the General replied with a sceptical look as he watched the eccentric Gestapo officer leave. He sat back down in his chair, and placing his elbows on the desk, and his chin on his clasped hands, he began to think. He then picked up the receiver of his telephone, and began to dial… 'Hello, put me through to Jakob Jansen's Food shop.'

•

Jakob was at the counter eating a crumbly biscuit when the phone rang in front of him.

'Hello, Jakob Jansen's Food Shop,' he answered, dropping biscuit crumbs down his black tie.

'Ah, Mr Jansen, it's the General here.'

Jakob dropped his biscuit on the counter, 'General! Er, how are you this morning?' he asked tentatively.

'I wish to speak with Eva, get her, will you?'

'Yes, right away, General.' Jakob hesitated, then he laid the receiver down on the counter, and went through to the back.

'Pssst, Eva!' he called through the kitchen doorway. Eva was having breakfast with Angelina at the table, both were wearing identical black silk dressing gowns, they both looked up at him. Jakob thought they looked like two incredibly attractive fashion models sitting there, but he told himself there was no time for those kinds of thoughts now.

'It's the General,' he whispered aloud, 'he's on the phone.'

'Oh, excuse me Angie,' she said as she stood up and glided out of the kitchen. Jakob joined Angelina at the table.

'Hello General?'

'Eva, how are you? Where did you disappear to last night?' The very question Eva had been dreading, since she decided to follow the others out the front door and desert the General on his birthday.

'Ah, well I was a little shaken up about the explosion, so I was escorted home by a soldier who just took my arm. I had no choice but to leave with him, but he saw me back safely,' Eva had already pre-planned her answer.

'Oh, I see, well that was nice of him. Who was it?'

Eva was put on the spot; she hadn't counted on this question.

'Er, I never caught his name, and I doubt I'd recognise him again, it being so dark out and all,' she invented.

'I see. Well listen, Eva, as we were somewhat interrupted last night, I was wondering if you would like to—'

'General, I must tell you, I'm already involved with someone,' she blurted out, she knew what was coming and she had to tell him sooner rather than later. 'I wanted to tell you last night, but I just couldn't find the right moment.'

There was a moment's pause, which made Eva feel very uncomfortable.

'I don't quite know what to say… may I ask who?'

'It's Gary, General.'

'Gary?'

'Yes, you remember, you met him that time we were on the bench at the canal.'

'Oh yes, of course. So how long have you been seeing him?'

'Just a few weeks,' Eva replied sheepishly.

'And it's serious already?' the General said incredulously.

'Well, we have known each other since school here in Holland, if you remember, General?'

'Oh yes, of course. And you're happy, are you?' he asked in an almost fatherly way.

'Yes I am.'

'Right, well, I suppose that's all that really matters. I'll er, see you around then Eva, take care.'

'Goodbye General.' She heard him put the receiver down. She too replaced the receiver and stood on the spot for some time, her mind deep in thought.

•

'Jakob, you are happy with me, aren't you?' Angelina asked him as he spread butter on a slice of bread.

'Well of course I am,' he said absent-mindedly, trying to get the butter in the corners.

'And you're happy with us and the way things are going?'

'Yes, yes, yes,' he said impatiently.

'And you do love me, don't you?'

'Well of course I do, why do you ask?' he began to cut his sandwich in half.

'Because I'm pregnant!'

'Oh, is that all, I don't see how that's—' Jakob froze, his sandwich half cut. He glared in disbelief at Angelina.

'You're what?' he asked slowly.

'I'm going to have your baby,' she clarified.

The moment was tense, neither spoke, they just stared into each other's eyes, Angelina waiting with anticipation for his response. Then, Jakob's face slowly began to broaden into a smile, relieving Angelina of any doubts she was having.

'Oh Angie, tell me it's true,' he turned his whole body to face her. She nodded, smiling, and they embraced.

'I love you,' he whispered in her ear.

'And I love you, but listen,' she added as they released

each other. 'What about your wife?' she asked with a grave face.

'We'll cross that bridge when we come to it,' he reassured her, and they held each other once more.

Eva came into the kitchen.

'Well, I have some good news,' she said as she pulled up another chair opposite them.

'So do we,' Angelina smiled.

'But you first,' Jakob said to Eva.

Eva half smirked and half frowned at them both; she knew they were both excited about something.

'OK,' she said slowly, 'well my bit of good news is, the General has no problem with Gary and me being together, and he doesn't appear to suspect anything about our involvement in the explosion.'

'Oh, that's brilliant,' replied Jakob.

'Great news,' said Angelina unconvincingly.

Eva rolled her eyes but with a smile. 'Go on then, what are you both bursting to tell me?'

'We're having a baby!' they both replied in unison.

Eva opened her mouth wide and cupped her hands together, her eyes darting from one to the other.

'Oh congratulations, I'm so happy for you,' she squealed and hugged them both in turn. 'But I must ask, what about Rini?' she added as she sat back down.

'I think a divorce is long overdue,' Jakob smiled at Angelina, who beamed back at him.

NINE

OFF THE RAILS

October 17, 1940

Otto was using the radio down in the cellar, dimly lit by the one candle he always had on his desk. A man with a British accent was talking to him, just about audible through the static.

'I repeat, there's going to be an "Express" passing by you full of "Might" for you to take care of; it will be passing your way at "numbers seventeen and fifty-five" tonight, do you understand?'

'Message received and understood, over and out,' Otto replied with confidence. He switched off the radio, and proceeded cautiously in the dim, flickering candle flame, over to the cellar stairs.

•

Jakob, Gary, Angelina and Eva were all sitting around the kitchen table, chatting and eating their cereal. Angelina was the only one not yet dressed, still in her black silk dressing gown, and her long, waist-length dark hair was not yet attended to, not that Jakob minded this look.

'All I'm saying, Angie, is to go carefully in your condition,' said Jakob through a mouthful of bread and jam.

'But Jakob, I can hardly say "no" when Rini asks me to take a stack of tins down to the basement,' Angelina told him.

'Well at least you're only in the early stages at the moment,' Eva said consolingly.

'Morning all,' said Otto as he entered the kitchen. He pulled up the chair at the end of the table and leaned forward in his usual business-like manner.

'Right, now listen everyone—'

'Nope, no, no!' Jakob cut him off with half a smile.

'What?' Otto asked innocently.

'Well usually when you say, "Right, now listen everyone" it usually ends with us in some death-defying situation,' Gary added. The girls sniggered.

'Don't be silly, and just listen,' Otto began. 'Now, a train will be passing by Amsterdam at five-to-six tonight, it will be filled to the brim with German officers, and I'm talking really high-ranking officers, including the SS. It will be up to us to make sure the train does not reach its destination.'

'You mean destroy the railway?' asked Jakob doubtfully.

'No, he means destroy the train itself,' said Gary. Jakob's eyes grew a little wider.

'You see, if we destroy the tracks, the German officers on the train will just find other means of getting to their destination, but if we destroy the train, we take out the German officers,' Gary explained. Eva gave him an impressed and seductive look; he smirked back.

'OK, so here's what we do,' Otto began. 'Eva, we'll need you to butter up the General, and steal his keys to his armoured car. You will then give the keys to us, and we will use his armoured car to destroy the train. We will then return the armoured car, and you must then return the keys to the General, without him being any the wiser.'

Every face in the room was looking at Otto as if he'd gone mad.

'I can assure you, it's perfectly plausible,' he added.

'So, when do you want me to do this ridiculous task?' Eva asked straight-faced.

'Well, whenever you like really, quarter past five, half past five, just as long as we make it to the railway by five minutes to six. Oh, and Jakob, Gary and myself will be outside waiting for the keys, so don't be too long,' Otto answered.

'So what exactly is she going to have to do?' Gary asked, feeling protective of Eva.

'Whatever it takes, Gary, this is war,' Otto replied.

'Well, I refuse to go too far with the General,' Eva put her foot down.

'Then how do you suppose we get the keys?' asked Otto.

'I have a plan,' Eva leaned forward and put her elbows on the table; everyone was all ears.

'Now, the General always keeps his keys in his jacket pocket...'

•

17:30. German Headquarters

Otto and Gary, dressed as German sentry, and Jakob in his regular white shirt and black tie, were all standing across the road from the German headquarters, and eyeing up the General's armoured car, which was parked to the right of the building. With them was Eva, who had just been running through the plan one more time.

'Otto, you know what to do,' she said. He nodded and began to jog over to the left side of the building, then went and hid behind it. Eva made her way over to the front doors of the headquarters, while Gary and Jakob stayed where they were on the other side of the road, chatting inconspicuously.

After knocking on the front door, Eva was surprised to see the General coming over to the door, and so soon.

'Eva!' he smiled. 'What're you doing here?' he greeted her.

'Well, to be honest, General, I felt so bad after our phone call the other week, when I told you I was seeing somebody else, and then there was the whole abandoning you at your party, and with the death of your friend, the Captain, I thought perhaps you could use a friend. So I was wondering if you just wanted to come out for a walk or something, maybe go for a drink?' It was working, she could see the General melting before her eyes.

'Eva, I'm honestly touched,' he smiled, 'I'll just grab my jacket.'

'No!' she called a little louder than she intended. 'I mean, it's such a warm night for the time of year,' she smiled innocently.

'Very well,' he nodded, and they left together arm in arm.

Otto watched from behind the building, as Eva and the General strolled down the street. Once they were out of sight, Otto went round to the front, and walked casually through the front door, watched by Jakob and Gary from the other side of the road.

The Great Hall looked very empty without all the tables and chairs, and was completely deserted of people, though the lights were all on.

Otto made a beeline for the elaborate stairs, situated in the middle of the marble floor, flanked by two long scarlet Swastika flags. His boots echoed loudly as he walked across the open floor and began to climb the stairs. Walking along the upstairs corridor, which could be seen from downstairs, Otto passed a couple of other German Privates, but they paid him no attention whatsoever, they just assumed he was one of them. He eventually came upon a door with a nameplate which read, 'General Klaus Schneider'. He checked the vicinity before entering. He opened the door slowly and peered inside, his eyes were drawn to the painting of Hitler, whose eyes pierced through those who dared look at it. He then noticed the General's jacket hanging over the back of his leather chair. Closing the door gently, and tiptoeing over to the jacket, he immediately began checking the pockets, nothing in the left, and only a cigar lighter in the right.

Knock! Knock! Knock!

Otto's heart jumped up to his throat; instinctively he ducked down behind the desk, and just hoped and prayed that whoever it was would go away.

Knock! Knock! Knock!

He held his breath. Suddenly the door opened. Otto's hearing had become hyper sensitive. The next sound was the sound of the door closing and retreating footsteps. Otto breathed a sigh of relief, and as he stood up, he accidentally knocked the jacket off the back of the chair; as it hit the floor, he heard a distinct jangle of keys. Frowning, he picked up the jacket again and checked each pocket, but nothing, he then thought about the inside pocket, and there they were. He scooped up the keys, put them in his own pocket, and exited the General's office.

Otto continued on back down the corridor as casually as he could, when he accidentally bumped shoulders with a real member of the German sentry coming round the corner. Otto's heart was back in his throat once again, but to his relief the soldier simply nodded. 'Heil Hitler!'

'Heil Hitler,' Otto replied, his voice a little shaky, but this apparently went unnoticed by the soldier who continued on the way he was going.

Gary and Jakob saw Otto heading towards the front door and, assuming he must've found the keys, began to head on over to the armoured car.

'Right, climb in you two,' Otto whispered into the night, once he'd opened the hatch at the back of the SdKfz 222 light armoured car. Gary was the first to climb in, followed by Jakob. Otto took a look around the vicinity, checking for Germans; he then checked his watch to see how they were doing for time. 5:45pm. Approximately ten minutes before the train would pass through Amsterdam. Otto climbed into the back.

It smelt brand new inside, with a multitude of controls, which confused both Gary and Jakob.

'OK, I will put my head through the top and operate the gun,' said Otto giving orders. 'Jakob, I'll need you to pass me the shells, Gary, you drive.'

'What?! And how do you expect me to do that?' Gary's raised voice echoed inside.

'Shhhhh!' they all told him.

'It's really very simple,' explained Otto, 'you won't be using all these knobs and levers. Accelerator there, brake there, steering wheel there. I mean, it's the same principle as driving a car.'

'Well, I just don't want us all to die because of my driving, I mean Jakob is about to become a father, I don't want his kid—'

'Gary! In the unlikely event that we die due to your driving, Jakob's child will grow up knowing what we died for. Now get going, for God's sake.' Otto rolled his eyes, Jakob turned away, bobbing up and down, trying to hide his laughter.

Gary reluctantly switched the engine on and pulled away, a little sluggish at first, but he got the hang of it.

•

17:52

Gary pulled the armoured car up on the grassy verge by a low five-foot fence, the only thing separating them from the railway line. The only reason they could see the railway clearly was due to the cloudless, moonlit sky. The entire wooded area was completely deserted, and they had a clear shot over the fence.

'So now we just sit and wait, I suppose?' Gary whispered as he switched off the engine. The whole area was deadly silent.

'Yep, as soon as the train passes, Jakob passes me one of those shells down there, I shoot, job done,' explained Otto.

'It sounds so simple when you put it like that,' Jakob added.

'It's very tight and cramped in here, isn't it?' Gary observed after a moment's silence.

'Well, it's the General's, isn't it, I doubt he uses it to socialise,' said Otto looking around the small interior.

'So how come you're not dressed in a German uniform then?' Gary asked Jakob.

'Because I'm too well known around this area,' Jakob explained.

'Yeah, if Jakob's caught with us two, well he just looks like he's accompanied us against his will, doesn't he? But if he's caught in a German uniform, well that'll wreak all kinds of havoc,' explained Otto.

'It's no good,' said Jakob twisting around, 'I can't hang on any more, call of nature, boys,' he told them as he clambered out the back. His feet trod on spongy grass as he ran round behind a thick tree trunk.

'Well, I just hope Eva manages to keep the General away from the headquarters for long enough,' said Otto looking at his watch.

Gary suddenly sat bolt upright, 'Do you hear that?' he asked fearfully.

Otto strained his ears, 'Yes, yes, I do, grab me a shell, Gary!' he ordered.

Gary lifted one of the heavy golden shells and passed

it to Otto, who slid it into the barrel. They sat in silence, waiting with dread and anticipation. The sound of the train was getting louder. Otto began to search for it in his sights. Suddenly the steam was visible in the moonlight, rising higher and higher into the air. And there it was, a large, magnificent black steam train came into view, and going at quite a speed.

Otto followed it in his sights, waited until the opportune time, and BANG!!! The whole armoured car shook, their eardrums rang, and in a blink of an eye, the magnificent great steam train was reduced to stationary, burning wreckage.

'Direct hit!' Otto called out excitedly, looking back at Gary who had just removed his hands from his ears.

Otto chuckled and said, 'I can actually feel the heat from the flames.'

But Otto's smile soon disappeared as they began to hear gunshots.

'Damn it, Germans!' Otto exclaimed. 'Gary get moving!'

'What about Jakob?' Gary said in panic.

'We've got no choice, now, get moving now, for God's sake!'

Gary reluctantly started up the engine and began to pull away, bullets clanging off the back of the armoured car.

Jakob saw the armoured car driving away; his insides did somersaults as he realised that Gary and Otto were deserting him. He dashed out from behind the tree and attempted to run after it, but the shout of 'HALT!' caused him to freeze in his tracks. With his heart pounding in his ears, and a sensation of dizziness coming over him, he raised his hands up. He slowly turned around to face an entire German sentry and stared down the muzzles of a dozen MP38s.

•

Eva and the General were walking arm in arm alongside the canal, the street lights shimmering in the water.

'I've had a lovely evening, Eva.'

'Me too,' she looked up at him and smiled.

'So you see I'm not all bad, I suppose women are my weakness, I see a pretty girl, and I'm immediately wrapped around her little finger,' he explained.

They walked around the corner, and to Eva's relief she saw the armoured car safely parked up. But to her horror, the back hatch opened up and she realised they'd only just pulled up.

'Er, General!' she stopped where she was, causing the General to turn and face her, exactly where she wanted him, facing away from his car.

'What is it?' he asked.

'I just wanted to say that I have also had a really nice evening, and that I'm glad we can be friends,' she smiled, as she looked around the General's arm to see Otto and Gary exiting the armoured car, and tried to hide her concern for the fact that Jakob was nowhere to be seen.

'I feel the same,' he returned the smile.

Eva was now doubly worried, as she saw Otto coming over towards them, but also noticed Gary had wandered off in another direction.

'Well, I suppose we'd better get going, General.'

'Eva, I've told you, it's Klaus,' the General corrected her.

She smiled, but before she could respond, 'Eva! How are you, it's lovely to see you again,' Otto extended his hand to her as he approached. The General turned to see who the stranger was.

'I'm very well, thank you,' Eva replied, completely perplexed, that was until she felt what Otto had concealed in his hand as she shook it: the car keys. They shook hands as casually as possible as the keys were handed from one to the other. As Eva took them, she was frantically formulating a reason in her mind as to why this German Private would know her name. She had it.

'Oh, of course, Klaus, this is the lovely soldier who escorted me home on the night of your party,' she nodded subtly to Otto so that the General wouldn't see.

'Oh yes, I remember you telling me, how do you do?' The General extended his own hand and they shook politely.

'Well, I must be off, back on duty any minute,' Otto lied, and nodded to them before departing.

'He must be quite new, I don't recognise him,' said the General, watching him leave.

'Oh, yes he is new, he told me. I expect you have seen him before, but perhaps you couldn't recognise him in the dark or something,' Eva tried to convince him.'

'Possibly,' he replied before turning his attention back to her.

'Well, I really must get back, Eva, but it's been a pleasure as always,' he bent down to kiss her cheek, and lingered there a little too long before finally pulling away. 'Until next time,' he smiled and turned around.

Eva knew what she had to do, and she only had one

shot. She threw the keys at the General's feet as he walked away, but he didn't seem to hear them.

'Oh, Klaus!' she called, scuttling over. 'You dropped these.' She bent down and picked them up.

'Oh, thank you, Eva. That's funny, I could've sworn I left them in my jacket pocket,' there was a brief, uncomfortable pause as the General considered this.

'Well, goodnight, Klaus, until next time.' She stood on tiptoe to kiss his cheek, and then walked away without looking back.

After only a few strides, Eva heard quick footsteps walking up behind her. She whizzed around ready to defend herself when, to her relief, she saw Gary approaching.

'Oh Gary,' they embraced immediately. 'Thank goodness you're OK, but where the hell is Jakob?' she asked.

Gary looked down at the ground as if he'd just heard some awful news. 'I've got a horrible feeling that Jakob is no longer with us.'

'What?!' Eva exclaimed, her thoughts jumping straight to Angelina, and her fatherless, unborn child.

'That's not necessarily so!' called a voice from behind them.

They looked into the darkness; Otto was approaching them.

'What do you mean?' asked Eva.

'As we speak, Jakob will be in the hands of the Gestapo,' Otto explained, as he joined them in the middle of the empty road under a street light. 'Which leaves us with a very big problem,' he continued. 'If Jakob can't hold out to their torture, which he probably won't, then he will reveal everything. The fact that we were the ones who attempted to assassinate their beloved Fuhrer, that you, Gary, are a British spy, that you, Eva, have joined the Allies, that I am Otto of the Dutch Resistance, that we have a radio down in the cellar of Jakob's shop, that it was my idea to assassinate the General with the cyanide capsule, that it was the Resistance who killed the Gestapo officer, that you two got rid of those forged notes, that we were responsible for the death of Captain Fritz Muller, everything. All our insecurities laid utterly bare.'

Gary and Eva looked as though the world as they knew it had just ended.

'We have to break him out of there,' Gary said decisively.

•

Jakob was sitting on a cold concrete floor, surrounded by three stone walls, the fourth consisting of multiple vertical metal bars, and within these bars was a door. He was sitting like a schoolboy, elbows resting on drawn-up knees. He was cold and shaking, but his mind was on other things. What were they going to do to him? Why had Gary and Otto deserted him? What would happen to Angelina and his baby if he was no longer around? And the one that he'd been kicking himself for, why was he so keen on being a part of this mission, when he didn't really need to go? Although he comforted himself by reminding himself that Otto wanted all three of them, in case something happened to either of the others, just as a precautionary backup.

Jakob was disturbed from his thoughts by the sound of footsteps making their way towards him. First, he saw the shadows, then he saw the people. Gestapo Officer Schultz was escorted by one of the guards to Jakob's cell. The door made of iron bars was unlocked and pulled back by the guard, the clang of the keys echoed loudly.

'You! Come with us!' called the guard. Jakob began to move but Herr Schultz interrupted.

'No, no, this will do just fine, you may leave us,' he told the guard, who nodded, then locked the door behind them and retraced his steps.

Jakob just stayed where he was, looking up apprehensively at the sinister Gestapo officer.

Schultz picked up a small abandoned wooden stool in the corner and placed it down in front of Jakob without saying a word. He removed his long black mac and placed it over the stool before sitting down. He simply leaned forward and stared at Jakob unblinkingly. Jakob's breathing was becoming noticeably faster, try as he might to disguise it, he just had to break the silence.

'Sir, could I start off by saying that I know nothing of any interest to you,' he said defensively.

'You were a witness at a crime scene where seventeen German officers lost their lives; tell me again that you know nothing of this incident,' Schultz began in a creepy, monotone voice.

'Honestly, I don't know anything,' Jakob pleaded.

'I'm afraid I don't believe you, and if you don't start talking, you will be experiencing high levels of pain,' Schultz said menacingly.

Jakob was thinking hard about what to say next, but Schultz spoke again.

'You were spotted by a German armoured car, which was responsible for the deaths of the seventeen German officers, and you live with a German, do you not? A spy? Could it not be that this spy is a double agent?'

Jakob was shocked to his core; how could this Gestapo officer know such things? Did he know all of what he said? Or was he just bluffing? But before Jakob had time to answer, Schultz had grabbed Jakob's chin, squeezed it between his thumb and forefinger, screwed up his own face and growled, 'You will talk!'

Jakob was in panic mode. 'Yes, I do have a German spy staying with me, her name is Eva, and she's renting a room upstairs, but we hardly talk, you understand, I don't know anything about her,' Jakob blurted out in sheer fright.

Schultz suddenly let go of Jakob's chin; he had a puzzled look on his face.

'Eva? Not the attractive blonde?' Schultz asked, clearly quite surprised.

'Only as a lodger,' Jakob replied, rubbing his chin.

'Tell me more about Eva,' Schultz said with a hungry look about him.

'I don't know anything.'

'*Talk!*' Schultz shouted at the top of his voice, but this merely made Jakob start to feel angry.

'Look! I can't tell you about someone I hardly nod to in the morning, can I?' he replied. Where this sudden and temporary burst of confidence came from, he had no idea.

Schultz stared back for a moment, before realising that Jakob had a point and simply nodded.

'So, tell me about tonight, what were you doing there? And what did you see?'

•

Eva, Gary and Otto were sitting around the kitchen table with Angelina and Rini. They'd just told them about what happened to Jakob.

'Oh Christ,' Angelina clapped her hands to her mouth, 'well we have to do something, what can we do?' No sooner were the words out of her mouth, than she realised she'd best hold back on her concern in front of Rini, who was already giving her a suspicious look, as Angelina peered at her over her cupped hands.

'I don't know yet,' Otto confessed.

'Will he be tortured?' Angelina asked, much more composed this time.

'It's highly likely, yes,' Otto couldn't lie.

'But what if he cracks under interrogation? He could drop us all in it, it would be the end of life as we know it,' said Rini, concerned.

'And what about Jakob!' Angelina shot to her feet and looked angrily at Rini, who was taken aback by this sudden outburst.

'I beg your pardon?!' Rini retorted, now getting to her feet.

'You heard me!' Angelina shot back, hands on hips.

'Not now,' Eva whispered through gritted teeth looking up at Angelina, trying to calm her down, but Angelina was having none of it.

'You've never cared about Jakob; all you've ever cared about is your precious business!' she shouted.

Gary and Otto were watching from the other side of the table, as if watching an intriguing film. Eva was looking down with her head in her hands caught between the two.

'You spiteful baggage, you take that back!' Rini shouted back.

'I don't see why I should, he should've left you years ago, you were never right for him!' They were both now red in the face.

'You jealous bitch! What's the matter, fancy him yourself, do you?!'

'Oh, I more than fancy him, *I've been seeing him!*'

The room went deadly silent, Gary, Otto and Eva were mentally preparing themselves to intervene if things got physical.

'*What?!*' Rini shouted at the top of her lungs, shattering the temporary silence. She looked like a raging bull.

'You heard,' Angelina now spoke with a calm and steady voice. 'We've been seeing each other, we've been sleeping together, and I am now carrying his baby,' she held her tummy, not yet showing any sign of a pregnancy.

'*You cow!*' Rini's arm swung over Eva's head, and slapped Angelina, whose long dark hair rushed through the air as her head swung to the side. Eva quickly stood up between them and put her hands out to stop them getting any closer to each other. Angelina held this pose for a few seconds, her face totally hidden by her beautiful long, dark hair. She then reached up to slowly take the hair out of her face, and draped it over her shoulder, revealing a deadly smirk as she looked back at Rini, and then whispered, 'And he couldn't get enough of it.'

'*You bitch!!*' Rini made an attempted lunge at Angelina, who had curled her own hand into a fist to defend herself, but as Eva turned her back, she managed to cover Angelina with her body, while Gary and Otto shot over to Rini to hold her off, and due to her stocky frame, even Gary and Otto had difficulty. They managed to pull a kicking and screaming Rini out of the kitchen and into the hallway, and with Gary and Otto still dressed as German soldiers, it made the whole thing look quite menacing.

'OK, quiet now, Rini!' Otto attempted to get over her shouting and cursing.

'Rini, calm down!' Gary told her. 'Then we can let go.'

Rini finally stopped yelling and tugging, she began to pant like a woman having contractions as she tried to calm herself down. Admittedly, Otto and Gary thought she looked more angry than upset; it seemed Angelina was right, she was only ever interested in his money. Gary and Otto slowly began to release their grip on Rini's arms.

'I think it would be a good idea if you went and packed your things,' Otto told her. She looked at him, thunderstruck.

'You do realise she's the one who's been carrying on with my husband? She's the one who should pack, *the pair of them!*' she hollered in the direction of the kitchen.

'Look, I'll find you somewhere comfortable,' Otto suggested.

'Why can't you understand…?' she stopped and saw the looks on both Otto's and Gary's faces.

'You knew, didn't you?' Her face in shock, she looked at them both in disbelief. 'You bastards, you both knew.'

'We all knew for a very long time,' said Otto authoritatively, 'look, you two weren't right for each other, anyone could see that.'

'I see,' Rini replied quietly, 'well don't bother about finding me a place to stay, I'm going to stay with my sister in Utrecht.' She pulled back the long red curtain and proceeded to climb the stairs.

Gary and Otto looked at each other and blew out a sigh of relief before entering back in the kitchen.

Eva had her arm around a quietly sobbing Angelina, as they sat back in their seats.

'It's OK,' said Gary walking over, 'she's packing her bags as we speak, she's going to stay with her sister, apparently, in Utrecht.'

'Gary, I have a plan to help Jakob,' Eva looked up at him, still consoling Angelina. 'But I can only do this alone, so I need you to stay here with Angelina, is that OK?'

Gary looked apprehensive but finally succumbed. 'Yes of course it is.'

•

19:42

Eva was once again strutting along the road to the German headquarters, the cold night air lashing at her legs. She knocked on the door, and after some time waiting, she saw a man approach on the other side whom she did not recognise.

'Madam?' he said as he opened the door, presumably a little surprised to see a visitor so late.

'I've come to see Klaus,' she said, hoping that if the man knew they were on first-name terms, he would be persuaded to let her in.

The man did indeed look a little startled to hear the use of the General's first name,

'Please step inside,' he said opening the door wider.

•

Jakob was still sitting on the cold concrete floor, still being questioned by the pacing Gestapo officer. But Jakob no longer looked cold, or even frightened, instead he looked half dead as he was leaning against the cold stone wall. His nose was bleeding profusely, and one of his eyes had swollen up into a black and purple balloon.

'And what do you think your wife would do, if she ever found out about this sordid affair with your twenty-six-year-old assistant? Not to mention your unborn child?' Schultz asked in a creepy, provocative tone.

'My life wouldn't be the same again,' Jakob said, but he didn't sound like himself at all, his nose was filled with blood, and may very well have been broken.

'Exactly, Mr Jansen, so let's have a few more answers shall we?'

'I've told you everything,' Jakob mumbled.

'Shut up!' Schultz delivered a nasty slap across Jakob's face.

•

Eva was sitting across from the General at his desk.

'So you see Klaus, Jakob couldn't have had anything to do with that train, he always takes his evening walks along that railway, he wasn't in this armoured car that the Gestapo say they used, and he wasn't even wearing a disguise of any kind, which you would've thought would be necessary to avoid detection, he was simply in the wrong place at the wrong time. So do you think you might be able to put in a good word for him?' she asked the General with a purposefully helpless look on her face.

The General leaned back in his chair and surveyed Eva for a moment, before breaking into a smile.

'Well, I suppose it couldn't hurt, after all, who else is going to sell me my favourite brand of water?' he smiled and reached for his telephone receiver.

•

Pain seared through Jakob's mouth as blood sprayed the stone wall, followed by a noise that sounded like a small stone had been thrown across the floor. Jakob felt the fresh bloody gap between his teeth with his tongue, and realised it was his tooth he'd heard on the stone floor.

'I will ask that again,' said Schultz in a deadly calm voice, 'Who-was-Anton?'

Jakob, on his knees, leaned against the stone wall, spitting blood from his mouth so that his words could be heard clearly. 'He used to live in Amsterdam… he was a member of the Resistance… but he was moved to England where he was killed in an air raid,' Jakob struggled.

'Good, that is what I was led to believe happened to him.'

Both Jakob and Schultz were distracted by the approaching footsteps.

'Excuse me Herr Schultz,' the same guard who had let him in had approached. 'An urgent telephone call for you.'

'Tell them I'm in the midst of an interrogation!' he barked.

'It's General Klaus Schneider,' the guard explained.

This caught Schultz's attention. 'Oh, very well,' he replied and he left with the guard, who locked the cell door behind them, leaving Jakob alone in a bloody mess, on the cold concrete floor.

•

Rini stomped down the stairs carrying her bulging suitcase, Gary and Angelina looking on from the kitchen doorway. Rini turned to them.

'I hope you're happy, coming between a husband and his wife,' she said spitefully, and left for the front door without saying another word.

Angelina began to sob once more as the door closed behind Rini.

'Look don't worry,' Gary put a comforting arm around her. 'She's just playing the victim, everyone knows they didn't love each other, we all know she was only with him so she could get her hands on this place. And Eva picked up on the fact that they weren't in love back when we first arrived here.'

This made Angelina crack a subtle smile, whether it was the mention of her friend Eva's name, or the fact that Eva knew what she'd been wondering for a long time, Gary saw that it had cheered her up somewhat.

•

Jakob once again heard footsteps approaching his cell; he realised his luck wasn't getting any better when he saw it was Herr Schultz returning.

'Right, you're free to go.'

Jakob's ears must've been playing tricks on him.

'I'm sorry, what did you say?' he asked, trying in vain to wipe his bloody nose clean on his already bloodstained shirt sleeve.

'You're free to go, the General put in a good word for you.'

Jakob was thankful but also very confused. Why would the General help him? *Unless of course, Eva*, he thought.

'I feel I must apologies,' explained Schultz. 'I had no idea you were helping the Germans, you should have said sooner, oh and please, use the bathroom to clean your face up before you go.'

Jakob couldn't believe his ears or his eyes, for the Gestapo officer had just smiled for the first time to Jakob's knowledge, and what was all this about helping the Germans? Jakob slowly got to his feet, using the wall for assistance, and made his way over to the cell door. Before exiting, he turned to face Schultz. 'Am I really free to go just like that?'

'Well, not quite yet, I have a favour to ask first,' Schultz walked up to him. 'There are stories circulating that the British have been bailing out of their aircrafts, wandering the Dutch countryside, and have been taken in by Dutch civilians. If you could keep your ear to the ground, Mr Jansen, I would be most appreciative, I could even see that you get a medal,' Schultz said casually.

Jakob, his nose and mouth dripping blood all over the floor, stared in disbelief at the Gestapo officer, before finally replying. 'Sure, I'll do that,' he said and was escorted out by the guard.

•

Back at the shop, Gary, Otto and Angelina were all sitting around the kitchen table with a cup of tea each, eagerly anticipating the return of Eva for any news.

'No, it's no good, I have to go and look for her,' Gary said as he stood up. But Otto tugged at his arm, forcing him to sit back down.

'Calm down, Gary, look, all we can do right now is wait for her to get back, she'll be fine, she's a smart woman, Gary,' he said consolingly.

Gary reluctantly picked his cup back up and took a sip of tea.

'Oh, I do hope she comes back soon with some news,' Angelina said, nervously fiddling with tips of her long hair.

Almost on cue the back door opened, and in walked Eva looking very pleased with herself.

'Eva, thank God,' Gary stood up and went over to hug her.

Eva was a little surprised. 'Gary, what's the matter?' she asked in his ear.

'Nothing now you're back, I was worried, you know, thought something might've happened.'

'Oh Gary, you and your imagination,' she replied as they released each other.

'When you two have quite finished,' said Angelina, 'is there any news on Jakob?'

'Angie, my friend,' Eva smiled and went over to hug Angelina, who could tell that this must mean good news. 'I've managed to sway it for Jakob, if he's not been released yet he soon will be.'

'Oh Eva, that's fantastic, thank you so much,' and Angelina stood up and threw her arms back around Eva.

'But Angie, listen to me,' Eva said with a tone of such seriousness, it made Angelina release her. 'Jakob has been gone for some time, what I'm saying is, he may not have come away unscathed, he was in the hands of the Gestapo after all,' Eva warned her.

Angelina calmed herself, nodded, and then said, 'But we do have some good news for him when he gets back.'

Eva frowned and looked around the kitchen. 'Where's Rini?'

Angelina smiled, 'That's the good news, the old battleaxe has gone for good.'

Eva stood open-mouthed and looked at Gary.

'I'll explain later, dear,' Gary smiled, and winked at Angelina who smiled back.

All of a sudden, the back door opened again, and to everyone's amazement, Jakob walked in with a cut across his nose, a swollen black eye, a tooth missing, and a puffed-up lip, but the blood had been cleaned up.

'Oh my God! Jakob!' Angelina swept over to fling her arms around him, as everyone else looked on, horror-struck at his appearance.

They stayed there for quite a while in each other's arms, eyes closed tight and just cherishing the moment.

'Oh Jakob,' Eva put her hands to her mouth, her eyes taking in his face.

'Well don't all look at me like I'm an alien, you should have seen me earlier before I cleaned up,' he joked, which surprised everyone in the room.

Angelina pulled back and looked at Jakob properly for

the first time. She reached up and gently put her hands either side of his face, causing him to wince slightly.

'Oh Jakob, what did they do to you?' tears began to fill in her eyes.

'Honestly Angie, it's worse than it looks, it was a maximum of three blows to the face, and I'm proud to say that I gave very little away, anything I did tell was of very little importance.' He then looked over at Eva. 'Eva, how can I ever thank you?'

'How did you know it was me?' she asked with a curious smile.

'Who else could've persuaded the General to get me off?' he grinned, as Eva laughed. 'But there are a couple of things I'm confused about, what was all this about me helping the Germans?' He too smiled curiously.

'Well, I managed to persuade the General to put in a good word for you, but just as he started dialling, I sort of told him about how you were… assisting me with my spy work… well he was very impressed, and it worked, didn't it?' she hesitated at Jakob's shocked face, but thankfully it broke into a smile.

'Well, yes, it certainly worked,' he said thankfully.

'So what was the other thing?' asked Eva.

'What other thing?' he asked.

'You said there were a couple things you didn't understand, that was one, so what's the other?' Eva asked.

'Oh, I was wondering where Rini was?'

'We'll let you explain this one,' Eva smiled at Angelina, and she ushered Gary and Otto out of the room.

Jakob and Angelina held each other as if they were in the middle of a dance.

'We got into an argument about you, Jakob. I was right, she didn't love you, she as good as admitted she was only interested in your business, that's the only reason she got angry when it all came out about me and you… and our baby,' they continued to hold each other in the same dance pose, her hands over his shoulders, his hands round her tiny waist.

'So she's gone then, she's really gone,' he said as his face broke into a smile, but he winced because of his swollen lip.

'Yes, she's gone, now you can get a divorce and we can finally get married.'

Jakob looked meaningfully into her eyes, pulled her close and rested his chin on top her head.

'The minute I am able to,' he replied.

TEN

THE BRITISH ARE COMING

November 8, 1940

Jakob and Angelina were in the middle of a rather large shop dedicated to newborn babies, blue and pink everywhere. There were clothes, toys, jars of baby food, even a variety of prams out on display. There was a warm, cosy atmosphere about the place, one would hardly know there was a war on.

'Look at this, Jakob,' Angelina said, holding up the tiniest pink jumper Jakob had ever seen.

'Oh, you've already decided it's going to be a girl then?' he joked, his face almost completely recovered from his run-in with the Gestapo.

'Don't be silly, I'm just saying, can you imagine?' she smiled.

'Not at that price I can't.'

Angelina grinned and put it back on the rail.

'Anyway, you're only two months gone,' Jakob added casually as they continued browsing.

'Correction, I told you two months ago, when I found

out I was apparently already six weeks gone, that makes me three and a half months gone already.'

'OK, OK,' Jakob held his hands up, 'what about this then?' he picked up a little boy's pullover.

Angelina looked at it with a slight frown, 'You're right, much too early.' She smiled and they made their way towards the exit.

•

'So, what're your plans for today then?' Gary asked Eva, as he was buttering his toast at the kitchen table.

'Well,' said Eva, as she sat down opposite him with her freshly made cup of tea, 'I thought I would go upstairs in a little while, take off all my clothes and jump into bed, care to join me?'

Gary missed his mouth and got butter all up the side of his face, much to Eva's amusement.

'What are you after?' he said through narrowed eyes, as he wiped his face clean with a cloth.

'Nothing, I was joking.'

'Oh, now that's a shame, seeing as we've got the entire place to ourselves right now,' Gary finally took a successful bite of his toast.

'It'll have to wait until much later, I'm afraid, I have a feeling that today is going to be another eventful day,' Eva said into her cup as she raised it.

Right then the back door opened and in came Otto, closely followed by a very tall stranger, with a brown moustache surrounded by a week's worth of stubble, a brown hat and suit, and a beige overcoat similar to Gary's.

Gary and Eva looked up in surprise; the stranger removed his hat and nodded with a smile, while Otto closed the door behind them.

'Where's Jakob?' Otto asked, looking a little concerned.

'He's out shopping with Angelina,' Gary explained, wondering why this was necessary.

'Er, OK, Gary and Eva, meet Flight Lieutenant Gatehouse,' Otto gestured to the stranger.

'Hello, hello,' he shook each of their hands in turn.

'Take a seat,' Otto pulled out a chair for him.

'Flight Lieutenant?' Gary asked.

'Yes, but please call me George,' he said as he sat at the table.

'As in British?' asked Eva, more interested than concerned.

'Yes, yes, yes, as in he's a downed British airman,' Otto clarified as he sat in his own chair, 'and don't worry, he's been cleared by London.'

'So what happened? How did you find him?' asked Gary, his curiosity getting the better of him.

'Well,' George began, 'I was flying over Amsterdam dropping leaflets, when all of a sudden, Bang! Bang! Bang! I was being shot at by the German anti-aircraft guns, shot the tail of the plane clean off and sent me spinning, the whole world outside my window was whizzing past in circles. I had no choice but to bail out, landed in a field east of Amsterdam. We were trained to lie low by day and travel by night, so that's what I did, I drank milk from the cows, and ate berries from the hedgerows. I was then fortunate enough to bump into Otto here, and after about a thousand questions, he brought me here,' he smiled at Otto.

'Well, I had to be sure, you could've been anyone,' Otto explained.

'Yes I know. So, who's this Jakob chap I've heard you mention?'

'He's the owner of this place,' Gary explained.

'Oh… so who're you two?'

'The less you know about any of us the better,' explained Otto.

'Oh, fair enough,' George shrugged.

The back door to the kitchen opened again, and in came Jakob and Angelina chatting, but the chatting came to an abrupt halt when they saw the stranger sitting at their kitchen table.

'Ah, Jakob,' Otto got to his feet quickly, 'allow me to introduce Flight Lieutenant George Gatehouse of the RAF; George, meet Jakob and his girlfriend, Angelina.'

'Hello there, nice to finally meet you,' George stood up and shook their hands.

'Jakob, George needs a place to stay for a short time, just until I can find a way of getting him back to England, would it be OK with you if he stayed here for a night or two?' Otto asked hopefully.

'Well…' Jakob hesitated and looked to Angelina.

'Well, of course he can,' Angelina rolled her eyes.

'Oh, thank you so much,' George smiled.

'Right, George, come with me down to the cellar, we'll get on the radio and see if we can get you back to England,' Otto beckoned George to follow him.

'Well, it was nice to meet you all,' George said as he picked up his hat and followed Otto.

'And you,' they all called after him.

'He seems nice,' said Gary approvingly.

'He may be nice, but he's also a problem,' said Jakob gravely.

'How'd you come to that conclusion?' asked Angelina.

'Have you got "baby brain" already?' said Jakob, 'I'm a Dutchman in Nazi-occupied Holland, hiding an Englishman in my shop, that's the problem.'

'But Jakob, it's only for a couple of days at the most,' Eva added reassuringly.

'I hate to say it, but he has a pretty good point,' said Gary, 'the past couple of months, there's been a lot of downed British airmen around Amsterdam, and those locals that have been taking them in have been shot, or worse, tortured.'

'Yes, he's right, and I have been asked by that Gestapo officer, Schultz, to keep my ear to the ground about all of this, and now I'm one of the ones doing it.' Jakob wiped his brow with frustration.

•

'Right you are, over and out.' Otto switched off the radio and turned to face George sitting next to him in the dim, candlelit cellar.

'We move tonight,' Otto told him.

'Tonight?' George sounded disappointed.

'What's the matter? Don't you want to get back to England?' said Otto, a little confused.

'Well, yeah, but, oh I dunno, I suppose I just wasn't expecting to go back so soon, that's all, I wanted to stay here for a bit, see the sights.'

'George, this is war, not a holiday,' Otto told him sternly.

'Yeah, I know,' George said sulkily. 'So, how's it going ahead then?'

'All in due course, I have to check on my disguises first,' Otto said as he got out of his seat and wandered over to a cupboard in the corner, his shoes echoing on the dark, dusty concrete floor. He was watched curiously by George, who was surprised to see that, in the darkest corner of the room, Otto possessed a cupboard filled with all sorts of interesting clothing, ranging from various German uniforms, to a doctor's outfit, even a Dutch policeman's uniform.

'How the hell?' George said as he wondered over to where Otto was standing at the cupboard.

'Don't ask,' said Otto firmly, 'don't ask and I won't have to kill you,' he smirked as George approached, mouth open.

'But this is fantastic!' George seemed rather excited.

'Well, they come in useful, particularly the German Private's uniform, which coincidentally, is the one I shall be using tonight.' George went to open his mouth for another question, but Otto stopped him by putting a finger to his own lips. 'No more questions now, just do as I say, and everything will be fine,' he said as he went over and laid out the German Private's uniform on his desk, ready.

•

22:00

George was in the kitchen saying his goodbyes, his moustache now standing out more clearly, due to the absence of the stubble. Otto was waiting by the back door in his menacing German Private's uniform.

'Well, goodbye everyone, it was lovely meeting you all, no doubt we'll meet again in the future. England won't stay on the other side of the Channel forever, you know, you mark my words.' Everyone smiled back. 'Good luck with parenthood you two,' he winked at Jakob and Angelina. 'Gary, Eva, best of luck.'

'And to you, George, hope to see you here in the future, when the tables turn,' said Gary confidently. George nodded and smiled, and he left with Otto.

The smell of the night air hit them hard and it took a moment for their eyes to adjust from the kitchen light to the pitch darkness outside. They walked round to the right, and down the side alley to the front of the shop, where they were met by a military truck.

George found it rather intimidating to see the white outline of the black German cross on the side of the door.

'So why couldn't they send a plane or something then?' George whispered into the night air.

'Too risky,' Otto explained. 'Last time we tried that, a friend of mine was forced to bail out, and now the Germans have tightened up security, you probably wouldn't be alive to bail out.'

George began to look a little doubtful about what he was about to do.

'Well, we can't stand around here chatting all night, get in the back, and use the hay to cover you completely,' Otto explained. George took a last look around the area before deciding it was time to go. Otto climbed into the front, started the engine, and pulled away, smoke billowing out the back.

•

'So, why didn't Otto just send for a plane like he did with Anton?' Angelina asked Jakob.

'Oh, they don't do that anymore, apparently, due to the Germans tightening up security or something. It's far too dangerous now; we were lucky not to have gotten caught last time, especially the length of time it took us to walk him to the field.'

Eva frowned at this.

'Because he'd been shot in the leg by the General,' Jakob explained.

'Really?' Eva was surprised at this news.

'Yep, to be fair he did try to poison the General,' Jakob continued casually.

Eva's jaw dropped.

'It was Otto's plan,' Jakob continued. 'You see, he put a cyanide pill in a bottle of the General's favourite water, and it all spiralled out of control from there really.'

'We missed all the fun, Gary.'

Gary smiled at her. 'So, what became of Anton?' he asked.

'Well, the last time I heard about him was when he told us about Hitler passing by our way, in fact I think you two were already here by then. If I were to take a guess, I'd say he's probably working for MI5 in London right now,' Jakob explained.

•

The countryside was completely deserted, nothing but a moonlit sky shining down on silhouettes of trees and hedgerows. Otto could barely see the sides of the road even with his lights on; he could only tell how close the hedge was on his right side, according to how loudly it brushed the side of the vehicle. It was so quiet out that the engine sounded extra loud to Otto. It seemed it was going to be an easy straight run to the coast, until Otto could make out shadows in the distance, shadows beyond where his headlights currently reached. As he drew nearer, he realised there was a roadblock up ahead, and the shadows were that of a German sentry. Great, what was he going to do now? What if they wanted to check the back? They usually did.

Otto slowed to a stop and wound down his window.

'Papers please,' said the soldier dressed exactly like Otto.

Otto produced his identity papers from his inside pocket and handed them to the German soldier. Otto noticed the gun the soldier was carrying in his holster, and if he wasn't much mistaken, a Walther P-38 too, arguably even better than the Luger. The soldier studied Otto's identity papers through narrowed eyes. He looked up at Otto, then back to the papers. *What's taking so long?* Otto thought. The papers were made by Anton, and they had always served him well in the past.

'Step out of your vehicle, please,' he told Otto. *This can't be good*, he thought as he opened the door and stepped down to the ground. As Otto closed the door behind him, the soldier told another soldier standing nearby to go around to the back and check what he was carrying.

'I'm not actually carrying anything,' said Otto, 'I've just delivered a load of ammunition.'

'We will see,' said the Private, who just stood there waiting with Otto for the other Private to come back round to the front. Otto noticed how, rather unnervingly, the Private kept a hold of Otto's identity papers, the papers being the only thing that Otto could see clearly given the pitch darkness of the surroundings.

The German Private that had been searching the vehicle came back into view, and walked slowly over to Otto and the other Private with a very smug look on his face.

'Would you like to tell us why you are transporting an Englishman in the back of this truck?' he said quite loudly. The other Private spun to look directly at Otto with suspicious eyes.

Otto noticed himself stop breathing for a second, his mouth suddenly very dry. *This is it*, he thought, *this is the end of the road*. Now it was his turn to go where Jakob had been just a few weeks ago, only he wouldn't be as lucky as Jakob. Otto's head was swimming with images of himself being tortured by the Gestapo. He saw his fingernails being pulled out, he saw himself being beaten badly, he saw himself screaming in pain, and then he saw Jakob, Gary, Eva and a pregnant Angelina being tortured to death if he ever revealed any of their secrets.

Otto followed them round to the back where lay, to Otto's complete surprise, George's dead body half concealed by the hay. He appeared to have a major head injury, with blood all over his head. Jakob tried not to show his confusion, as he thought of a reason as to why he had a dead body of an Englishmen in the back of his truck. *And that was another thing*, thought Otto, *how could they possibly know he was British?*

'My apologies,' the Private said, and handed Otto his identity papers. Otto, now with even more confusion to conceal, gladly took his papers back.

'Damn Englishmen,' he said, 'it's quite obvious what has happened,' he said to the other Private. 'This is obviously another Englishman who was shot down, injured, roamed the countryside, and tried to seek shelter in a truck; trouble is, they never recover from their injuries, so they just die in their sleep,' he turned to Otto. 'I've seen this a lot recently, he probably climbed in when you finished unloading your ammunition.'

'I expect so, yes,' Otto tried to appear innocent.

'Well, I suppose we'd better find out who he is,' said the Private in charge, and he opened the back hatch and proceeded to climb in.

'Ah, no,' Otto called out, 'er, I'll do it, it's my truck he's squatted in.'

Otto clambered on inside, watched closely by the two soldiers, and went over to George. Otto knew he had no choice but to look inside his pockets, as the other two were watching. He knelt down next to George, his back to the prying eyes of the Germans, and froze in shock as he saw George's hand slip into his trouser pocket and pull out some identity papers. Otto took them and had a quick look; the name on them said James McDonald. He also noticed other false information on them. He looked to George, who gave him a wink. Otto stood up and handed the identification papers down to the soldier outside. He stood there for some time looking them over.

'OK,' he said and handed them back to Otto. 'Would you like our help to dispose of the body?'

'Er, no, no, I'll take it on and burn it when I get back,' Otto tried to appear casual.

'Very well, goodnight to you, Heil Hitler.'

'Heil Hitler,' Otto replied as the other two strolled back to their positions at the roadblock. Otto looked back at George.

'Tomato sauce,' George smiled, pointing at his head.

Otto smiled and shook his head. 'I have to get back to the wheel, or they'll wonder what the hold-up is… you had me going then, you know,' Otto told him. George grinned back as Otto climbed down outside and closed the hatch, and before they knew it, they were well clear of the German sentry.

•

Back at the shop, Gary, Eva, Jakob and Angelina were continuing their previous conversation around the kitchen table.

'… and I remember,' Jakob continued, 'when I was walking on down by one of the canals, and I bumped into a group of German soldiers for the first time, my heart was in my mouth. I was so glad to hear Anton's voice calling me, and that's when he told me, he said, never make eye contact with the Germans, as it leaves you open for conversation, and I never forgot that.'

'Sounds like a very wise man,' said Eva.

'Yea he was, although he was very young,' Jakob explained. 'He was also the one who left behind that spare German uniform.'

'Oh, the one Otto uses?' asked Gary.

'That's right, yeah,' Jakob confirmed.

'What about the one Gary's worn before? Eva asked.

'Yeah, he left that behind too,' Jakob smiled, 'he was a crafty sort, but very loyal.'

•

Otto and George could see the reflection of the moon shimmering on the surface of the vast, black ocean. The air was bitter, but the smell of the sea was inviting as they sat on the beach, knees drawn up under their chins, holding their legs tight to keep warm.

'How much longer, Otto? I'm freezing my boots off,' said George shaking.

'The submarine is due any minute now,' Otto told him, who seemed to be in a world of his own.

'You all right there, Otto? You look as if you're deep in thought,' George observed.

'I was just thinking, we're facing the North Sea, the same ocean a friend of mine once crossed, he escaped to England to avoid the German General, Klaus Schneider,' explained Otto.

'Oh, I've heard of Schneider, nasty piece of work in Amsterdam, transferred from Poland,' said George.

'So it's not just mainland Europe who've heard of him then?' Otto said with a tone of surprise.

'Oh no, no, no, back in England, we know all about his infamous tactics of loosening the tongue for information, not to mention the ill treatment of the Jews, especially in Poland. Just the mention of his name sparks fear into those who hear it,' George admitted. Otto nodded.

'So tell me, where did that tomato sauce come from? Not to mention those papers you gave me?' Otto asked, looking very impressed.

'You're not the only one who has forgers,' George smiled, 'and the tomato sauce? Good question, it just happened to be there in the truck, don't ask why, somebody obviously left it there.'

Otto smiled and shook his head.

After just a few minutes, Otto spotted something in the water, something rising to the surface while coming inland.

'It's here,' Otto called and pointed out to sea.

'And about time too.' George got to his feet while squinting at the submarine's metallic exterior glinting in the moonlight.

'Well, I suppose this is goodbye,' said George, holding out a hand.

'I suppose it is,' Otto said, shaking it. George turned and made his way down to the submarine. Just as half his feet disappeared in the water, he turned back to Otto and called out, 'Tell the others I'll be back, and that England will never desert them!'

'I will, good luck, George!' Otto called back before turning to walk back up the beach, and back to the parked truck.

•

'Well, we'd best be off to bed,' said Jakob, standing up from the table with Angelina, 'we'll say goodnight to you two.'

'Goodnight then, Jakob, night Angelina,' said Gary and Eva.

'See you tomorrow,' Angelina replied as they disappeared into the hallway.

'Well, looks like it wasn't such an eventful day after all,' Gary smirked at Eva.

'On the contrary, I didn't say who it would be an eventful day for… but it certainly was an eventful day for Otto and George,' Eva replied.

Gary looked at Eva. 'Fancy making it an eventful night?' he grinned.

Eva tilted her head up and to the side, and looked down at Gary, 'Yeah all right then,' she smirked as she grabbed Gary's hand, stood up, and made their way over to the hallway, where Gary turned out the kitchen light as they left.

ELEVEN

DIGGING FOR VICTORY

Stalag VI J, Krefeld, Belgium.
December 3, 1940. 07:35

Wing Commander Thorne of the RAF was a tall, slim, middle-aged man with a dark grey moustache and grey hair poking out from under his blue cap. His hands were clasped behind his back as he paced the perimeter fence, glancing up every so often at the guard in the watchtower.

From out of nowhere, a small stone was thrown over the fence, which landed right at Wing Commander Thorne's feet. Checking the guard at the watchtower hadn't noticed, he knelt down on the pretext of tying his shoe, picked up the stone, put it in his pocket and walked on to his barracks.

Inside the barracks was rather homely, especially in the rooms where everyone slept in bunk beds. There were pictures and photos on the walls, some of family from home, some of friends in the army, others of film stars, including Celia Johnson and Betty Grable.

'I've got a reply, men!' Thorne called out to everyone in his posh voice, as he turned the corner and walked into a room with two bunk beds. He sat on the bottom, presumably his own, while others from the barracks crowded around him, some sitting up in bed, others from other rooms.

Thorne unwrapped the paper around the stone tied with an elastic band and read aloud.

'It's going ahead.'

The men looked at each other.

'Is that it?' one of them asked.

'Well, they couldn't reveal too much in case the stone was seen, in which case our cover story was going to be that the play we're rehearsing was going ahead. I mean, they couldn't very well prove otherwise, could they?' explained Thorne.

'So they're continuing the digging of the tunnel then?' the man in the bunk above him asked a little sleepily.

'That's right, although if my sources are correct, and as you know I don't tell you men everything, but it would seem the Dutch Resistance will be taking over from the Belgian Resistance at the other end of the tunnel, meaning we continue from our end, they continue from theirs, and eventually we will meet up, twice as quick, nice and easy,' Thorne said confidently.

'The Dutch Resistance? Why?' asked another.

'I don't tell you everything,' said Thorne sternly, 'I just hope the Belgians are back in time to give us our false papers.'

•

Otto strolled into the kitchen where Jakob, Angelina, Gary and Eva were sitting, having breakfast around the kitchen table, which was full of the usual: bread, jam, ham, bowls of muesli, yoghurt, and cups of coffee.

'Morning all, I've got a bit of a different day for you gentlemen today,' Otto said as he joined them at the end of the table.

They all looked on with mild interest.

'We are going to Belgium for a day or two,' he smiled.

'Nope! No way am I going to Belgium overnight,' Jakob said flatly, buttering his bread.

Otto's smile faded, 'Why not?' he asked.

'Because I have my business, a pregnant girlfriend, and I have to try and sort out a divorce before the new year if I can,' Jakob explained.

'Well, if you let me finish, I will tell you why we are going to Belgium. The Belgian Resistance would like us to finish a job that they started, as they are busy elsewhere at the moment, something to do with an… ammunition lorry or something,' Otto mumbled while feeding himself a spoonful of muesli.

'So what's the actual reason for us going there?' asked Gary.

Otto finished his mouthful of food and continued. 'Well, they want us to go to Stalag VI J Prisoner of War Camp in Krefeld, and complete the tunnel they were digging outside the camp. Now this tunnel is to meet up with another tunnel, which is being dug from inside the camp by the escape committee, and they will join to make one. The prisoners will then pick an opportune time to escape, by which time, the Belgian Resistance should be back to give them their false papers, so that they can hopefully escape to Switzerland if all goes to plan,' Otto said casually and continued with his muesli.

They were all looking at Otto, awestruck.

'Well, if I did go, I'm coming home tonight, there will be no staying overnight,' Jakob put his foot down. 'Will you two be all right looking after the shop alone?' Jakob asked Angelina and Eva.

'Yes of course, no problem,' they replied.

'Good, that's settled then, we should get going soon if you want to get back tonight though,' Otto added.

•

Midday, Angelina was writing in the notebook on the counter, when the bell tinkled, signifying that someone had entered through the door. She looked up and saw the General with a briefcase in his hands.

'General! How nice to see you,' Angelina called out, hoping that Eva would hear her from the kitchen; she did.

'Good afternoon, er, Angelina isn't it?' he smiled pleasantly as he strolled over.

Eva took off her heels, and crept round to the hallway to listen in.

'I love the Christmas decorations,' the General said as he observed the decorations around the shop ceiling, 'most festive.'

'How can I help, General?' Angelina asked, sounding bored.

'Well, actually, I was wondering if Eva was around?'

'Oh, er...'

'I'm here,' Eva walked casually into the kitchen. 'Klaus, how nice to see you,' she smiled and pecked the General on the cheek.

'A pleasure as always,' he smiled.

'So, what can I do for you, Klaus?' she asked, noticing the briefcase.

'Would you mind leaving us for a while?' the General asked Angelina; she nodded politely and exited through to the hallway.

'Eva, you remember how, a few months ago, I put in a good word for Jakob for you? And got him released from the Gestapo?'

'How could I forget?'

'Yes, well, I only did that for you, you know I'd do anything for you, if it had been up to me he'd still be there now. Anyway, I believe one good turn deserves another, I would like you to look after this for me,' and he placed the briefcase on the counter.

'May I ask what's in it?' Eva asked tentatively.

The General opened up the briefcase and Eva's jaw dropped. It was packed with jewellery, gold chains, necklaces, bracelets, rings, rubies and diamonds.

'They belonged to Jews who are now in labour camps,' the General said casually. 'I need someone I can trust to look after them for me until the end of the war.'

'But Klaus, they're searching all around here for downed airmen, what if they should find this?'

'Don't worry, you live with Dutch, they'll just get the blame instead of you,' he said callously.

Eva looked outraged, 'Klaus, I can't let that happen, I told you how much Jakob means to me.'

'OK, OK, I was joking, look, when the time comes for this area to be searched, I will personally have a word with the Reich Commissioner Seyss-Inquart and have him put in a little recommendation about this shop, how's that?' the General bargained.

'Fine, that's fine,' Eva finally agreed.

'Good, I will leave this in your hands then,' he smiled and turned to walk away.

'Klaus!' Eva called as he opened the door and turned back to her. She chose her words carefully. 'Why shouldn't you be found with them? Surely nobody would dare question you?'

'Because they belong to the Fuhrer, they're officially missing, but I'm keeping them for myself,' he winked at Eva and left.

Eva was frozen on the spot.

'Did I hear that right?' asked Angelina as she came into the shop.

'Yes, I'm afraid so.'

'All of this jewellery belonging to those poor Jews, and now Hitler is looking for it, and you have to look after it all for that evil pig?' Angelina clarified.

'Ever thought of becoming a spy yourself, Angie?' Eva grinned. 'Well, I've got no choice,' she said, closing the briefcase, 'I'm going to have to do as he says and take care of it.'

•

Jakob, Gary and Otto were all dressed in dark green overalls, sitting in a dirty old truck, parked outside Krefeld Prisoner of War Camp. The camp looked massive, multiple barracks inside a nine-foot-high perimeter fence, with watchtowers at each corner, each containing a guard with a sub-machine gun.

'Why did I agree to come?' Jakob said, staring round at the guards in the watchtowers.

'Just relax, we're workmen, they won't bother us,' Gary reassured him.

'Right, let's go, men,' Otto told them, and they all jumped down from the truck and went round to the back where their tools were waiting for them, wrapped in a large white sheet. Otto pulled the hatch down, collected the tools in his arms, and led them on a short walk through three-foot-high grass, until they came to a small wooden hut in the middle of the field. Gary opened the door to reveal an old, decrepit toilet in the middle.

Otto placed the tools down on the floor as Jakob closed the door behind them.

'This is it; this is the where the tunnel is,' Otto grinned.

'Where?' said Gary and Jakob looking around the five-by-five-foot shack.

'Under here,' he pointed down at the toilet, then bent over to grab a hold of the toilet, and simply lifted it aside to reveal a deep, dark hole in the ground.

'Wow! So this leads into the camp then, does it?' asked Jakob looking down the hole, his voice echoing.

'Well, it will do when it's finished,' said Otto, 'we'll be digging from one side while the prisoners dig from the other.'

'And what pretext are we here on?' asked Gary.

'We're fixing the toilet, of course,' said Otto. 'Right, anyone got a light?'

'You're not stopping for a cigarette now?' asked Gary incredulously.

'No don't be silly, I want a torch to see where I'm going down there,' Otto explained.

'We're not working by torchlight?' asked Jakob.

'No, I want torchlight to find the light switch down there,' said Otto.

'You mean they've actually got electricity down there?' Gary asked.

'Apparently so, yes, so let's get going. I'll get the rope,' said Otto, as he took out a long piece of rope from inside the white sheet and began to tie one end to a metal bar, which was part of the wash basin. Otto was the first to descend down the hole, gripping tightly on the rope. He was followed by Gary next, then Jakob, who was carrying the wrapped-up sheet containing tools.

'Got that torch?' Otto asked. Gary handed him the torch, and he shone it around looking for the switch. Next minute there was a small click, and the tunnel was lit up. An electrical system of lights had been cleverly set up; they ran the length of the ceiling, which was only four feet high, so they all got on their hands and knees and crawled along.

'This is clever and everything, but I can't help but feel a little claustrophobic,' said Jakob crawling along behind them, dragging the tools alongside him.

'Claustro-what?' asked Otto, concentrating on finding the end of the tunnel.

'Claustrophobic; it's a fear of confined spaces,' Gary explained, their voices echoing in the tunnel.

'Look, there's nothing to it, Jakob, we'll just be digging for a few hours, and then we would've done our bit, wouldn't we? Then we can go home, knowing that we've lent a small help to the Allied effort.'

'Well, that's something, but I didn't realise we were going to have to crawl,' Jakob moaned.

'Well, of course, it's quicker to build it this way, isn't it?' Otto explained. 'The way I hear it, all tunnels leading out of camps now are getting narrower and narrower height-wise; you mark my words, soon you'll have to go along on your bellies.'

'It's all right for you two, you're young, I'll be fifty in a few short years,' said Jakob, struggling on behind.

Finally, they stopped. Otto had found the current end to the tunnel.

'Looks like they've left us a few containers,' said Otto picking one up and showing them.

'Well, it's not as if the toilet's working, I suppose,' said Gary.

'Don't be thick, Gary, these are to fill with earth,' Otto explained. 'OK, let's start digging, shall we? Jakob, pass the tools.'

•

A couple of hours later, after taking it in turns to dig and fill up the containers and empty them in the entrance, Otto stopped digging.

'Shhh, do you hear that?'

'What?' asked Gary, now pausing. 'Jakob, stop digging,' he whispered back to Jakob.

'What is it?' Jakob asked.

'I think I can hear the prisoners digging from the other side, means we're close,' Otto said excitedly.

Gary and Jakob listened, and they could indeed hear the voices from the prisoners coming from somewhere up ahead.

'Keep digging,' Otto told them.

It was only minutes later when the earth fell away in front of Otto's eyes, exposing four very dirty, and very British-looking faces, all staring awestruck back at Otto.

'I don't believe it,' said Otto smiling back at Gary. 'It's the British.'

Gary and Jakob looked around Otto.

'Wing Commander Thorne of the RAF,' said the middle-aged man, with the bristling grey moustache and the blue cap, extending his hand.

'Otto of the Dutch Resistance,' Otto replied shaking his hand, 'and this is Gary and Jakob,' Otto gestured behind him.

'Gary?' Thorne queried. 'You're British, are you?'

'That's right, yeah,' Gary clarified.

'Ere boys! We've got another one from dear old Blighty over here,' Thorne called back to his men, who were all crouched on the ground behind him.

'All right, Gary!' they all called out in unison.

'Well look at that, would you?' Thorne said, observing all the electrical lights along the upper walls. 'Never thought of that our end, did we?' he chuckled, raising his gas lamp.

All of a sudden, and apparently to all of their surprise, at least two men's voices could now be heard, coming from the outside entrance to the tunnel behind Jakob. They all froze to listen.

'Hello!' one of the voices called.

Jakob chanced a look behind him and saw movement at the other end of the tunnel. He thought he could see dark green overalls like theirs in the dim light of the tunnel.

'Who is it, Jakob?' Otto asked with a tone of panic.

'I don't know, but they're not German,' Jakob replied.

'Not German? Then who the hell—'

'It's OK, don't be alarmed, it's only us, we're the Belgian Resistance,' the man in front said, as they approached Jakob. 'Ah, I see you've already been introduced to Wing Commander Thorne.'

'Yes, all the pleasantries have been done,' Thorne smiled, 'have you got our identification papers?'

'Right here, pass these down the line, will you?' the man handed them to Jakob, who passed them on to Gary, then to Otto and onto the British.

'OK, listen up everyone,' said the Belgian, 'we have five spare overalls at the tunnel entrance, so here's the plan. The two of us and you three,' he said referring to Jakob, Gary and Otto, 'will leave this place and go about our business, at which time the guards will have swapped over, leaving it free for you five gentlemen to leave wearing your overalls,' he said referring to the British. 'The new guards on duty will just think you're us,' he explained.

Moments later, the two Belgians, Jakob, Gary and Otto were climbing out of the dark tunnel and into the shack with the toilet. Once they were all out of the hole, one of the Belgians pulled the toilet back over the top to hide the tunnel, so now it all just looked like a regular outside toilet. Otto opened up the door and they exited. The cool breeze had hardly brushed their faces when…

'HALT!'

They all stopped in their tracks; the hairs on their necks and arms stood on end.

'What are you five doing?!'

They all turned and saw a German soldier on the other side of the wire fence, brandishing an MP34.

'Er, we're just the workmen, we're in the process of fixing the outside toilet, remember?' one of the Belgians called back.

'Why are you taking so long with it?' asked the guard.

'Well, we have nearly finished, not long now,' the other Belgian called back.

The guard looked over his shoulder and saw the sentry changing hands. 'Count yourselves lucky, I'm off duty,' he said and, to their relief, he walked away.

'What was his problem?' asked Otto slowly lowering his arms back down.

'I don't know, but that was too close for comfort,' muttered Jakob, 'let's get out of here.'

•

Eva came down the stairs and into the kitchen, where Angelina was behind the counter, sitting on the stool and doodling in the notebook. The street light outside came on as the daylight began to fade.

'So where did you hide the briefcase?' asked Angelina.

'Up in my room for now,' Eva replied, looking drained.

The bell tinkled as the door opened. They looked up and saw the Gestapo officer, Schultz, enter the shop carrying a briefcase. Angelina automatically had flashbacks of Jakob's bruised and battered face at the hands of this Gestapo thug.

'Merry Christmas to you ladies.' He smiled his sinister smile under his black hat and made his way over to the counter. 'I would like to speak to Eva alone,' he said in his creepy monotone voice, as he placed the briefcase on the counter.

Angelina looked at Eva with an expression which they could both read in each other, they were both getting the uncomfortable feeling of déjà vû.

'I'll just slip into the kitchen.' Angelina smiled politely and exited the shop.

'What is this all about?' Eva asked, eyeing the briefcase.

'I need you to hide this for me,' he said, patting the black leather briefcase.

'Why, what is it?' she asked cautiously.

Schultz fiddled with combinations and opened the briefcase to reveal jewellery and money filled to the brim. It looked like he'd just robbed a bank and then a jewellery shop. Now Eva was certainly feeling déjà vû, as she stared at it in horror.

'Lots of jewellery and 1,000 Guilders, all taken from Jews and to go to the Fuhrer, but all in good time. In the meantime I need you to hide them here until I ask for them back,' Schultz informed her.

'Yes, Herr Schultz,' she agreed reluctantly. She had the distinct feeling that, just like the General, Schultz wanted these possessions for himself.

'Good, I'll be in touch,' he said softly as he gazed at her, his eyes in shadow under his hat. 'Heil Hitler,' he nodded and turned to leave.

Eva was speechless, staring at the contents of the briefcase.

Angelina, hearing the bell tinkle once more, came back into the kitchen and stopped in her tracks.

'Oh my God, not another fortune belonging to the Jews?' she asked with a mixture of shock and disgust.

'I'm afraid so,' Eva replied as she walked round and closed the briefcase. 'I won't alter this, I don't know the combination,' she said to herself as she lifted it off the counter. She carried it out into the hall. She stopped by the long red curtain separating the stairs from the hallway with a hopeless look in her eyes, and she put the case down; she then turned back to Angelina. 'Angie, would you take a walk with me? I need some air and I don't want to be alone,' she asked, tears beginning to fill her blue eyes.

'Oh of course, we'll have to lock up,' Angelina replied as she reached under the counter for the keys. 'Here, you lock up and turn that closed sign around will you, Eva, while I write a quick note to Jakob in case he's back before us.'

•

An hour or so later, Jakob, Gary and Otto came bustling in through the back door, chatting and laughing.

'Oh, I'm glad that's over,' Jakob said as he reached round for the light. 'Where is everyone?' Gary asked as they all stepped into the light of the kitchen.

'I'll see if Angie's left a note in the notebook, she often does,' said Jakob as he went through to the shop. Gary and Otto followed him when Gary noticed the briefcase at the bottom of the stairs.

'What's this then?' he said, picking it up, Otto by his side.

Gary opened the case and their faces dropped. 'I don't believe what he's doing,' said Gary fuming.

'What is it, Gary?' asked Otto, looking puzzled at the contents.

'That bloody General, he's passed forged money onto Eva before. Well, I'm doing with this what I did with the last lot,' Gary said angrily.

'It's OK, they've just gone out for a walk apparently, they'll be—' Jakob came back to the hallway and stopped abruptly as he too spotted the contents of the case in Gary's hands.

'You remember that forged money the General gave Eva months back? I think he's back to his old tricks,' Gary slammed the case shut. 'I'm dumping this in the canal, I'll see you all later,' he said as he turned to leave out the back way.

TWELVE

A FRIEND FROM THE PAST

A few moments later, Eva and Angelina came in through the back door, to be greeted by Jakob and Otto, both sitting at the table with a glass of brandy each.

'Jakob, how did it go?' Angelina asked, wrapping her arms around him.

'Well, as far as we know, it was a complete success,' he replied, his arm around her waist.

'Where's Gary?' asked Eva as she closed the door, looking from Jakob to Otto.

'He's gone to chuck the briefcase in the canal,' Otto replied casually, sipping his brandy.

Eva and Angelina exchanged horrified looks. She quickly disappeared into the hallway, but came back very slowly, her expression hadn't changed. 'It's gone,' she told Angelina.

'What's the matter?' asked Jakob noticing the looks on their faces.

'That briefcase contained jewellery and money, once

belonging to Jews who've now been deported to labour camps, but now belonging to Hitler,' Eva explained.

Jakob and Otto were now the ones exchanging horrified looks.

'The Gestapo officer, Schultz, gave it to me to look after,' she added.

'Oh my God.' Jakob looked to Otto for help, hoping he'd come up with an idea as usual, but Otto was looking just as bewildered. The silence was almost unbearable but was unexpectedly broken by Gary coming in through the back door.

'Hi,' he smiled at Eva, 'how are you?' he walked over to her and put his arms around her, but she did not return the gesture. Gary noticed and pulled back to look at her.

'What's the matter?' he asked her, then he looked round at the others' expressions. 'What's happened?' he looked back at Eva with a feeling something had gone terribly wrong.

'Did you throw a briefcase in the canal?' Eva asked him quickly.

'Yes, I did, for your sake!' Gary replied defensively.

Eva strolled over to a chair, pulled it out, sat down and put her face in her hands.

'Look, will someone tell me what the hell is going on?' Gary demanded.

Angelina walked up to Gary, put her hand on his arm, and spoke in a quiet, almost motherly voice.

'Gary, that particular briefcase was given to Eva by the Gestapo officer, Herr Schultz. It's meant for Hitler. Eva was supposed to be keeping it safe for him,' she explained calmly.

Gary was stunned, speechless, as he tried to take all this in. 'I'll go and retrieve it at once,' he said desperately.

'Retrieve it?' said Jakob incredulously. 'It's at the bottom of the canal, the money will be soaked through and useless.'

Gary looked completely helpless; he kept looking at Eva for support, but that wasn't going to happen; she was the one who could suffer thanks to his hot-headedness, and he knew it, unintentional though it was.

'All right, wait a minute,' said Otto as he got to his feet, 'I've got an idea, Gary, go and get the briefcase back.'

'But the money will be ruined,' Gary replied helplessly.

'Never mind the money, I'll sort that, you go and get that jewellery back,' Otto ordered.

Gary left at once through the back door.

'What have you got in mind, Otto?' Eva asked in a weak voice.

'I'm going to use the radio,' he said as he made his way to the hallway, he turned back for a second and said, 'I need to speak to an old friend.'

•

Gary felt a very strange feeling in his stomach as he walked alongside the canal; he didn't know what it was, but he didn't like it. Was it guilt? Was it panic? He didn't know, but he did know that if he was successful in retrieving that briefcase, then at least half of what he was feeling would be gone.

He thanked his lucky stars, when he got to the spot where he'd put the case in the water, for it was completely devoid of any street lights, it was in the shadows, and after gazing around the area, appeared to be currently deserted.

He removed his beige overcoat first and laid it on the bank; he then proceeded to simultaneously remove his shoes and socks while keeping his eyes peeled for passers-by. He then rolled up his trouser legs and proceeded with caution into the icy waters of the canal. It was so cold that he felt like he had pins and needles in his feet, and as he stepped in deeper, the pins and needles travelled up his legs.

Gary felt around with his feet for any sign of the case, but all he could feel were stones and what felt almost like seaweed.

'Oh, come on, it must be around here somewhere,' he muttered to himself, as he kept a constant visual on his surroundings. He had a horrible feeling that it must have drifted deeper into the canal. He walked in as deep as he could, ignoring his trousers now getting soaked as the water travelled up his thighs. He was conscious of the noisy ripples he was making, echoing in the dead of night. But then something else broke the silence. Gary froze, and not because of the temperature of the water, but because he heard the unmistakable sound of jackboots; a German sentry was on their way, the footsteps getting louder.

'Oh, you've got to be kidding me,' he whispered to himself, seeing his own breath escape his mouth. He knew what he had to do, he had no choice, he took a deep breath and secreted himself under the surface of the water. His whole head filled with searing pain, and he could hear nothing, not even the Nazi jackboots; instead it felt like someone had placed a pillow over both ears: deathly silence. As he waited until he thought the German sentry had marched by, he opened his eyes ready to go back up to the surface, when a wave of excitement washed over him;

he could see the case sitting on the canal floor. Careful not to create ripples on the surface, he slowly, struggling against the current, made his way over to the briefcase. He picked it up, turned around, and made his way slowly back to the surface again. As he broke the surface, the sound of jackboots was clear once more, only this time they were fading away. Gary took a quick look around before bringing the case to the surface, then proceeded to put on his socks, shoes and coat.

•

Otto came walking into the kitchen with a satisfied expression.

'So who was it you had to get hold of, Otto?' asked Jakob curiously, Angelina perched on his lap.

'Anton,' he replied simply.

'Anton? As in…' Jakob nodded, prompting Otto to confirm.

'Yes, Anton, our old friend, and more to the point, forger,' Otto added.

'Oh I see, so Anton is going to be forging the money?' Eva asked with genuine interest.

'Yes, that's the good news at least,' said Otto.

'So what's the bad news?' asked Angelina.

'The bad news is that it's going to take him at least a week to do it, so let's just hope that Schultz doesn't ask for the case back before that time,' Otto explained.

Gary came bursting through the door out of breath and soaking wet, his hair in his eyes, his shirt sticking to his body, but he had the case.

'Well done, Gary, well done my son,' said Otto taking the case.

'Oh Gary,' Eva said, suddenly looking all motherly, 'you are absolutely saturated, come on, let's take you upstairs and get you washed and dried,' she said, taking his wet hand and guiding him through to the hallway.

Otto knelt down and opened the heavy wet case on the floor – luckily the combination hadn't been moved – and he opened the case.

'Urgh, absolutely soaking. The jewellery is perfectly fine, thank God, but the money has had it, straight in the bin with that lot, it's probably...' Otto stopped and studied the money.

'What is it, Otto?' Jakob asked as he and Angelina looked on.

Otto looked up at them, mouth open in shock, 'This money is genuine.'

'It's what? It can't be, that's why Gary chucked it in the canal, remember?' said a confused Jakob.

'Well, maybe because he was angry, wasn't he, he obviously didn't notice, he just assumed they were fakes like the last lot he told us about, the ones from the General,' suggested Otto.

'Well, I suppose it makes sense they should be genuine, if they once belonged to Jews, and now they belong to Hitler,' Angelina interjected thoughtfully.

'Yes, but you would've thought that Schultz would've swapped them for forgeries, wouldn't you, you know, keep the genuine ones and give Hitler the forgeries,' Jakob added.

'Well, who's to say that's not still his plan, he could be

getting forgeries made right now, while he gets Eva to take care of this lot?' Otto suggested. 'But let's not speculate yet,' he added, 'because hopefully, in about a week or so, we'll have a thousand Guilder in perfectly forged notes, courtesy of Anton.'

•

December 10, 1940. 23:58

The almost-full moon was shining silently in the pitch-black sky, overlooking the large field in which, Gary, Otto, Jakob, Angelina and Eva were looking up at the skies, and waiting. Otto and Gary were dressed as German Privates. their story for being out after curfew should they get stopped and questioned was to say that they and Eva, who was known by the General to be a German spy, had caught Jakob, Angelina and Gary out after curfew, and were escorting them back.

'I can't wait to see him again,' said Jakob, his face lit up by the moonlight.

'May 16th, I think it was, the last time we saw him,' confirmed Otto.

'Has it really been seven months already?' asked Angelina.

'Well, he sounds like a very nice man, I'm only sorry I missed him by a margin,' said Eva.

'He was the best,' said Otto.

And finally, there it was, the sound of plane in the distance. Otto got out his torch and began to wave it across the field, hoping to attract the pilot's attention. The sound of the engine was getting louder; everyone was facing the skies. After a few minutes a plane came into view over the treetops and it flew lower and lower until the wheels scuffed and bounced along the ground.

Everyone ran over to the plane as it came to a stop. They saw a man in the cockpit waving at them; he was wearing a helmet and goggles and was unrecognisable until he pulled back the glass roof and removed his goggles.

'All right everyone!' he called.

To hear Anton's voice was like having sunshine break through thick cloud to warm the face.

'Anton! How are you, my man?' called Otto.

'It's great to see you,' added Jakob.

'Really great to see you,' Angelina nodded.

'It's great to see you all too,' Anton said, carrying a briefcase as he clambered down on to the soft grass.

Anton and Otto hugged and slapped each other's backs in affection.

'Jakob,' Anton said with his arms open.

'Good to see you, my friend,' said Jakob as they patted each other's backs.

'Angelina,' Anton smiled as he embraced her.

'Er, Anton, may I introduce Gary, British intelligence,' said Otto.

'Pleased to meet you, Gary, I've heard all about you,' said Anton as they shook hands.

'Likewise, but don't worry, I won't tell,' Gary joked.

'And this is Eva, Gary's girlfriend,' Otto introduced.

'Eva?' Anton frowned while shaking her hand.

'I was sent here from Berlin. I was a German spy, but then I met Gary here, and to cut a long story short, I'm now on your side,' she smiled.

'You picked the right side,' Anton returned the smile.

'So, where's Rini?' Anton asked innocently.

The others exchanged uncomfortable looks.

'Well, Rini and I are no longer an item,' said Jakob looking down at the black ground where he could barely see his own feet.

'Oh, I'm sorry to hear that,' Anton said, taken aback.

'No, no, don't be, we fell out of love years ago, it was inevitable, but I'm with Angelina now...'

Anton's jaw dropped with a slight smile.

'And we're having a baby,' Jakob added.

'What?! I did not see that one coming. Well, congratulations to you both, I really mean that,' Anton smiled at them both.

'Er, I hate to break this up, but is that the money you've got there, Anton?' asked Otto.

'Oh yes, one thousand Guilders,' Anton handed over the case.

'Thanks Anton, we are forever in your debt,' Otto replied.

'I'll hold you to that,' Anton grinned as he began his climb back into the cockpit.

'Will you be all right getting back? I seem to remember last time you getting caught in an air raid, and you had to ditch in the North Sea, and then got picked up by a submarine,' Otto joked.

'Don't remind me,' Anton replied putting his goggles back on, 'no, I'll be all right, I'm flying myself this time,' he grinned.

He switched on the engine and the front propeller fired up.

'Goodbye for now!' Anton called out above the engine.

'Take care, Anton!' they all called out as the plane began to move along the ground. The plane picked up speed and was eventually airborne.

Everyone waved, and Anton responded by rocking his plane from side to side, as it was silhouetted in the moonlight.

THIRTEEN

HITLER'S ON THE PHONE

December 11, 1940

'The approaching train is the eight-thirty-four to Utrecht, that's the eight-thirty-four to Utrecht,' said the lady's voice coming through the speaker at the train station.

The platforms were very busy, with both Germans and civilians alike.

Angelina was sitting on a bench on one of the platforms, staring around and absent-mindedly rubbing her small baby bump with her hands, as a large black steam train began to roll into the station. Suddenly, the sound of chatter was drowned out by the sound of pistons. She looked over to her left through the crowd of bustling people and saw Eva making her way over to her. She sat down next to Angelina.

'It's done,' said Eva.

'The case?' asked Angelina.

'Yes, the case, it's in the storage compartment on the train bound for Berlin,' Eva explained.

'Job done then. Come on, let's go home,' said Angelina, and they both got to their feet and merged into the crowd.

•

Many hours later

'Have a nice day, madam,' said Jakob as he handed the lady her change over the counter. The lady smiled and turned to exit through the door. Just as she exited, just before the door could fully close again, the General entered.

'Ah, General, how nice to see you, and how are you?' Jakob asked with convincing politeness.

'Mr Jansen,' the General replied as he strolled over to the counter. 'And how have you been since that terrible ordeal with the Gestapo?' the General asked most curtly.

'Oh, that is all forgotten, General, thanks to you,' Jakob smiled.

'Don't thank me, thank Eva, she's the one who told me how valuable you apparently are to her work, as hard as that is to believe. I'd do anything for that woman,' the General replied thoughtfully. 'And talking of Eva, she's not available to talk to by any chance, is she?'

'Oh yes, of course, I'll just get her,' Jakob said and went through to the back and called her. 'Eva, the General wishes to see you.' The General heard him call. Next minute Eva came in from the back, and Jakob stayed in the hallway to listen in.

'Eva, and how are you?' he asked, bending down to kiss her cheek.

'I'm well thank you, Klaus, and you?'

'Oh, fine, fine, I just wanted to enquire about the briefcase, is it safe?'

'Perfectly safe, General, it's safely hidden in my room,' she told him reassuringly.

'Excellent, now then, I—'

The telephone started ringing.

'Excuse me, General,' Eva said apologetically, and lifted the receiver.

'Jakob Jansen's Food Shop,' she answered.

The General listened in.

'Eva, it's Herr Schultz, listen to what I say. You're not going to believe this, but I've just had the Fuhrer himself on the phone.'

'The Fuhrer?!' she gasped.

'Listen, he had that money in that briefcase examined—'

'Ah, I can explain that, you see—'

'It doesn't matter,' he cut her off again, 'it was my intention to tell you to put it on the train anyway, the point is, he has discovered that the money in the case was fake, forgeries.'

'Oh really?' Eva replied trying to sound genuine, knowing it was the money Anton had printed.

'Yes, you see I was intending to give the Fuhrer forgeries while I took the real money,' said Schultz.

Eva was shocked and confused; this meant that Otto was wrong, and Gary was right, the money was fake. It suddenly dawned on Eva that they had replaced forgeries with forgeries.

'I have the genuine money with me here in the office. I told the Fuhrer I gave the case to you, and now he wants you to speak with him over the phone, so you can use the one in my office, and Eva, don't even think about telling the Fuhrer what I've told you, because I will be standing right here next to you,' he threatened.

The General snatched the phone from Eva.

'This is General Klaus Schneider!' he barked.

'Oh, er, General Schneider, please allow me to explain—'

'Any telephone call to the Fuhrer made from Amsterdam can be made from my office, authorised by Seyss-Inquart himself. Eva will escort me to my office now, and make the telephone call from there,' the General slammed down the phone, and looked at Eva. 'Taking another's possessions is one thing, but giving forged notes to our beloved Fuhrer crosses the line. Do not worry, my dear, just tell the Fuhrer what you know,' the General added.

Eva nodded, her nerves on tenterhooks. She poked her head around the doorway to let Jakob know that she was just about to leave with the General.

•

Officer Schultz of the Gestapo was frantically packing clothes from his wardrobe into an open suitcase on his desk.

There was a knock at the door; it opened and the doorman stood in the doorway holding a cup and saucer. 'Are you going somewhere, sir?' the doorman asked.

Schultz stopped what he was doing and looked up. 'Ah, Herman, I don't think I want the tea now.'

'That's fine, sir… er, you seem in an awful hurry.'

I'm sorry, Herman, but I'm a little busy,' Schultz continued to pack.

Herman left and closed the door behind him.

Schultz then took a black briefcase from the wardrobe, put it next to the suitcase on the desk and opened it. He smiled menacingly at the thousand Guilders' worth of genuine notes.

•

'Please take a seat, Eva,' said the General, as he placed his hat on his desk and took a seat, while Eva sat on the other side.

The General lifted the receiver and went to dial the number, but paused and looked at Eva. 'Are you ready?' he asked her, Eva nodded.

He dialled the number, while Eva waited, butterflies in her stomach.

'General Klaus Schneider of the… yes, that's the one. I wish to be put through to the Fuhrer, tell him Eva Van Houten has important information for him.' He passed her the receiver. She took it slowly, put it to her ear and waited.

'Hello,' said a voice, Eva froze, she recognised the voice from the newsreels. 'Hello,' the voice of Adolf Hitler spoke in her ear again.

'Eva,' the General prompted her.

'Hello?' she finally managed, struggling to keep her composure.

'Eva Van Houten? I believe you have some information for me regarding my money,' he asked.

'Yes, mein Fuhrer,' she looked to the General, and mouthed the word 'water', at which the General opened the drawer in his desk and took out a bottle of his favourite water. He opened it and passed it to her; she took a sip right away.

'I'm waiting,' he replied in her ear.

'Pardon me, mein Fuhrer,' she composed herself. 'Officer Schultz of the Gestapo dropped by yesterday. He gave me a briefcase full of jewellery and money; he said he wanted me to hide it for him. He said he wanted to keep the money for himself, despite him knowing it was meant for you. I couldn't bring myself to do this, and so I sent it to you on the train. Only this morning, he rang me to tell me they were forgeries.'

There was a slight pause.

'Very well, put the General back on the line,' he told her. Eva passed the receiver back to the General. 'He wants to talk to you,' she whispered.

'Mein Fuhrer,' the General said with confidence. 'Yes, mein Fuhrer, I can vouch for Frau Van Houten, I was present when the exchange took place… yes, mein Fuhrer, I suspect Herr Schultz has the genuine money in his office as we speak… yes mein Furher… well would you like me to take care of it, mein Fuhrer? Very well… thank you, mein Fuhrer, goodbye.' The General replaced the receiver and looked at Eva.

'Well? What did he say?' Eva asked, intrigued.

'Well, I think Herr Schultz has bothered you for the last time.'

A wave of relief fell over Eva. 'Why did you tell him you were there?' she asked.

'To get you off the hook, of course, as a thank you. You said you'd put his case on the train, but you did not mention mine; that is the sort of loyalty I admire, Eva. I trust you still have my case well hidden?'

'Of course, Klaus.'

'Good, because while Schultz's case was full of forgeries, mine are genuine, and when the search for it has been called off, I shall take it back.'

'Well, thank goodness that's over,' Eva said, standing up.

'Are you leaving already?' he asked.

'Yes, I need to get back and have something a little stronger than that water,' she smiled.

'I understand,' the General smiled back, 'well at least let me see you back?'

'OK,' Eva agreed.

They entered the cold street, and walked slowly side by side, as a few flecks of snow began to float down from the sky.

'I would like to thank you again, Eva, for not mentioning my briefcase.'

'Well, that's what friends do, and thank you, Klaus, for saying you were a witness.'

'That's what friends do,' he smiled down at her.

Next minute, they heard the sound of jackboots.

'What's going on over there?' the General mumbled to himself.

Two German guards marched around the corner, as if on a mission, and burst through the front doors of the Gestapo headquarters.

Schultz was still busy packing his suitcase when he had the shock of his life as the office door flew open with a bang. Schultz looked up from his suitcase to see two German guards standing in the doorway, aiming their MP34s at him. He stood up straight and looked them in the eyes from his side of the desk, fear etched on his face for the first time. The guards opened fire, spraying him with bullets. He got blown back, his lifeless and bloody body slumped in his chair.

Eva and the General were still outside when the guards exited the Gestapo headquarters. They marched with authority in their direction. Eva was sure they were coming for her, but they marched on past.

'Did you hear the firing?' Eva asked the General. 'Shall we take a look?'

'Yes, let's see what's going on,' the General agreed, and they made their way over to the Gestapo headquarters. As the General entered, followed by Eva, a woman Private came hurrying down the corridor from the other end to them, and peered inside Schultz's office. She clapped her hands to her mouth, let out a scream and dashed past Eva and the General. They continued on to Schultz's office to take a look. The General looked round the corner first; he showed no emotion as he saw the dead body of Schultz slouched in the chair, he simply shook his head. Eva then looked round and, much like the lady before her, she clapped her hands to her mouth, but she managed to contain her screams.

'Oh my goodness, why would anyone do this?' she said, more to herself than to the General.

'Isn't it obvious? All it took was one telephone call from the Fuhrer. But, of course, they will still be searching for the case,' explained the General.

'Maybe not,' Eva said, as she quickly walked over to the briefcase on the desk.

'Is that what I think it is?' asked the General.

Eva turned the case around to show the General.

'My God,' he said in surprise as he went over to the case. He closed it and handed it to Eva.

'Eva, take this case and put it with the other one in your room. When the war is over, we will take one each,' he told her excitedly.

'I don't know if I could take this for myself,' said Eva feeling guilty.

'What do you mean?' he asked, surprised.

'Well, it rightfully belongs to… the Fuhrer,' she caught herself.

'Eva, listen to me,' the General looked at her seriously. 'If the Fuhrer gets this money, he's only going to spend it on more architecture and autobahns, but we will deserve it, you will certainly deserve it, Eva,' he tried to persuade her.

Eva nodded reluctantly; she knew she was taking money belonging to the Dutch Jews.

'OK, now go, put it with the other case and say nothing to anyone, and I will try and make sure the shop is exempt from being searched. No promises, mind you.'

'OK, I'm gone, I'm gone,' she replied, and she took the case and exited the office. The General looked back to Schultz slumped in the chair. 'Merry Christmas, you bastard.'

FOURTEEN

GERMANS IN THE CELLAR

January 12, 1941

Jakob, Gary, Angelina and Eva were all gathered around the counter, listening to the wireless.

'... but naturally the bombing continues. In London yesterday, fifty-seven people were tragically killed, and a further seventy-nine were injured, as a German bomb landed right outside the Bank of England, totally demolishing the underground station below, and leaving a great 120-foot crater in the ground. In other news...' Jakob switched off the wireless.

'I think I can safely say that we are still at the beginning of this terrible war,' Jakob said as he looked down at Angelina's ever-growing tummy. 'Six months gone already; what sort of world are we letting this one be born into?' Jakob shook his head.

'It's going to take time, Jakob, but we will win through,' Angelina consoled him gently rubbing his back.

Otto came into the shop from the back.

'Bad news I'm afraid, everyone,' he explained. 'I just got off the radio, Hitler is sending yet another Gestapo agent to Amsterdam; his name is Ludwig Von Braun. He's ruthless, and his sole purpose for being here is to find the two missing cases and return them to Hitler.'

'Oh, you're joking. I have to see the General right away,' Eva said, looking concerned. 'I'll see you later.' She pecked Gary on the cheek and made to exit the shop.

'The search is imminent,' Otto explained, 'he will search every building in Amsterdam, and will stop at nothing until those cases are found. It might be a good idea to persuade Eva to deliver both cases anonymously by train.'

'Or we could just hand them over to this Gestapo officer?' suggested Gary.

'Don't be ridiculous, we'll all be up against the wall facing a firing squad,' Otto explained.

'But the General knows about the cases, there's no way he will give up his case,' said Jakob.

•

Eva opened the unlocked front doors to the German headquarters, and marched across the marble floor, making a beeline for the stairs that started in the centre of the hall. As she reached the top of the stairs, she turned left and marched along the corridor.

'Excuse me, miss, you can't just...' called a man's voice from an office to her left, but she completely ignored him and continued on. She eventually came to the office of General Klaus Schneider. She knocked on the door.

'Come in,' he called.

Eva opened the door and entered.

'Eva, what an unexpected surprise, how can I help?' the General got to his feet.

'We have a problem,' she said urgently as she pulled up a chair opposite. The General sat back down.

'The Fuhrer is sending a new Gestapo agent to Amsterdam. His name is Ludwig Von Braun; he is ruthless, and his sole purpose for being here is to retrieve those cases and return them to the Fuhrer. Apparently, he will stop at nothing until he finds those cases.'

The General looked stunned.

'Eva, how did you come by this information?' he asked.

'I'm a spy,' she shrugged.

'This is excellent work, Eva,' he told her, leaning back in his chair and clasping his hands together deep in thought. 'We need to think of a place to hide these cases, somewhere they won't think of looking,' said the General thoughtfully.

'But Klaus, they will be searching everywhere, the butcher's, the florist's, Jakob's shop, they'll even search here,' explained Eva in mild panic.

'Perhaps, but not a nunnery.'

'A nunnery?' asked Eva, confused.

'Yes, that is the last place they will think of looking,' he got to his feet and began pacing. 'Yes, we will take the cases to the nunnery on the outskirts of town and tell the Reverend Mother to hide them until the end of the war. We will tell her that we are collaborators, and that we are trying to prevent the cases falling into the hands of Hitler,' the General explained, still pacing.

'So, shall I go and get the cases now?' Eva asked.

'Yes, and I shall come with you,' he added as an afterthought.

Moments later, they arrived at the shop. Jakob had just finished serving an elderly man at the till, when he looked up in surprise to see Eva entering with the General.

'Hello Jakob,' Eva smiled, walking past a second customer.

'Eva, General,' Jakob nodded.

'I'll be right down, Klaus,' she said as she made her way out back.

The silence between the General and Jakob was most awkward.

'So, how are you these days, General?' Jakob asked, trying to make conversation.

The General turned to Jakob with an emotionless expression.

'That's not really any of your concern, is it, Mr Jansen?' he replied lazily.

Jakob didn't know how to take this unnecessary sarcasm, and just kept his head down and pretended to be searching for something in the writing pad on the counter.

'You!' said the General randomly. Jakob looked up to see the General approaching the only customer currently in the shop, a middle-aged man with dark wiry hair and a protruding nose, who froze in his tracks.

'Let me see your papers,' the General ordered.

The man slipped his hand into his trouser pocket, pulled out his necessary identification and handed it to the General, who snatched it with a loathing look on his face.

'Jew,' he whispered, and he opened the door and threw the man's identity papers into the street, 'get out, you piece of filth,' the General said, looking at the man as if he were something nasty on the bottom of his shoe.

The man looked over to Jakob.

'He won't help you, because if he does, I'll shoot him.'

Jakob felt his heart beat a little faster as fear rose up in his stomach. He went back to his writing pad, as the man simply left the shop with fear etched on his face. The General turned back to Jakob.

'I'm surprised at you, letting filth like that enter your shop. Don't let me see that again,' the General warned him. Jakob simply kept his head down and neither of them spoke again.

The uncomfortable silence didn't last long, as Eva came back into the room carrying the two cases, which didn't go unnoticed by Jakob.

'Ah, Eva, I'll take those,' said the General and she passed him the cases.

'I'll get the door,' Eva opened the door for him. Eva nodded to Jakob as she left, hoping to communicate that she knew what she was doing. Jakob went straight into the kitchen, where Gary, Otto and Angelina were chatting.

'Otto, Otto!' he called urgently, as he walked up to him. 'I don't know what Eva's got in mind, but she's just given both cases to the General and they left.'

'Do you think she could finally be getting rid of them and putting them on the train for Berlin?' asked Gary.

'Only if she's managed to persuade the General first,' Otto replied. 'No, I think, with the knowledge that Amsterdam is to be searched, they've taken the cases to hide them somewhere, until the General decides he wants them back.'

'Well, should one of us follow them to see where they're hiding the cases?' asked Jakob.

'No, Eva will let us know when she comes back,' Otto explained.

•

Eva and the General arrived at the nunnery; tall black iron gates separated them from the long gravel path, which in turn separated a flower-decorated garden, leading up to the oak doors of an imposingly large but elegant nunnery.

Eva opened the gate for the General, who was still carrying the cases. She let the squeaky gate swing back with a clang. Their feet crunched on the gravel with each step. They arrived at the tall oak doors, enclosed by a large stone archway. Eva knocked, and a short moment later they heard the clanging of the handle being turned from the inside. The door slowly opened to reveal a nun's head poking round.

'Yes?' she said.

'Good morning,' smiled Eva, 'we wondered if we could speak to the Reverend Mother?'

'Come inside,' said the nun, and she opened the heavy oak door wider to admit them inside.

The interior was very much like that of an ordinary church, the stained-glass windows with colourful designs, the rows of pews on either side, separated by an aisle leading up to the altar. There was a damp, musty smell in the air, as their steps echoed through the building.

'Wait right here,' the nun smiled, 'I will fetch the Reverend Mother for you.' She exited the main hall through a small doorway.

'I hope this works,' Eva's whisper echoed.

'Of course it will, it would never occur to them to search a nunnery,' the General replied confidently.

An elderly nun entered through the little doorway through which the other nun had exited.

'Good morning, I am the Reverend Mother, how may I help you?' she asked; she looked so old and frail.

'Good morning, Reverend Mother,' the General smiled, 'we were wondering if you could hide these cases for us? The Germans are looking for them.'

'And are you not German?' she asked inquisitively.

'Er, well, yes we are, but I suppose you could call us collaborators, we're collaborating with the Allies. You see, these cases really belong to poor Jews, we are hoping to return them to those particular Jews once the war is over,' the General explained.

'Well, I'm sure you're both aware that we are not a part of this war, we have chosen to remain ignorant to it. However, it would not be Christian-like to turn a blind eye with regards to this. Very well, I shall keep them safe in my office,' she said.

The General handed over the cases. 'Reverend Mother, thank you so much, thanks to you, those poor innocent Jews will have their belongings returned.'

'Are you sure you're OK carrying those?' asked Eva.

'Fine thank you, dear,' she turned to face them from the doorway, 'and may God be with you,' she said, gravely before exiting.

•

Jakob was stood looking through the blinds of the front door.

'Have you sorted everything, Otto?' he called back over his shoulder.

'Everything is fine,' Otto replied, coming into the shop from the hallway.

'No, everything is not fine,' said Jakob. Otto detected worry in his voice. 'The Gestapo have just entered the butcher's.'

Otto rushed to the window beside Jakob and observed trough the blinds.

'Jakob, get away from the door, if they see you, they'll know you've got something to hide,' came Angelina's voice as she entered the shop.

'She's right,' said Otto backing away. He and Jakob joined Angelina over at the counter.

'I never thought it would come to this, my shop being searched by the Gestapo for Jewish belongings wanted by Hitler.'

The bell jingled. Everybody looked up in fright, but were relieved to see it was only Eva.

'I see the Gestapo have started their search,' Eva said as she strolled over to them, removing her woollen gloves.

'Yes, and we're probably next,' said Jakob anxiously.

Gary entered from the back, sweeping his side parting with one hand. 'Eva, what have you done with the cases?' he asked.

'The general and I have taken them to the nunnery,' she replied casually.

'The nunnery?' said Jakob incredulously.

'What did I tell you?' Otto smirked. 'I told them you'd

probably taken them to hide them in an undetectable place.'

'Yes, but I'm having second thoughts about it all,' said Eva, 'in fact I'm considering going back to retrieve them and putting them on the train.'

'Wouldn't the General become suspicious if Hitler suddenly called off the search for the cases?' asked Otto.

'Well, not really, I could just say the Gestapo searched the nunnery, found the cases and put them on the train for Berlin,' she said while deep in thought. 'In fact, that's exactly what I'm going to do now.' She'd made up her mind and exited through the front door.

'Right, I'd better get out of sight,' Otto said suddenly.

'What? Where are you going? The Gestapo are going to be searching here soon, I might need you with me,' said Jakob nervously.

'Jakob, when the Gestapo come searching, they're going to search upstairs too. They will see four rooms, one being a storage room, and they will wonder where I sleep,' explained Otto.

'Yeah, why do you sleep in the cellar, by the way?' asked Gary as if he'd only just noticed.

'The radio,' Otto said simply, 'I have to be at hand day and night.'

'Oh,' Gary still looked confused.

'Right then, I'm off,' said Otto as he made his way out back.

'They're on their way over now,' said Angelina in an urgent whisper, as she peered between the blinds. She stood to the side as the door was pushed open rather violently by a Gestapo officer, a very tall man, as tall as the General at six-foot-four. He was dressed in a black hat, and a long black leather mac. He held the door open for two German soldiers who stormed in.

'Begin upstairs,' the Gestapo officer ordered.

They marched past the counter with their MP40s slung over their shoulders and made their way through to the back.

Jakob pretended to be writing in his pad on the counter, while Angelina made herself look busy stacking the shelves.

The Gestapo officer walked slowly and deliberately over to Jakob, and he just stared at him in silence until Jakob finally looked up at him.

'Good morning, proprietor,' he said in a deep voice, 'I am the Gestapo, my name is Ludwig Von Braun, that's Herr Von Braun to you.'

'Good morning, officer, please feel free to look around, we have nothing to hide do we, dear?' Jakob said to Angelina, his voice trembling.

Angelina looked over while she was on the first step of a stepladder, and simply shook her head.

'Good, because if anything of any interest to us is found, particularly two cases full of money and jewellery, you will both be shot on the spot and your bodies burned, do I make myself clear?' the Gestapo officer said in a deep threatening tone.

'Crystal clear, Herr Von Braun,' replied Jakob, trying in vain to stop his voice from quivering.

'Good,' said Von Braun, as he walked slowly over behind Angelina, who was stretching up high bringing tins forward on the top shelf. He was looking at her up and down, her long, thin, silk-stockinged legs, her protruding posterior through her short, tight, black satin skirt, her long dark hair swaying about her tiny waist.

'Is this your daughter?' asked Von Braun sincerely.

'No, that's my... wife,' Jakob chose his words carefully.

Angelina played along and turned around to reveal her ever-growing baby bump. Von Braun took one look at it and walked away.

The two German soldiers returned to the shop.

'Nothing so far, Herr Von Braun,' one of them told him.

'Well, don't just stand there, keep searching. Try out the back, I'll come with you,' he told them, and he too walked through to the back. Jakob and Angelina looked at each other, horrified.

'*Stand up!*' one of the soldiers shouted, pointing his MP40 at Gary at the kitchen table, who shot to his feet with his hands in the air, trying his best to keep his face neutral and hide the fear he was feeling. The two soldiers searched high and low, through drawers and cupboards.

Von Braun frowned at the floor as he crossed the hallway; he doubled back and began stamping his foot on the floor. Jakob and Angelina exchanged worried looks.

'Is everything OK, Herr Von Braun?' asked Jakob innocently.

'Remove this carpet,' he told them at once.

Angelina cast Jakob a horrified glance. Jakob gave Gary in the kitchen the same kind of look, but surprisingly for Jakob, Gary subtly nodded his head, his hands still raised. Jakob frowned back, uncertain.

'Come on, I said remove the carpet now,' Von Braun repeated. Jakob looked back at Gary who nodded a little more obviously. Jakob finally bent down and began to roll the carpet back, revealing the trapdoor to the cellar.

'Is this the entrance to a cellar?' Von Braun asked.

Jakob looked at Gary, who again nodded subtly back.

'Yes,' Jakob replied.

'Why do you cover it with this long carpet?'

'Er… well…' Jakob was thinking hard, 'because there is often a draught that comes through, and so we put the carpet over to stop it coming into the shop.'

Von Braun didn't look convinced; he knelt down and hovered his hand over the edges of the door. 'I feel no draught,' he said simply, 'open it up.'

Jakob looked back at Gary. Angelina noticed this exchange of silent communication. Gary nodded once more, and Jakob reached for the handle and lifted open the door. Von Braun squatted down and peered inside.

'You two, search down in the cellar,' he called to the two soldiers. They came marching over and began to climb down the steps one by one. Gary finally let his aching arms down, as he watched Angelina and Jakob exchange worried looks, while the two soldiers descended down into the cellar.

Moments passed. Jakob and Angelina didn't dare to look at each other, through fear of being watched by the onlooking Von Braun. Jakob was just waiting for the inevitable. Down in the cellar was a radio belonging to a member of the Dutch Resistance. The cellar also contained a mattress, clothes and various other belongings of the same Dutch Resistance fighter.

'There's nothing down here but stacks of food and drinks!' came a voice from the cellar.

'Very well, up you come, we will continue our search

next door!' Von Braun called back. The soldiers climbed back out of the cellar and followed Von Braun to the front door where they left without another word.

Jakob breathed an audible sigh of relief, 'Oh that was too close for comfort,' he said.

'Oh Jakob,' Angelina wrapped her arms around his neck.

Gary wandered over to them in the hallway.

'What was all that nodding for? And why didn't they find anything?' Jakob asked perplexed.

'Yes, I was wondering that,' Angelina said, releasing Jakob.

'Otto removed the radio and all his other belongings,' Gary said simply.

Just then the back door opened and in came Otto.

'You missed all the fun,' said Jakob.

'Not exactly, I was outside listening in the whole time,' said Otto, joining them in the hallway. 'So, they found the cellar, then, did they?' he said as he rolled the red carpet back over it.

'Yes, where the hell could you have hidden that great big radio?' Jakob asked astonished.

'It's in Eva's room,' Otto shrugged.

'But they would've found it in there,' Angelina frowned.

'They most probably did, but they would've assumed it was her radio, wouldn't they?' Otto gave a one-sided smile.

'Oh, very good,' Jakob nodded, smiling.

'There is one problem though,' added Gary. 'The Germans now know we have a cellar, and that it could be used in the future for hiding things.'

'Well, we'll cross that bridge when and if we come to it; in the meantime, we're in the clear,' Otto said, as if that were an end to it.

•

Eva was once again at the train station, standing beside a great big, black beauty of a steam train that had not long rolled in. Eva was in mid conversation with the train guard; he was carrying two cases.

'Thank you so much for this, sir,' she told him over the sound of the train.

'You're welcome, miss, I shall put them under lock and key until we arrive in Berlin,' he replied, stepping onto the train with the two cases. Eva stepped away from the train as it began to slowly pull away, creating a lot of noise and smoke which filled the entire platform, engulfing Eva as she walked on and merged with the crowd.

•

The Gestapo had reached the gates of the nunnery.

'Her Von Braun, I don't think this is really necessary, is it? I mean, it's a nunnery,' said one of the soldiers, looking highly doubtful.

'I've told you before, the first rule is to suspect everyone. Open the gate,' Von Braun told them.

The two soldiers reluctantly opened the tall, black iron gates, and marched noisily up the gravel path, followed by Von Braun.

One of the soldiers hammered on the large oak door. 'Open up, the Gestapo demand entry!' he called.

The door opened to reveal the frightened face of the Reverend Mother. The soldiers burst in as she jumped to the side, a hand clasped to her mouth muffling a slight scream.

'I apologise for them, Sister, they're young and keen,' Von Braun explained as he stepped inside the door. 'We're simply looking for two cases that belong to our Fuhrer; if we find nothing, we'll be on our way.'

'Two cases?' queried the Reverend Mother.

'Yes, why? What do you know of this?' Von Braun asked. They were barely inside the door, unlike the soldiers who had started searching between every pew.

'Well, a man came in for them earlier.'

'A man? What man?'

'A young man, around middle twenties, slim, average height, dark hair, said his name was Anton.'

'Anton?' Von Braun frowned; he'd heard that name before from somewhere.

'That's correct,' the Reverend Mother replied.

'OK men, time to go now!' he called over to them, his voice echoing around the old building. 'Thank you, Reverend Mother.' He nodded curtly, and stepped back outside, followed by the soldiers.

•

Eva arrived back at the shop through the front door.

'Eva, you're back, what happened?' asked Angelina from behind the counter.

'It's done, Angie, the cases are on the train to Berlin as we speak,' Eva told her as she joined her behind the counter. 'Meaning Hitler will receive the cases and call off the search.'

'Oh, that's brilliant.'

'So did they search here?'

'Yes they did, and would you believe it, we actually had Germans in the cellar.'

'What?! But what about the radio?' Eva asked, flabbergasted.

'Otto hid it in your room in plain sight, so when they found it, they simply thought it was yours, they obviously know about you being a German spy and living here,' Angelina shrugged.

'Oh I see, well, it looks like we can finally start getting back to normal,' said Eva.

'Well, not exactly normal,' Angelina smiled, 'my wedding dress has arrived, it's upstairs right now.'

'Show me,' Eva said excitedly, and she took hold of Angelina's hand as they ran out to the hallway.

'Jakob, watch the till a moment!' Angelina called out, as she and Eva ran up the stairs laughing like schoolgirls.

FIFTEEN

OR FOREVER HOLD YOUR PEACE

February 14, 1941. 14:00. St Mary's Church

Jakob and Otto were dressed very smartly, each in a dark grey suit, white shirt and black tie. They stood at the end of the gravel path by the tall, black iron gates. The weak winter sun shining down on the church grounds was the only thing keeping them warm in the chilly breeze. The smell of the flowers in the graveyard wafted invitingly their way.

The last of the congregation had entered the church.

'I am all of a shiver,' complained Jakob.

'You'll be fine,' said Otto straightening Jakob's tie, 'just keep calm and carry on, as they say in England,' he joked.

'Oh, very funny Mr Best Man.' Jakob rolled his eyes as Otto finished with Jakob's tie, and then took to straightening his own.

'Just calm yourself,' said Otto, 'one day this will be an old and beautiful memory. You've got a good one in Angelina, you know.'

'Yes, I know,' Jakob agreed.

'Right, are you ready?' asked Otto.

'I don't think I'll ever be ready,' Jakob replied, his nerves apparent.

Otto chuckled and placed his hand on Jakob's back as they walked up the gravel path to the large oak door.

The sound of echoing chatter met their ears as they entered. Only the front few pews were occupied; this was clearly a very carefully chosen, select few guests; those friends and family who mattered most. Heads turned as Jakob and Otto made their way between the aisles, up to the frontmost pew on their right.

'Oh please, let's get this over with,' muttered Jakob as they took their seats.

'I'd have thought you'd be OK with this; you've done it before,' said Otto.

'Only once, and that was over twenty years ago,' Jakob exclaimed.

Suddenly, as the sound of the organ filled the church, the chatter died instantly.

'Here we go.' Jakob took a deep breath.

The sound of the church door shutting caused the whole congregation to turn to face the back. Jaws dropped as their eyes met the stunning image of Angelina, beginning to make her way down the aisle in a long white tight-fitting lace dress. She wore long white satin gloves that came just above the elbow, and she carried a bunch of red roses clutched to her chest. Her lace veil obscured her features, while her long dark locks were bundled up majestically above the veil.

It wasn't until she got closer to the altar that Jakob noticed it was Gary who was giving her away, and Eva, who was holding the dress up at the back, was her bridesmaid.

'Go on, Jakob, get in position,' Otto nudged him.

Jakob got to his feet and stood at the front to face the priest.

Angelina joined Jakob at the altar; they turned to face each other, the look on their faces speaking louder than any words possibly could. This was it, the day they had long been waiting for.

Eva, Gary and Otto took their seats on the front pew. Gary struggled to avert his attention from Eva, who was wearing a long, figure-hugging satin dress, which was a pale shade of blue; it shimmered as she moved. They smiled at each other before turning their attention to the priest.

The priest, an elderly gentleman in long purple and golden robes, opened the Bible in his hands and began.

'Ladies and gentlemen,' his voice echoed around the church. 'We are gathered here today to witness the joining of Jakob Jonas Jansen, and Angelina Fleur Koelman, in holy matrimony. Before I begin, are there any persons here present who can show just cause as to why they might not be joined together? May they speak now or forever hold their peace.'

'I can show just cause!' a lady's voice echoed from the back of the church. The priest looked up in mild shock, while everybody's attention turned to the lady standing at the back in plain clothes.

Jakob and Angelina looked as though they'd seen a ghost. Gary, Otto and Eva, however, looked angry at her nerve.

'Rini,' Otto muttered under his breath.

'May I ask who this woman is?' asked the Priest.

'I'm the groom's ex-wife,' Rini said confidently as she began to walk down the aisle towards them.

Eva got to her feet, put her hands on her hips, and gave Rini the ultimate death stare.

'Stop right there, Rini, you are not ruining this wedding!' Eva told her, her blue eyes blazing through a dark border of eyeliner.

'My God, they've got you as a bridesmaid? Well, there is a war on, I suppose, we've all got to make do,' Rini retorted, though she did stop where she was when Eva told her to. Eva made to storm up to Rini, but Angelina held her arm to stop her.

'Just get out of here, Rini, we are not married anymore!' Jakob barked.

'The world doesn't revolve around you, Jakob. I didn't come here for you, I came here for her,' Rini pointed unexpectedly at Eva, prompting Gary to get to his feet and stand by her side.

'I don't know what your game is—' Gary began, but Rini interrupted.

'And you,' she pointed at Gary. 'These are the ones I was talking about!' Rini called out behind her.

A man came round the corner in plain clothes, pointing a Luger at Gary and Eva. An audible gasp rang through the congregation.

'What the hell is going on?!' Gary demanded as he and Eva were forced to raise their hands. The man walked slowly past Rini and made his way over to Gary and Eva, his gun constantly pointed at them. Rini followed him now that she felt more confident.

'Who in God's name is this?' Jakob demanded.

'This is a German spy,' said Rini, 'a genuine German spy, unlike this hussy. Feel free to shoot them, Hermann, this one is the collaborator who claimed to be a German spy, and that one is her boyfriend, who just happens to be a British spy, have fun,' she grinned.

The German spy stopped a few feet short of Gary and Eva, and surveyed them, Luger still pointing at them.

'You spiteful cow!' Angelina raised her voice. 'Just because Jakob chose me over you!'

'That's got nothing to do with it, you're welcome to him, and I don't know what you're wearing white for, not with that!' she pointed at Angelina's baby bump.

Eva, whether through anger or strategy, took a step towards Rini.

'You've got no chance, hussy,' Rini grinned, as the German spy changed his aim slightly, and pointed his gun directly at Eva, and Eva alone, his face expressionless.

'She's got every chance in the world,' the German spy looked to his side and saw Otto pointing Otto's own Luger at him, mere inches from his head. The German spy was clearly in deep thought; he could point his gun now at Otto, but by the time he did this, Otto could shoot.

Rini looked on with confusion; how did Otto suddenly get there? When a moment ago he was sitting beside Gary?

The Priest and most of the congregation also appeared to be wondering this.

The German spy, after careful consideration, and a little prompting from Otto who held out his hand, finally decided to hand over his gun. As he placed the gun in Otto's hand, the spy unexpectedly swung his opposite fist across the side of Otto's face, taking Otto by surprise, and causing him to fall sideways onto a couple on the pew, and causing him to drop both guns. The spy made a grab for one of them, but Otto managed to kick it over the other side and under a pew. The spy made another grab for it, but Eva kicked him hard in the head with her high heel, causing him to hold his head in pain, while Eva quickly picked up the gun. Otto, having lost the other gun under a pew somewhere, dived at the spy, and bowled him over onto the concrete aisle way. Everyone gasped, including the priest, who was clutching his Bible and looking on horrified. Eva held one hand out behind her to signify to Gary, Jakob and Angelina not to interfere.

Otto had the spy on the floor in a headlock, but Eva noticed the spy put his hand inside his jacket pocket and pulled out another Luger, forcing Eva to make a split-second decision.

BANG!!!

The spy suddenly stopped struggling, as blood began to seep through his white shirt.

'Somebody call an ambulance!' called the priest.

'Don't bother,' Otto replied placing two fingers under the spy's jaw, 'he's dead.' Everyone gasped, this was not the scene everyone was expecting to see today. A dead German spy in the middle of the aisle, Eva pointing a Luger at him while dressed like a mythical goddess, making her look like some kind of superhero. Jakob, Angelina and Gary looking on in disbelief. The Priest was absolutely awestruck, and the congregation felt lucky to be unhurt.

Otto got to his feet. 'Where's Rini?' he asked, looking round.

'She must've run for it,' said Gary.

'There she is!' Eva saw Rini's head disappear from the church doorway. Eva took off her heels and broke into a run, Luger still in hand. Gary decided to go after her, while Otto picked up the limp body of the spy under the arms, and proceeded to drag him all the way back down the aisle, and out of the church door.

'Carry on!' Otto called back to the priest as he closed the door behind him.

'You may continue,' Jakob said to the priest, but he was looking at Angelina, as they smiled into each other's eyes. 'Let's get this done,' he whispered to her.

'Er, yes, right,' the priest stuttered. 'Let us continue!' he called over at the people, who were all muttering to each other in disbelief about what they'd witnessed.

'Ahem!' the priest cleared his throat loudly to gain full attention once again. The people did their best to compose themselves.

•

'Stop! I've got a clear shot, Rini!' Eva shouted as Rini stopped at the church gates. She turned to face her with her hands raised. Eva walked slowly over to her, treading carefully as her bare feet walked the gravel path. Gary stayed by the door and observed. When she got close enough, smack! Eva punched Rini with a full swing across the façe. Rini collapsed in a heap at the foot of the gates; she was knocked out cold.

Otto dragged the body of the German spy around the corner of the church out of sight, then went to go back inside the church when he noticed the scene by the gates.

'She didn't shoot her, did she?' Otto asked Gary.

'No, just knocked her out,' Gary smirked, which Otto returned as he re-entered the church.

•

'Who has the ring?' the priest asked.

'Here, I have the ring,' Otto called out. Walking down the aisle, he marched up to Jakob and handed him the ring.

'Now repeat after me,' the Priest began.

•

'Gary, do you think you could lift her onto your shoulder? I have a plan,' said Eva.

'What about the wedding?' Gary groaned as he began to lift Rini up off the ground.

'They'll be fine, we've got a job to do.'

•

'And do you, Jakob Jonas Jansen, take thee, Angelina Fleur Koelman, to be your lawful wedded wife?'

'I do,' said Jakob, looking longingly into Angelina's eyes.

'Then I now pronounce you husband and wife,' the Priest smiled, 'you may now kiss the bride.'

Jakob and Angelina gazed lovingly into each other's eyes as they inched closer for a passionate kiss. The congregation cheered and applauded; it was almost as if the earlier incident had never taken place, that wedding atmosphere was in the air once more.

Otto gave them the thumbs-up as they proceeded to walk slowly down the aisle hand in hand, smiling and acknowledging their friends and family on either side.

•

Gary and Eva arrived round the back of the shop with Rini still out cold. Gary lay her down by the back door.

'I hope nobody saw us,' he said, looking back up at Eva.

'Don't worry, if anyone did, they'll just assume she's either drunk or not feeling well, nobody would care either way, now give me the keys.'

Gary reached in his pocket and passed her the door key.

'So what's your plan?' he asked her, as she began to unlock the back door.

'We change our clothes as if we never went to a wedding, I call the General round, and tell him that she shot the German spy at the church, and that she was the one who took the cases from the Nunnery, and that she intended to keep them for herself, the spy found out and he sent the cases to Berlin by train, and this was her motive for shooting him.' Eva just hoped the General and Von Braun never discussed who took the cases from the Nunnery.

Gary gaped at her. 'That's brilliant.'

'Not quite, we just have to hope that those people at the church don't go gossiping,' Eva added as an afterthought as she paused in the doorway. 'If all goes well, however, it'll be her word against mine, and the General will believe me and he'll put her in a labour camp. Now, bring her in here, will you?'

'Don't you think that's going a bit far? A labour camp?' Gary asked as he lifted her in through the door.

'Gary, she made Jakob's life a misery, she attacked a pregnant Angie, she gate-crashed a wedding with the hope of killing both of us, she's turned into a collaborator. Plus, you don't think she would've really left Jakob and Angie alone, do you? And on top of that, she would've told the spy about Otto, the radio, Anton, the assassination attempt on Hitler, everything,' she explained as she closed the door.

'Yes, perhaps you're right,' Gary agreed.

Eva quickly grabbed an orange ball of string from the kitchen drawer. Gary sat Rini in the nearest kitchen chair. Eva tied Rini's hands to the arms of the chair, while Gary tied her ankles to the legs.

'Stay with her, Gary, I'm calling the General,' Eva told him as she rushed out of the kitchen.

Rini began to groan as she slowly lifted her head up. Her eyes blinked open, recognition was visible on her face as she looked about the kitchen, and then she finally saw Gary standing to her side.

'What am I doing here?' She went to move and realised she was tied to the chair. 'What do you think you're going to achieve?' She struggled, a note of panic in her voice.

'Don't even try to free yourself, it's not going to happen,' Gary told Rini to his right, the hallway to his left. His attention was suddenly diverted as Eva glided in like a model, her long, blue satin dress shimmering as she walked, her hip bones protruding through the tight, figure-hugging material, her blue eyes focused on Rini, just like Gary's were focused on Eva, but for a very different reason. She stopped in front of Rini; she took a wide stance, one hand on her hip, the other loose by her side with a Luger in her hand.

'You German whore,' Rini said callously.

Slap! Eva swiped her across the face.

'You're about to go where you belong, you bitch,' Eva said calmly, she then looked at Gary. 'You'll be OK in those clothes, but I'd better change, General Klaus Schneider is on his way,' she emphasised, looking at Rini, whose face dropped.

'No, don't change, you look gorgeous, plus you're dressed how you normally dress anyway,' Gary smiled at her.

'Perhaps you're right,' Eva agreed.

'When the General gets here, I'm going to tell him everything,' Rini said in a smug voice.

'Go ahead, he'll believe me anyway,' Eva smiled sarcastically.

'Why did you do it?' asked Gary. 'Why did you stay with Jakob?'

'We fell out of love a long time ago, anyway, he's the one who cheated with that tart, I did a lot for Jakob when I was with him.'

'The most I ever saw you do for Jakob was make him a cup of tea,' Eva replied incredulously.

Rini spat at Eva; it caught the bottom of her pale blue dress. Eva stayed calm, and simply took a cloth from the kitchen unit and wiped it clean with one wipe. She then took another chair, placed it to the side of Rini's, sat down and crossed her legs, gliding her dress up over her knees, which didn't go unnoticed by Gary.

'The General is going to destroy you,' Eva said, rather seductively, Gary thought.

Knock! Knock! Knock!

'I wonder who that could be?' Eva said sarcastically, as she got to her feet and exited the kitchen.

At this point, Gary decided to step out the back door. Rini strained her ears to listen.

'Klaus, come in, she's through the back,' came Eva's voice.

The General entered the kitchen, followed by two guards, and Eva tagging on behind. They were confronted by an angry, struggling Rini.

'Stop struggling,' said one of the guards, and he pointed his Schmeisser inches from her head. Rini was too irate.

'You German pigs!' she shouted, and spat at the guard who looked taken aback, and looked at the General for guidance.

The General simply took the chair Eva had sat in, put it in front of Rini, and sat facing her. He leaned forward and said very calmly and quietly, 'If you do that again, I will personally shoot you right now where you're sitting.'

Rini couldn't hide her fear as she looked into the General's cold blue eyes, magnified creepily through his glasses.

'What has she told you so far?' he asked Eva.

'Whatever that bitch says is a lie!' Rini snapped.

'Silence!' the General shouted in her face; he then looked back to Eva.

'Well, Klaus, those cases at the nunnery, they're gone, she took them,' Eva said very convincingly.

'What cases?' Rini said, outraged.

'Quiet!' the General shouted again.

'She wanted to keep them for herself, but a spy caught

her. He took the cases and put them on the train for Berlin, so she found the spy and shot him. You'll find his body up at the church where she crashed a wedding, Jakob's and Angelina's wedding, she thought she'd kill two birds with one stone.' Eva found herself adding details that she hadn't planned to say, but something told her that, by the way the General was looking at her, she was going to get away with this tissue of lies.

'Have you gone mad?! Untie me this instant!' Rini struggled with the ever-tightening string.

'I assume you were a bridesmaid?' the General asked.

Eva didn't expect the General to notice any change in her dress sense, but obviously he just knew. She felt there was no point in denying it.

'Yes, I was a bridesmaid,' she smiled.

'You look incredible,' the General looked her up and down as she blushed.

'Oh, for God's sake! Are you actually going to believe this cow?!' Rini snapped.

The General didn't pay her any attention, he simply gazed at Eva and said softly, 'Yes I am, take her away,' he told the guards as he stood up from his seat.

'*No, no! Stop it! Get off me you bastards!*' Rini shouted at the top of her lungs as she was hoisted up by the guards, still attached to the chair, and carried through the front and out of the shop. '*You bitch! I'll get you for this!*' her voice carried in from outside.

The General stood in front of Eva, mere inches between them.

'You look so teasing right now,' he said in a low voice, his eyes travelling the length of her body.

'Thank you,' she said, attempting to keep eye contact, a tone of embarrassment in her voice.

He put his large rough hands on her bare smooth shoulders, subtly massaging her collarbone with his thumbs.

'You know how I feel about you, don't you?' he whispered, stepping ever so slightly closer. Eva nodded, standing as still as a statue. 'If you ever need me for anything… anything, I will be all yours,' he leaned in and kissed her so gently on her cheek she barely felt it. She could feel his breath on her neck, but he didn't stop there, she then felt his lips on her neck. First, he kissed so gently it was almost a tickle, then she distinctly felt him give a subtle suck on her neck as he moved down to her collarbone. Eva closed her eyes and tilted her head back; her breathing was becoming rapid. He roughly grabbed hold of her waist and pulled her sharply towards him, so they were pressed together. His lips moved down to her smooth bare chest. He could feel her heart beating against his lips, which then moved down to her firm cleavage. He could feel the cushioning of her breasts as he pushed his lips into them. He breathed in deeply; she had the scent of heaven. She then felt his large, hot hands clasp tightly around her rear through her tight satin dress and squeeze firmly.

'Klaus, I'm sorry, I can't, I'm so sorry,' she said apologetically, as she grabbed hold of his hands to pull them away and took a step back.

'I'm sorry,' the General replied with his hands raised momentarily, 'I just couldn't resist, I apologise, Eva, I really do,' he said most sincerely.

'It's just that I'm with Gary. I mean you're attractive, of course, but given the situation—'

'Please, say no more, Eva, my fault entirely, forgive me, I have to get going,' he said, and with that he exited through the kitchen and made his way out through the shop.

Eva composed herself. She pulled down her risen dress around her hips and pulled it up around her cleavage.

She jumped as the back door opened and in came Gary.

'I saw the General leave around the front,' he told her. 'So how did it go, did they believe you?'

'Yeah, I think so, looks like Rini will be giving Jakob and Angie no more trouble.' She gave a weak smile.

'Well come on then, let's get to the reception,' Gary smiled and took her hand.

SIXTEEN

LUST AND MONEY

February 17, 1941

The room was dark despite it being daytime, it was pouring with rain outside, the curtains were drawn and not a single light was on. The silhouette of a young, slim naked woman was rising and falling in repetition, she was moaning loudly with pleasure, as was the middle-aged man under her, whose wrists were handcuffed to the bedframe above him. Her long, loose wavy hair was bouncing in time to her rhythmic tempo. Her breasts, so firm and pert, were hardly moving. Her soft skin shone with perspiration. The man's eyes grew wider, and his breathing grew heavier as his moaning grew louder.

The woman slowed down and leaned forward, her smooth flat torso on his round hairy stomach, her firm breasts pressing into his hairy chest, her long hair dangling in his face as she planted her plump lips on his. She then swung her leg over him as she stepped off the bed and onto the floor. She rummaged for something in his jacket lying on the floor, walked round to the foot of the bed and raised her right arm, pointing a gun at him.

He stared at her in disbelief, like a deer in headlights.

'Wait, what are you doing? You said if I told you everything, you'd let me go.' Fear was easily audible in his voice as he struggled to sit up, his wrists still handcuffed to the bedframe.

'I lied,' she said in a seductive voice.

BANG!

A fresh hole appeared in his forehead, and blood splattered all up the wall behind him as he lay staring, motionless.

•

Eva came in through the front door of Jakob Jansen's Food Shop; she held the door open for an elderly lady customer to leave. The sound of the heavy rain became apparent during the few seconds the door was open.

'I've been invited out to a party tonight,' she said as she made her way over to Jakob at the counter, removing her headscarf. 'It's over at the German headquarters, do you remember? Where the General had his birthday party?'

'How well I remember,' Jakob said gravely, 'my heart was pounding through my chest holding that ladder for Gary and Otto, knowing they had a grenade on them, and that we could've been caught at any moment. I'm not likely to forget that in a hurry.'

Eva smiled. 'I'll go and tell the others,' she said as she made her way out back.

Gary and Angelina were sitting at the table chatting; Eva came in and hung up her black fur coat on the coat stand.

'All right, love?' Gary smiled.

'I've been invited to a party tonight by the General,' she informed them as she strolled over and took a seat. 'It's at the German headquarters.'

'Oh, you mean the place where we blew up the General's bedroom that time?' Gary smiled.

'Yes, Jakob has fond memories of that too,' Eva grinned. 'So where's Otto?'

'Down in the basement as usual,' Angelina replied, sounding bored.

'He spends half his life down there on that radio,' Eva replied.

Miraculously, Otto walked into the kitchen at that very moment.

'Ah, talk of the devil,' Eva smiled.

'What?' he asked.

'We were just saying how much time you spend on your radio, that's all,' Gary grinned.

'And it's just as well I do,' said Otto pulling up a chair, 'listen to this, I've just received news that one of our Resistance members was killed earlier this morning by a German spy.'

They all wore expressions of shock and concern.

'But this wasn't just any old German spy,' Otto continued, 'this is a woman, her name is Heidi Eichmann.'

Their shocked expressions intensified.

'Apparently, no woman has a patch on her beauty, and she uses this beauty to wrap men around her little finger, she beds them for answers, and then she shoots them,' Otto explained.

'Oh my God, and she's actually here in Amsterdam?' asked Gary.

'Apparently so,' Otto replied.

'I wonder if she'll be at the party tonight?' Eva muttered, deep in thought.

'What's this?' asked Otto.

'The General is holding a get-together this evening at the German headquarters,' Eva explained.

'Well, if she is, get every bit of information on her you can; our lives may depend on it,' Otto said most seriously.

•

17:55

The bell jingled as the front door opened, and in came the General.

'Ah, good evening, General, all ready for your party tonight?' Jakob asked politely.

'Why do you ask? It's not as if you're invited,' he replied sarcastically, taking a bottle of his favourite water off the top shelf to his right.

Jakob tried not to show how unnecessary he thought the General's comment was.

'Not long now, just over an hour to go,' the General said as he strolled over to Jakob with some change, which he placed on the counter.

'Thank you, General.' Jakob placed the money in the till.

'I take it Eva is coming?' the General asked.

'Oh yes, she's looking forward to it.'

'Good,' the General replied, and made to leave with his bottle, when the bell jingled again as the door opened. This time, the Gestapo officer Ludwig Von Braun entered with his two guards.

'General Klaus Schneider, it's a pleasure to finally meet you.' Von Braun held out a black-gloved hand.

'Ludwig Von Braun, I presume?' the General replied, shaking his hand.

They stood almost eye to eye, with the General just having the edge in height and build.

'That's correct, it's nice to finally meet my match, I've heard the stories,' Von Braun added in a whisper as he winked at the General, then made his way over to the counter.

'Mr Jansen, is it?' he asked as he approached Jakob.

'Er, yes that's right,'

'I want some cigarettes, that blue packet down there will do,' he said.

'Yes, Herr Von Braun,' Jakob replied and retrieved the blue packet.

Von Braun placed the money on the counter, 'Keep the change,' he said, and he took the cigarettes and turned away. He noticed the General was still standing by the door watching him and his guards.

'Everything all right, General?' he asked as they stood face to face once more.

'I just wanted to invite you to my party tonight at the German headquarters, seven o'clock, you would be most welcome,' replied the General.

'That's very civil of you, General, yes, I'll see you at seven,' Von Braun nodded and left with his guards.

'You know,' the General began as he stared after the Gestapo officer with narrowed eyes, 'I can't put my finger on it, but there's definitely something not right about that man,' and with that, he too left the shop.

'Goodnight, General,' Jakob chuckled.

•

Otto was once again disguised as a German private, standing guard outside the General's office, with his MP40 slung over his shoulder. He looked like a genuine German guard.

The red-carpeted corridor was as quiet as a grave, until a door opened up directly opposite Otto. His jaw dropped at the sight that greeted him; he even screwed up his eyes tightly and looked again, just to make sure this wasn't a dream or a hallucination. But no, she was still there standing in the doorway, just staring back at him, while wearing nothing but an open, black satin dressing gown. Her firm, pert breasts were fully on show, as was her flat, smooth torso and her long, slim legs, with no attempt whatsoever to cover any part of her person. Otto distinctly felt his heart beat faster. What was he seeing? She looked provocatively at Otto, with her smoky green eyes peering through her long, wavy blonde hair. Otto just stood there in shock; he couldn't believe his eyes, had he unknowingly died and gone to heaven?

She beckoned him over with her index finger, her nails long and painted red. Otto looked left and right to check the coast was clear, then walked across the corridor to her. She said nothing as she stood aside and allowed him to enter.

•

Back at the shop, Jakob saw something on the floor by the front door. Curious what it could be, he wandered over to take a look.

'What's that?' asked Angelina as she came in from the back.

'Looks like somebody's dropped their wallet,' said Jakob, picking it up and examining it. 'Must be Herr Von Braun's or the General's,' he said as he opened it up.

'Oh no it's not, there's a picture of Eva inside, it's Gary's.' He rolled his eyes. 'Could you call him, Angie?'

'Gary! We found your wallet!' Angelina called over her shoulder.

Gary came in from the kitchen, 'No it can't be,' he said brandishing his wallet, 'I've got mine right here.'

Jakob and Angelina exchanged curious looks.

'Then why does this wallet have a picture of Eva in it?' asked Jakob.

'Eva? Let me see,' Jakob handed Gary the wallet.

'Who's been in the shop within the last half-hour?' Gary asked, examining the photograph.

'Well, the only men have been Herr Von Braun and the General.' Jakob replied.

'It has to be the General,' Angelina said with confidence, 'he has a crush on Eva.'

'Angie, don't go jumping to conclusions,' Jakob told her.

'I'm not,' she replied defensively.

'No, it's all right, she's right,' Gary said sounding

defeated, 'Eva told me how a few days ago the General had come onto her.'

'What?' Jakob couldn't believe his ears.

'It's OK, Gary,' said Angelina sympathetically, 'she told me too, she was curious to see how far he'd go, but she couldn't take any more, so she soon put a stop to it.'

'I can't believe it,' said Jakob astonished, 'what a total and utter creep.'

'Yes, I know, but she also said that he's not the type to push if she didn't want to. He may fancy her, but he also respects her,' Gary admitted.

'So it has to be the Generals' then?' Jakob said, looking for confirmation.

'Probably. Eva will be back in about three hours' time, we'll see then,' said Gary.

•

Eva drew all the men's attention in her black, see-through lace dress hanging off one shoulder. Her matching black lace underwear could just about be seen in a certain light. A split up one side revealed her long pale legs as she glided across the marble floor. Her long blonde locks were loose, and hid one side of her face as she tilted her head.

'Eva!' she heard a man's voice call out from the bar. She looked over and saw the Gestapo officer, Ludwig Von Braun, beckoning her over.

'Ludwig,' she smiled as she approached him and sat on the stool beside him.

'I would offer to buy you a drink, but I see you already have one,' he smiled.

'I'm afraid the General beat you to it,' Eva replied, taking a sip of her champagne.

Von Braun eyed Eva with hunger. 'Eva, you look absolutely ravishing tonight,' he told her.

'Thank you, and you look well,' Eva replied.

'I want you to know that not a day has gone by that I haven't thought about you,' he said seriously.

'Oh Ludwig, I thought you would've moved on by now,' she said, taking another sip from her glass.

'Never; when you left Berlin, I was in a terrible state, I didn't know which way to turn. Luckily, I had my friends here to keep me on the straight and narrow,' he said, referring to his guards on his other side, looking very different in their suits and bow ties.

•

Otto, topless and lying on his back with his head propped up on the pillow, watched as the luscious blonde sat completely naked at her dresser, and applied red lipstick to her pouting lips in the mirror. The dim lamp by her side, the only source of light, gave her naked body a warm glow. She then stood up slowly, stepped into a carefully placed red silk dress on the floor, and slid it slowly up her body, becoming taut across her hips, then finishing off at the breasts, as the top of the dress squeezed them together. Saying nothing, she turned around to reveal her long sexy back, holding her long hair round the front out of the way. Otto instinctively got off the bed and walked over to zip her up. When the zip reached the top, he couldn't help himself; he placed his lips on her warm back, kissing her protruding shoulder blade. But she unexpectedly turned around and told him in a rather cold voice, 'Get dressed and get out,' and she simply turned around and walked out of the room. Otto couldn't believe his ears; who was this woman? She'd just slept with him, taken him to heaven, and now she was dropping him like a bad habit. Otto decided to quickly get back into his German uniform and work all this out later. But as he slid his trousers on, something didn't feel right. He checked his pockets. 'Oh no, my wallet!'

•

Meanwhile, Von Braun was beginning to get closer to Eva; he was holding her hand on her lap.

'… and night after night I dream about you, about what we had, don't you miss what we had, Eva?' he asked pleadingly.

'But Ludwig, we were over before I left.'

'Only by a couple of weeks.'

The General was standing over the other side of the hall when he happened to look across and see how close Von Braun and Eva were sitting. He put his glass down on the nearest table and walked into the centre of the hall. He clapped his hands loudly.

'Ladies and gentlemen, could I have your attention for a moment please?!' he called out. The violinists in the corner stopped playing, and the chatter died down as all attention was on the General.

Otto walked along the corridor and came to the landing at the top of the stairs, giving him a bird's eye view of the great hall, where he could clearly see the General in the centre.

'I have an announcement to make,' the General continued. 'The reason you were all invited here tonight, was because I wanted you to all bear witness to something special. For a little while now, I have been getting quite close to a particular woman, a perfect example of German womanhood, a goddess among women, a blonde bombshell whom I fell in love with at first sight.'

The hall was dead silent, everyone was intrigued as to where all of this was going. Otto's eyes were darting from the General to Eva and back. Eva was simply motionless with anticipation, while beside her, Von Braun was looking on with minor curiosity.

'Some of you will know what I'm talking about,' the Generals' eyes landed on Eva as he scanned the room. 'Some of you will not. Ladies and gentlemen, please allow me to introduce my bride-to-be, Fraulein Heidi Eichmann!' he called out. Everybody began to clap as he gestured to the top of the stairs.

Otto looked to his left and did a double take as he saw the sexy blonde he'd just slept with glide down the stairs in a figure-hugging red silk dress. Eva looked over to the stairs, and she suddenly realised she had competition. This was indeed as the General had said, 'a goddess among women'. She was tall, slim, a perfect shape with a body to die for. She sailed over to the General, the tight red silk of her dress bursting around her hips, while her breasts almost spilled over. Her long blonde hair billowed out behind her as she walked.

The claps turned to cheers and whistles as she approached the General; she took his face in her hands and proceeded to kiss him passionately in front of all the spectators.

Otto's jaw was on the floor, while Eva looked a little uncomfortable. Just the other day the General was forcing his intentions on her, and now he tells the entire congregation that he's been with this woman for 'a little while now'.

'Thank you, thank you,' the General called out waving his hand; the cheering died down.

'Heidi, my dear, do you have anything to say?' he asked her.

Heidi looked around at the people; she wore a confident, even narcissistic expression.

'As my darling Klaus has already announced, I am indeed his bride-to-be.' Some cheers followed this. 'And as you can all tell by my name, I am in fact the niece of Adolf Eichmann.' More cheers erupted. Otto's face was an expression of astonishment.

'I would like to thank you all for coming, please drink and be merry!' She smiled broadly and caused the biggest cheers yet by wrapping her long thin arms around the General's neck and planting her red lips on his and not letting go. Everyone watched as he placed his large hands on her tiny twenty-four-inch waist, their lips remaining locked.

•

A little later, Otto arrived through the back door of the shop. Jakob, Angelina and Gary were chatting at the kitchen table. They all looked up, momentarily surprised, until they realised it was Otto in his German disguise.

'Otto, how did it go?' asked Jakob.

'I have good news and bad news,' Otto replied as he pulled up a chair, and placed his helmet on the table. 'I found out who Heidi Eichmann is, the one who killed the Resistance member this morning. The bad news is, she just so happens to be the future wife of the General, the niece of Adolf Eichmann, and I slept with her.'

'What?!' they all gasped simultaneously.

'That was before I knew who she was,' Otto added as a defence, 'she just beckoned me into her room and seduced me, just like that.'

'But why? As far as she was concerned, you were a German,' said Gary.

'Yeah, it's not like she expected to get any information from you,' added Angelina.

'She slept with me so she could steal my wallet,' Otto explained.

'Your wallet? Are you sure you didn't just leave it behind?' Gary asked inquisitively.

'Gary,' Jakob tutted, 'as if that wallet belonged to Otto,' Jakob rolled his eyes.

'As if what wallet belonged to me?' asked Otto totally nonplussed.

'We found this in the shop earlier,' Gary took the wallet out his pocket and handed it to Otto. Otto opened up the wallet and saw the picture of Eva.

'Er, I think you've just given me your wallet,' Otto smiled, handing it back.

Gary remained straight-faced and shook his head.

'You mean this isn't yours?' Otto asked, looking at the picture again.

'Nope, Jakob found it on the shop floor by the front

door, and not long before, the General was in the shop, and I do happen to know that the General does have a crush on Eva,' Gary explained.

'Well,' Otto said thinking, 'there is one other person it could belong to.'

'Who?' they all asked simultaneously.

'The Gestapo officer, Ludwig Von Braun; he was getting quite cosy with Eva at the party, I don't mind telling you,' explained Otto.

'Well, where is she now?' asked Gary, jealousy visible in his eyes.

'She shouldn't be too far behind me,' said Otto.

Right on cue, the back door opened, and in came Eva, in her black lace see-through dress.

'Do you know who this wallet belongs to?' Gary jumped up and showed her, clearly trying to bottle his anger. Eva was a little surprised at his behaviour.

'I have no idea, Gary,' she said looking at it, 'why?'

'Because there's a photograph of you inside.' He showed her, his hands a little clumsy in his impatience to get the photo out. Eva was completely dumbfounded.

'Gary, I'm confused, where did you find this?' she asked, utterly bewildered.

'Jakob found it by the front door, it has to be the General's, right?' asked Gary impatiently.

'No, this is definitely not the General's,' Eva replied, now taking out another piece of paper from the wallet; it was a shopping list. 'I recognise this handwriting,' she said, studying it; she had everyone's attention. 'This wallet belongs to Ludwig Von Braun.'

SEVENTEEN

DEADLY BACKFIRE

February 18, 1941

'OK, listen everyone,' Otto addressed everyone at the kitchen table while they tucked into their breakfasts.

'I stayed up all night writing a letter out in Von Braun's handwriting, using that shopping list as a guide. Now, this letter is a love letter, it's going to be from Von Braun to Heidi Eichmann. I plan on sneaking into the General's and Heidi's bedroom and planting it under their mattress. I just hope the General finds it before Heidi does.'

'Well, that's a great plan, Otto, but how do you intend on sneaking into the General's bedroom?' Jakob asked as he buttered his toast.

'Two things,' said Otto, 'my German uniform, and their absence.'

Angelina suddenly squirmed and held her stomach.

'More pains again?' asked Jakob sympathetically. She nodded. 'She's been getting these pains on and off since the early hours,' Jakob explained.

'It's OK, it's gone again,' Angelina sighed.

'I cannot believe you slept with her,' Eva said to Otto, while buttering her toast rather severely, 'don't you have any shame?'

'I've already told you, that was before I knew who she was,' Otto explained. 'Besides, she was gorgeous,' he added with a dreamy smile.

'She may be gorgeous, but she's pathologically evil,' Eva said matter-of-factly.

'I haven't seen her yet,' Gary smiled at Otto, which soon vanished when he caught Eva giving him a deadly stare.

'You wouldn't want to,' she said bitterly as she took a bite of her toast.

'Actually, you know, she's a bit like an evil version of you,' Otto joked.

'Oh, thank you very much,' Eva replied sarcastically whilst crunching. Gary found this highly amusing.

•

Otto was now dressed as a German Private, leaning against the lamp post, one hand in his pocket, the other holding his cigarette. He was facing the German headquarters and waiting for the General and Heidi to leave. After a few moments, there they were, the General and the beautiful Heidi leaving the headquarters arm in arm. Otto dropped his cigarette, stomped it out, and casually walked over to the entrance doors.

His jackboots echoed loudly as he marched across the marble floor, which was now completely void of any life, but last night had been packed out. He made his way over to the stairs that began in the middle of the floor, and he began to ascend. After passing several other German guards along the posh, red-carpeted corridor, he finally came upon the General's bedroom door. After confirming nobody was around, he opened the bedroom door and entered.

The General's and Heidi's room was much more luxurious than the one they'd blown up a few months ago further down the corridor. The carpet was thick and red, the bed had red silk sheets and a golden frame, the furniture was dust-free mahogany, and the scent of the room was that of Heidi's perfume. Otto opened the top drawer on Heidi's side of the bed; it was full of lingerie, satin and lace everywhere, mainly all black and red. Otto had a look through them. 'My God, she's a sex fanatic,' he muttered. He also came across stockings, suspenders, and a pair of handcuffs, which he noticed with his hawk-eye had what appeared to be a spot of blood on. Otto closed the drawer, pulled the letter out of his pocket, and went round the other side of the bed to place it under the mattress, but as he lifted the mattress to do so, his face dropped; he saw his wallet. Heidi had clearly put it there. He took out his wallet and checked its contents. His money was surprisingly still there. But why was it on the General's side of the bed? Perhaps it was a coincidence? Or maybe Heidi just wasn't thinking? Or maybe she'd given this a lot of thought; maybe she was attempting to frame the General? A hundred ideas flooded Otto's brain at once. He eventually decided to put the letter in the top drawer on the General's side of the bed, containing his many socks. Otto then went over and opened the bedroom door; he poked his head round to check the coast was clear and exited the room.

As Otto walked along the corridor, he had the shock of his life; he heard the voices of Heidi and the General coming from the other end as they climbed the stairs.

'How can I buy anything if I've misplaced my wallet?' he heard the General say.

Otto looked down at his bulging pocket, 'I was sure this wallet was mine?' he muttered, and he quickly tiptoed back to the bedroom. He opened up the door and stuffed the wallet back under the mattress. He heard their voices getting nearer as they approached the bedroom. Otto quickly lay down on his belly and slid under the bed until he was completely hidden by the long red silk bedsheets that draped onto the floor. Luckily, Otto could see right through the sheets that were draping on the floor.

'Wait here, darling, I'll find it,' Heidi told the General, and he waited outside the door while Heidi entered the bedroom. Otto got a close-up view of her silk-stockinged legs as she made her way over and lifted the mattress, but only momentarily, as if she didn't take the wallet, she just wanted to check it was still there. He then saw her open the top drawer, she paused and just stared at the contents, before reaching in and retrieving the letter Otto had just placed there moments before. To his horror, she began to read it, and just as she got to the end, she heard the General call.

'Have you found it yet?'

'Er, no,' she said and stuffed the letter inside her black fur coat. 'You must've dropped it somewhere when you were last out,' she replied.

'Oh, wait, I think I know where it must be,' said the General. At this response, Heidi exited the room and left with the General.

Otto slid out from under the bed and went to take his wallet when a thought struck him. If Heidi found the wallet missing, she'd most probably guess it was him who'd taken it, so he thought he'd play it safe and leave it where it was for now, so he too exited the room without the wallet.

•

As Heidi and the General walked down the street arm in arm, her heels echoing through the street, the weak February sun shining down on them, Heidi suddenly stopped.

'Oh, just a minute, I have to go in here,' she said, stopping outside the Gestapo headquarters and ruffling her hair.

'Why do you need to go in there?' he asked suspiciously.

'It's to do with work, now go, I'll catch you up,' she smiled and entered through the door. The General shrugged and slowly sauntered on through the cyclists and pedestrians.

Heidi came to a halt as she read the name on the door to her right-hand side: Ludwig Von Braun. She knocked.

'Come in,' she heard Von Braun's call. She opened the door and stepped inside. Von Braun was sitting at his desk; he looked up from his paperwork to see the most beautiful pair of legs in stockings, and a knee-high tight red skirt. He then looked up to see a gorgeous yet cunning face looking back at him.

'Heidi!' he smiled. 'Please take a seat,' he gestured to the chair opposite him at the desk.

'Thank you,' she replied as she accepted the seat. Von

Braun looked on with delight, as he watched Heidi sit down and cross her long legs.

'So, what can I do for you?' he asked as he leaned back in his black leather chair and observed her.

'It's more about what I can do for you,' she said as she lit a cigarette and blew a puff of smoke through her plump red lips.

'I'm listening,' he replied, his eyes focused on hers.

'I saw that note you wrote to me, I had no idea you were so talented with words,' she smiled seductively.

Von Braun was secretly confused but decided to play along.

'So, you liked it then?' he asked convincingly.

Heidi blew another puff of smoke across the desk. 'If you want to do all those things you mentioned in your note, I suggest you waste no more time about it, Ludwig,' she said in a soft seductive voice.

'Really?' Von Braun chose his words carefully. 'And to which part of the note in particular are you referring?' he asked.

Heidi uncrossed her long legs, stood up, walked around his side of the desk, holding eye contact until she was standing behind him. She wrapped her arms around him and whispered in his ear, 'The part where you said you can't wait to seduce me.'

Von Braun tried his best to hide his excitement, but he was liking where this was going. He quickly turned his chair to face her.

'Then let's waste no more time, Miss Eichmann,' he said with a deadly stare. He got to his feet as she stood up straight. He took hold of her waist, pulled her towards him and planted his thin lips on her plump red ones. He breathed in the scent of her perfume mixed with scent of her long blonde hair.

•

Otto arrived back at the shop.

'Not good, Jakob, not good,' he said as he walked up to Jakob at the counter.

'What do you mean? What happened?' Jakob asked, sitting on the stool behind the counter.

'Let's just say my plan backfired,' said Otto resting his elbows on the counter. 'That note meant for the General to find, so that he would have a right go at Heidi, which was payback for her stealing my wallet, was in fact found by none other than Heidi herself. I also found my wallet, but I couldn't take it because otherwise she'd have known I was there, and she'd come looking for me.'

'Well, unfortunately there's more,' Jakob added through gritted teeth.

'More?' said Otto looking hopeless.

'Not so much as five minutes ago, I had the General in here looking for his wallet.'

'What?! You mean that wallet belonged to the General after all?' Otto said in surprise.

'Yes, he obviously has very similar handwriting to Von Braun, which means that the General really does like Eva, despite the fact that he's going to marry Heidi, the niece of Adolf Eichmann,' explained Jakob.

Otto was quiet while he processed all this.

'My God, this war is beginning to get complicated. Any alcohol about? I think I need it.'

Jakob chuckled at this. 'Yes, help yourself, and have as much as you like, saves Angelina from being tempted by it.'

Otto laughed as he made his way out to the kitchen.

EIGHTEEN

PHOTOGRAPHIC EVIDENCE

March 17, 1941. 14:32

The rain was lashing down on their cold faces. The barn and the surrounding countryside was a war zone. The Dutch Resistance, shielded by the haystacks, were firing their MAS 36s at the Germans. There were about fifteen aside, including the General and Von Braun. Von Braun was firing his Luger at the Resistance. The smell of gunfire in the air was strong. Everybody was soaked to the skin and could hardly see their own guns in front of them for the pouring rain.

The General was dug into a ditch nearby where he was firing an MG42. He could feel its power as it vibrated his whole body, and the noise was deafening. His right knee and left boot were caked in wet mud. All of a sudden, he saw something land by his foot. He looked down and, with a surge of panic, he picked up the grenade and threw it over the hedge into the field behind him. The explosion that followed caused a shower of debris over the General, and several Dutch and

Germans looked over in his direction. This appeared to give one of the German soldiers an idea as he pulled out a grenade from his belt, unscrewed it, and threw it in the direction of the barn where some of the shots were coming from. The grenade exploded on one side of the barn; one entire wall was gone, causing that side of the barn roof to collapse.

During this distraction, the Dutch Resistance decided to retreat deeper into the countryside, but not before one Dutchman fired a shot with his Geweer M. 95 at the General's left thigh, and another at Von Braun's right shoulder. As the Dutch hastily retreated, several German soldiers came running over to check on the General and Von Braun, who were both lying on the wet muddy grass, rolling in agony, blood pouring between their fingers as they put pressure to their own wounds.

•

Otto came excitedly into the kitchen, where Jakob, Gary and Eva were sitting and chatting at the table.

'I've got some exciting news,' he smiled as he pulled up a chair at the end of the table.

'Don't tell me, you've finally managed to retrieve your old wallet?' Jakob chuckled.

'Very funny,' Otto didn't look impressed. 'I've just got off the radio, there was some heavy shooting earlier out at one of the barns, between some members of the Resistance and some Germans. Three of ours were injured, but three of theirs are dead, and two injured, and guess which two were injured,' he said, grinning like a Cheshire cat.

'Who?' they all asked curiously.

'The General and Von Braun,' Otto replied excitedly.

'No?' Eva clapped her hands to her mouth.

'Yes,' Otto said, not noticing her concern, 'he's laid up in hospital as we speak after being shot in the leg, and Von Braun likewise after being shot in the shoulder.'

'Well, that's cheered me up anyway,' Gary grinned as he took a sip of tea. Eva looked at him daggers.

'Well, what do you expect?' Gary continued. 'Two Germans who have the hots for you, they got what they deserved if you ask me.'

'Oh yes, you should go and visit them, Eva,' Otto explained, 'keep up the pretence, you know.'

'Oh I will, I'll go now to get a couple of cards from the card shop, I'll see you all later,' she said, and without a single glance at any of them, she got up and left through the back door.

'I think she's going off me, you know,' said Gary, staring into space.

'Oh don't be silly, she's got to keep up the pretence, you know that,' said Jakob.

•

While Eva was looking through the get-well cards on the shelf, she noticed Heidi being served at the counter. She too appeared to be buying two cards, and one was considerably bigger than the other. Eva got the distinct impression that Heidi was also going to the hospital to visit the General and Von Braun. She strained her ears to try and hear what she and the ageing shopkeeper were talking about.

'That's quite a size difference,' the old man joked, 'I'm

guessing one person is more important than the other?'

'The small one is for my husband-to-be, the big one is for my lover,' Heidi smirked. The shopkeeper chuckled as he assumed she was joking.

Eva noticed the same small card on the shelf in front of her, and a plan started forming in her mind.

•

The General was sitting up in his hospital bed wearing a hospital gown, his left thigh bandaged, the remnants of blood seeping through. The Gestapo officer, Ludwig Von Braun, was also sitting up in bed; he was topless, as his shoulder was bandaged and taped up. They were sitting opposite each other, though they couldn't see each other for the curtains around their beds.

Eva walked up to the desk in the reception area.

'Yes?' asked the uniformed lady behind the desk.

'Good evening,' Eva smiled, 'I've come to see the General, Klaus Schneider.'

'I'm afraid his wife-to-be has just gone through; if you like you could always come back later?'

Eva looked up and saw Heidi talking on the telephone attached to the wall, her two cards on the shelf beside the telephone. Eva nodded and smiled at the receptionist and made her way casually over to where Heidi was standing. Eva decided that this was the perfect opportune time to put her plan into operation. While Heidi was facing the other way talking on the telephone, Eva took her small card to the General out of her handbag, and replaced Heidi's card on the shelf with hers, and put Heidi's into her handbag, then casually walked back to the hospital entrance.

Replacing the receiver, Heidi picked up her two cards and proceeded to the ward. She was told by the receptionist, 'Third bed on the right.' Following her instructions, Heidi stopped by the third bed with the curtain around, placed the larger of the two cards in her handbag, and entered through the curtain.

'Hi sweetheart,' she smiled, planted him a gentle kiss, then sat in the chair beside his bed.

'Heidi, are you a sight for sore eyes,' the General replied, smiling.

'So how is it?' she nodded to his thigh.

'Well, I'll live,' he shrugged.

'Well, maybe this will cheer you up.' She reached into her handbag, pulled out the small card and handed it to him.

'Aw, you shouldn't have.' He smiled as he took the card out the envelope and began to silently read what was inside, observed by a smiling Heidi.

Dear Klaus, try not to show any surprise on your face, but this is Eva speaking, I'm sorry to inform you that Heidi has been sleeping with Ludwig Von Braun behind your back, and I have the proof. I'll meet you tonight, make sure Heidi isn't around. For now, it is important that you carry on as normal. Get well soon.

The General closed the card and looked at Heidi, 'Thank you, my love,' he smiled, and placed the card on the table at his other side, wincing in pain as he did so.

'Are you OK?' she asked him.

'Apart from my gunshot wound, I'm absolutely wonderful, my dear,' he smiled.

'Good, do you think you'll be out later?' she asked.

'Oh, I highly doubt it, they'll probably want to keep me in for twenty-four hours for routine checks, should be out around three o'clock tomorrow afternoon,' he explained.

•

18:00

Jakob, Angelina, Gary and Otto were all sitting around the kitchen table eating their dinner. The smell of chips mixed with curry, ketchup, mayonnaise and onions filled the air, along with the sounds of cutlery on plates.

'Any day now, isn't it, my love?' Jakob said to Angelina, who nodded with a mouthful of food.

'So, what are you hoping for then, a boy or a girl?' asked Gary.

'Well, we have discussed that, haven't we, and we really don't mind which,' said Jakob.

'But we have decided on names, haven't we?' Angelina added. 'Peter for a boy, and Carice for a girl.'

'Oh nice names, very nice,' Otto nodded, 'you never know, you could have one of each.'

'I hope not, we can only afford the one really, at present times at least,' Jakob explained.

'What about you and Eva?' Angelina asked Gary.

'Oh, well,' Gary felt a little caught off guard, 'well, we've decided against bringing a child into the world the way it is at the moment,' he smiled uncomfortably, but the moment he said it he felt he was being unwittingly sarcastic.

'We understand, son,' Jakob winked at him with a mouthful of chips.

•

Eva arrived back at the hospital; the same lady behind the desk caught her eye, who nodded at Eva to go through. She passed several nurses in white hats, and doctors in long white coats as she approached the correct ward. Three beds along on her right with the curtain drawn round she could just make out the General through the gap.

'Eva,' said the General as she entered; he winced as he attempted to sit up. Eva said nothing but pulled up a chair beside his bed.

'What is all this about Heidi cheating and you having proof?' he asked sceptically.

'I'm sorry, Klaus,' she said as she pulled two photographs out of her handbag and handed them to him, 'I truly am.'

'I don't believe what I'm seeing,' he said, studying them. The pictures showed Heidi in intimate positions with Von Braun.

'Klaus, you know how much I've always respected and admired you; I just couldn't let her make a fool of you any longer,' said Eva sincerely.

'No, it's you who's making a fool of me,' said the General, stuffing the photographs under his pillow.

'What do you mean?' Eva couldn't believe her ears.

'You can't have me because you're devoted to that Gary, so you won't let anyone else have me,' the General replied.

'Klaus, I don't understand, are you saying I somehow faked these photographs?' Eva sounded outraged.

'Oh no, they're genuine all right, but it's your intentions, Eva, I don't believe them to be honest. You see, this sort of thing she's doing with other men, it doesn't bother me, it was always supposed to be a marriage of convenience anyway, I wanted a beautiful woman, she wants money, it's as simple as that,' the General explained. Eva was in shock; she never thought the General would react like this.

'But Klaus, my intentions were to show you what sort of a woman you were going to marry, I didn't want her to make you look a fool. I thought you would believe me, I thought you respected me, I thought you liked me, I thought I was someone special to you, isn't that why you carry that picture around with you in your wallet?' she asked, and suddenly wished she hadn't after the look on his face.

'Oh, you mean this picture?' he said as he reached under the other side of his pillow and pulled out his wallet. He took out the photograph of Eva and threw it away; it fluttered to the floor on the other side of the bed. 'It means nothing to me,' he said nastily.

'Fine, well don't say I didn't warn you,' Eva said just as nastily. She got to her feet and exited through the curtain.

When she had stepped through, she noticed Heidi over at the reception. Eva had no choice but to dive through the curtain opposite, where she ended up face to face with Von Braun.

Von Braun let the top of his newspaper drop and fold over as he looked up into Eva's eyes.

'Eva, what a lovely surprise,' he said as he laid down his paper on the bedside table, careful not to move his opposite shoulder.

'He knows,' Eva replied as she sat in the chair beside him.

'About the photographs, you mean?' he asked. Eva simply nodded.

'Good, my plan is working, soon Heidi will be all mine,' he smiled menacingly.

'But there's one tiny problem,' Eva continued, 'he's still insisting on marrying her.'

'He what?'

'He says it's a marriage of convenience, he wants a beautiful woman, she wants money,' Eva shrugged.

'Which I have more than enough of, no, mark my words, she's mine,' Von Braun said quite confidently, 'and if he wants a beautiful woman, there's always the one he holds dearest to his heart,' he looked at Eva with a sly grin.

'But Ludwig, I'm taken,' Eva exclaimed.

'So you keep saying,' he picked up his paper again, 'but I do see something there when you look at each other,' he said while studying his paper.

•

Meanwhile, at the General's bedside, Heidi was putting some yellow flowers in a vase on the table. The General struggled as he tried to get out of bed.

'What are you doing?' Heidi asked him.

'I just need to visit the little boys' room that's all,' he gasped.

'Well, you know very well you can't walk, stay there, I'll go and find a doctor to bring a wheelchair,' Heidi said as she stepped through the curtains.

'Excuse me,' she called to the passing matron, 'could we have a wheelchair please, the General wishes to go to the gents?'

'Yes, certainly dear,' said the rather large middle-aged

matron, turning to one of the nurses at the other end of the ward. 'Nurse Clark! Could we have a wheelchair down this end please, the General wishes to go to the gents?'

'Yes matron,' the young nurse replied, as she took hold of the nearest wheelchair by the desk and wheeled it on down. After the nurse and the matron managed to hoist the General onto the wheelchair, Heidi sat on the end of the bed to wait for his return. She stared around idly, when something caught her attention, something poking out from under the General's pillow. As she pulled it out, she noticed they were photographs, she then noticed they were photographs of her naked, and kissing Von Braun. As her head was tilted down studying the photographs, her eye caught the picture of Eva on the floor. She went over to pick up the picture, then went to place all the pictures on the table, but to make room for them she first had to move the vase with the yellow flowers in, but in doing so she knocked the card on the floor, which landed open. Heidi noticed that the writing inside did not match her writing, nor was it the greeting she had put in her card. She picked it up and read it to herself. A look of enlightenment dawned on her face, which was slowly replaced by a look of revenge.

The General was wheeled back through the curtain. Heidi quickly hid everything behind her back, pretending to just be clasping her hands behind her. The matron and the nurse assisted the General back into bed. Once they had gone, Heidi rounded on the General and let loose.

'What the hell is this? And this? And these?' She raised her voice and threw the three photographs and the card on to the bed.

'This is all an attempt to break us up, my dear, but it's not going to happen,' the General replied quite calmly. 'Eva, the other German spy, she's just jealous, take no notice,' he added as he collected the three photographs and the card, and put them on the table to his side.

'So, are you not angry? Are you not confused?' Heidi asked, quite perplexed at the General's unusually relaxed attitude.

'Nope, because ours will be a marriage of convenience, I need a beautiful woman at my side, and you need money,' he said simply.

Heidi sat down in the chair beside him, crossed her long slim legs and said, 'I'm glad we're in agreement,' with a seductive tone.

NINETEEN

ONE PHOTO ON THREE DOORSTEPS

April 9, 1941. 17:45

The ambulance came screeching to a halt outside the hospital. The ambulance men got out and dashed round to the back to open the doors. One man pulled down the ramp while the other wheeled the bed down it. Angelina was holding her swollen tummy in pain, as a consoling Jakob ran alongside. The one who let down the ramp then ran over to open the hospital door, and they wheeled Angelina inside. They wheeled her past the reception area, and straight through to the maternity ward. They entered a room with a single bed, uncomfortable-looking white sheets and a little middle-aged stout woman who had just put down a clipboard she was reading, who smiled pleasantly at her.

'You'll be fine, Angie, you're in the best capable hands,' Jakob told her consolingly while kissing her hand as she was wheeled inside. Angelina, moaning in pain and clutching her baby bump, was transferred to the bed, while Jakob peered nervously through the small window in the door.

•

The sun was shining its last shine over Amsterdam before it began to set. Eva and the General were having a pleasant conversation, while standing on the bridge looking over the Amstel Canal.

'No, no, no, I really must apologise,' said Eva staring down at her own reflection in the water, 'I should never have let you see those photographs.'

'No, it's fine, Eva, if you hadn't shown me those pictures, I'd never have found out what she was like, and I would've gone through with that wedding,' replied the General.

'But you said it was going to be a marriage of convenience?' queried Eva.

'Well, perhaps that was just talk. It shouldn't be you apologising to me, it should be me thanking you,' explained the General.

'Eva!' they were interrupted by the approaching Von Braun, who's long black coat had one loose sleeve, as his arm was in a sling. 'Have you seen Heidi by any chance? I can't find her anywhere,' he asked.

'No, I'm afraid not, Ludwig,' Eva replied, looking over as he came closer.

'Perhaps she's with another man,' added the General as he lit a cigar.

'Listen General, the better man won, OK?' Von Braun replied as he stood a mere two feet from them.

'I'd say the better man had a close shave and is now free,'

the General said smugly as he breathed out a puff of smoke.

Von Braun ignored the General and looked to Eva. 'Would you accompany me in looking for her?'

'Well, I need to find my Gary, I can't find him either,' Eva explained.

'So shall we look together?' he proposed.

'OK, I'll see you later, Klaus.' She smiled at him and left with Von Braun.

The General nodded and watched them leave. 'Hmmm, I wonder?' he mumbled to himself as he blew out another puff of smoke.

•

Angelina's screams could be heard all down the ward. Jakob was pacing up and down outside, wishing it could all be over very soon.

'I want to stop for a while,' he overheard Angelina plead.

'OK, Angelina, get your breath back, my dear,' the midwife replied.

•

Gary, dressed as a German Private, was carrying a bottle of milk and a loaf of bread across the great hall of the German headquarters, following the beautiful Heidi as she too was carrying a bag of shopping. They walked past the stairs with the long Swastika flags hanging idle and came to a door at the far end of the hall. Heidi opened the door and Gary saw it was the kitchens. Heidi placed her shopping bag on the side unit.

'Thank you, Private Reinhardt,' she smiled as he placed the milk and bread beside her shopping bag.

'You're welcome, Miss Eichmann,' Gary replied, 'er, may I ask where the toilet is?'

'Follow me,' she smiled, and she brushed past Gary in the doorway and headed for the bottom of the stairs, which started in the centre of the hall. He followed as she began to climb the stairs, her slim, elegant hand sliding up the golden banister as she went.

'Second door on the left that way,' she said when they reached the top.

'Thank you,' Gary nodded and clicked his heels.

Heidi walked down the corridor in the opposite direction, and when she came to her room, the first thing she did was begin to undress.

The General had arrived at the headquarters, and now began to climb the stairs, limping ever so slightly as he did so.

•

Gary washed his hands in the bathroom.

The General reached the top of the stairs.

Gary began drying his hands.

The General walked along the corridor and eventually came to his office.

Gary opened the bathroom door and stepped out into the corridor.

Heidi opened her bedroom door and called to Gary.

'Reinhardt,' she whispered.

Gary took a couple seconds to realise this meant him; he turned to face Heidi.

'Could you help me with something?' she asked as she poked only her head out of the doorway.

'Yes of course,' Gary replied and made his way over to her.

When he entered, he looked around to see what the trouble might be, when he heard the door close behind him, and he looked round to see Heidi dressed in nothing but black stockings and suspenders. From the waist up she was completely naked. Gary couldn't believe his eyes, she was like a gift from God, every inch of her body was perfect, like a Roman goddess before his eyes.

'What's all this?' Gary asked, his voice coming out a little higher than intended.

'This is your dream come true,' she said in a seductive voice, and to Gary's delight or horror, he couldn't quite make up his mind, she walked slowly over to him, the dim light from the lamp rippling over her smooth skin as she walked. She stopped in front of him, her naked body inches from his German uniform. She wrapped her long thin arms around his neck. Gary's mind shifted to Eva for a second, and a pang of guilt dropped into his stomach. Heidi must've sensed this as she looked into his eyes. He felt her firm breasts press into his lower chest as she tilted her head and brought her lips to his ear, 'Just go with it,' she whispered softly, and before he knew what was happening, their lips were pressed together, as if he were under her spell. Gary reached down and couldn't deny how good it felt to grab a handful of cheek in each hand.

•

The General exited his office and limped along the corridor with a camera now hanging around his neck. He came upon his and Heidi's bedroom.

'I know what you're up to,' he muttered to himself, wincing, as he lowered himself onto one knee and looked through the keyhole. He could quite clearly see the contours of Heidi's naked back, her hair loose and gathered to one side with her head tilted, as she rose up and down. But he couldn't quite make out the man. He turned the handle on the door as quietly as he could and opened it ever so slightly. He poked his head through and raised his camera; he took one snap and quickly bought his head back around, closing the door as silently as he could.

•

While Eva and Von Braun were strolling along in mid conversation, they heard an urgent voice call out.

'Eva! Eva!' They looked round to see Otto in civilian clothing running towards them.

'Otto, what is it? What's the matter?' Eva asked as Otto stopped in front of her trying to catch his breath.

'Eva, you're wanted back at the shop!' he said urgently.

'Oh, right, I have to go, Ludwig, but good luck with finding Heidi,' she smiled at him and left with Otto; Von Braun merely nodded back.

Once they had rounded the corner of a building, Otto took a hold of Eva's arm. 'We'll go this way,' he told her.

'But the shop is the other way,' she queried.

'That was a cover for Von Braun, it's Angelina, she's giving birth at the hospital.'

'What?!' Eva exclaimed as they quickened the pace.

•

Jakob was fidgeting in his seat, one leg bouncing up and down on the ball of his foot, eyes fixed on his shaking hands as he tried to block out the screams coming from the labour ward.

A lady doctor walked past him; she was about to enter the ward when Jakob looked up at her and asked, 'Excuse me, doctor, but how much longer do you think?'

'Your baby will come when it's ready, Mr Jansen, the contractions are becoming more frequent, so I should hang on where you are if I were you,' she said as she entered through the door. Jakob sighed and stared at the floor.

'Jakob!' he heard and looked up to see Otto and Eva running towards him.

'Eva!' Jakob stood up smiling. They hugged and Eva asked how Angelina was doing.

'She's doing well, the contractions are becoming more frequent.'

'Won't be long now then,' said Otto sitting down. Eva and Jakob sat down beside him.

So, where's Gary? I thought he'd be here,' asked Eva.

'I have no idea, I thought he was with you, I haven't seen him all day,' Jakob replied.

'That's strange.' Eva frowned at the floor in deep thought.

•

The General was walking briskly across the busy road on his way to the Gestapo headquarters. He had the photograph of Heidi sleeping with an unidentifiable man in one hand, and a small rock in the other. He placed the photograph on the step outside the front door and put the small rock on top to prevent it from blowing away. The General then walked away as casually as if he'd just delivered a letter.

Moments later, the door opened and out stepped Von Braun. He did not notice the photograph by his feet immediately; only when he looked down to adjust the back of his coat collar did he notice it. He bent down to pick it up, then stood up straight and studied it while standing on the step. His face then slowly broke into a smile.

'Nice try, Eva, but I'm afraid it's not going to work,' he muttered to himself, and picking up the small rock as well, he walked across the road carrying both, passing cyclists and pedestrians, and headed in the direction of Jakob Jansen's Food Shop.

After arriving at the shop, he placed the photograph on the front step, weighed it down with the small rock, and walked briskly away.

•

Jakob, Otto and Eva were still waiting outside the delivery ward.

'Sorry! Sorry I'm late, I got held up,' called Gary as he entered the waiting area, looking as though he'd thrown his own clothes on in rather a hurry.

'Oh Gary, I was so worried about you.' Eva stood up and wrapped her arms around him. But before anything else could be said, they were all distracted by Angelina's sudden screams of pain.

'Keep pushing, Angelina, keep pushing, you're doing great,' called the midwife.

'Oh my God I think it's finally coming,' said an anxious Jakob.

'Calm down, Jakob, it's going to be fine,' Eva consoled him.

After some time, Angelina's cries were soon replaced by a different sort of cry.

Shortly after, the midwife opened the door and looked directly at Jakob.

'Congratulations, Mr Jansen, you have a beautiful baby girl, would you like to come and say hello?'

Jakob was speechless; he had literally lost his voice. He couldn't believe it; he was actually a father to a baby girl.

'Jakob, go!' Eva gave him an encouraging shove into the labour ward.

Jakob walked in on the strangest scene he'd ever witnessed. A tired and sweaty-looking Angelina, holding in her arms a tiny little person wrapped in a pink blanket. Angelina smiled weakly at him as he slowly made his way over. He looked into the face of his daughter. She was smaller than he'd ever expected, with the bluest of blue eyes, and her little curled fingers could just be seen poking out of the pink blanket.

'I'm so proud of you,' he whispered to Angelina and kissed her on her forehead. 'And you,' he added kissing his daughter's forehead; her skin was strangely soft and had an unusual but pleasant scent.

'Are we agreed on the name then?' he asked Angelina

hopefully. She nodded and smiled. Jakob looked down lovingly at his daughter. 'Hello Carice,' he whispered as his eyes began to fill up.

•

About an hour later, Jakob, Otto, Gary and Eva were on their way back to the shop, when Eva spotted something on the front doorstep. Hurrying ahead of the others, she bent down and picked up the small rock and looked at the photograph. She could quite clearly see Heidi pleasuring what appeared to be a German soldier; she could just make out the sleeve of a German uniform.

'What's that you've got there, Eva?' asked Jakob approaching her.

'Jakob, have you got a pen on you? I think this is the General's handiwork, trying to make me jealous,' said Eva looking convinced.

Jakob handed her a pen from his top pocket, and she proceeded to scribble down something on the back of the photograph.

'What's that you're writing down there, Eva?' asked Otto.

Eva handed Jakob the pen, then read aloud.

'Dear General, I cannot believe you would stoop this low. I don't care what you two do together. I knew you weren't over it.'

'What are you going to do?' asked Gary.

'I'm taking this to put on the step of the German headquarters,' she said simply, and off she went. Gary watched her for a while as the others went on inside.

•

Moments later, Eva reached the steps of the German headquarters; she placed the photograph down, weighed it down with the small rock then casually walked away.

After a few minutes the General came round the corner; he placed one boot on the step when he noticed the photo and frowned. Picking it up he saw some writing show through from the other side; he turned it over and read aloud to himself.

'Dear General, I cannot believe you would stoop this low. I don't care what you two do together. I knew you weren't over it.'

The General looked over the street towards the Gestapo headquarters. 'Well, Herr Von Braun, you certainly took that well,' he whispered to himself.

TWENTY

MIX-UP AFTER MIX-UP

April 10, 1941. 09:50

Eva, the General and Von Braun were all standing on the customer side of the counter in the shop, discussing the photograph. The General was standing in the middle holding the photo while all three of them examined it.

'I'm sorry, Klaus, I could've sworn this was from you,' said Eva.

'Yes, and I thought it was from you,' Von Braun said to Eva.

'Well, I thought it was you who wrote this on the back,' the General said to Von Braun.

Gary was listening intently from around the corner.

'So let me get this straight,' said Eva, attempting to clarify, 'Klaus, you took this photo yesterday of Heidi sleeping with an unknown soldier or officer, you then put it on Ludwig's doorstep to show him what she's like. Ludwig, you then looked at this photo thinking it was

Heidi with the General, and that I had taken it, and so you put it on the doorstep outside here. I in turn assumed it was from Klaus.'

'And here we are, trying to figure out who the man in the photograph is,' said the General.

'Well, I have no idea,' said Von Braun disinterested, 'and to be honest, I really don't care; all I wanted was a gorgeous woman on my arm and now I've got one, so if you'll excuse me,' he said and he made his way over to the front door. Eva and the General, both rather surprised at his attitude, watched him to the door. He put his hand on the handle but then turned back to them.

'Oh, by the way, Heidi and I are having a private wedding, just me, her, the priest and a couple of witnesses. We were hoping to have the reception held at the German headquarters if at all possible?'

Eva and the General exchanged looks.

'You're both invited, by the way,' Von Braun added.

'It would be an honour,' the General replied with a nod.

'Good, we'll see you at 18:00, Heil Hitler!'

'Heil Hitler,' they replied as Von Braun left the premises with a jingle of the bell.

Suddenly, Gary walked into the shop from the back; both Eva and the General noticed that something was bothering him.

'Gary, what is it? What's wrong?' Eva asked as he stood on the other side of the counter.

'I have a confession to make,' Gary said while looking down at the floor like a guilty schoolboy. 'The man in the photo,' he continued, 'it's me.'

Eva shook her head slowly in disbelief, her eyes like saucers. The General wasn't looking very impressed.

'But let me explain,' he said urgently, 'nothing happened.'

'Nothing happened?!' Eva raised her voice. 'How do you explain this?!' she slammed the photo onto the counter facing him.

'Yes, I know it looks bad, but I promise you, seconds later I was gone,' Gary pleaded.

'Actually, this is true, I can vouch for him,' said the General to Gary's surprise. Eva looked at the General completely nonplussed; even Gary was a little confused by this.

'After I had taken the photo, I limped along the corridor as quickly as I could and began to descend the stairs; as I did so I distinctly heard Heidi's bedroom door open and shut. I knew it was hers, it's the only door that has that particular squeak if you open it far enough. I also heard footsteps coming along the corridor; it must've been you,' the General explained.

'Well, thank God you were there to hear that,' Gary breathed a sigh of relief.

'But that doesn't explain why you were there in the first place?' The General narrowed his eyes suspiciously.

'I helped her in with some shopping, I then asked where the toilet was, she told me and I went, when I came out, she was just standing there… naked… I admit it was difficult to resist, but after a few moments I did resist because… because I love you, Eva,' Gary explained rather sheepishly yet sincerely.

Eva just studied the photo in deep thought, and then

looked up at Gary. 'Yes, I suppose it's her I should be angry with, not you.'

Gary gave her a subtle smile, but it was not returned. Again, Eva was in deep thought as she looked down at the photo.

'Now all I need is a plan of revenge,' she said darkly.

•

That afternoon, Heidi and Von Braun were sitting on one side of a wooden desk opposite a priest, while Von Braun's guards were standing present as witnesses. The room was dark, quiet and a little eerie; the only source of light was coming from a candle on the desk. Both Von Braun and Heidi were only in civvies, while the priest wore his long white robes and a purple collar. The priest looked down to his side and pulled a large heavy bible from his bag. Placing it on the table, he searched for a particular page, and after finding it, he looked up at Heidi and Von Braun and finally broke the silence. 'Shall we begin?' he asked simply.

•

Eva and the General were in the Great Hall of the German headquarters, organising everything. There were tables all around the outside draped in long white tablecloths, with polished glasses, serviettes and beautifully lit candles.

The General, wearing every medal he owned including the Iron Cross, was polishing some glasses, while Eva, wearing a long red silk and lace figure-hugging dress, laid out some cutlery.

'Are you absolutely certain your plan is going to work?' the General asked her.

'She is a disease of this city, Klaus, and you know it, she tries to sleep with Gary, she cheats on you, she cheats on Ludwig, she's a disease, and this,' she said as she dropped a small pill into a glass of wine, 'is the cure.'

The General watched her momentarily. 'Perhaps you're right.' He continued to clean the glasses.

•

Sometime later, chatter filled the hall as guests began to enter.

Eva took the glass of wine containing the pill over to the bar at the far end, her heels echoing on the marble floor as she walked. She placed the glass just around the corner on the bar out of sight; she noticed the barman watching suspiciously as he cleaned a glass.

'This glass is reserved for the lucky bride,' Eva smiled; the barman simply nodded in acknowledgement.

The entire guest list now seemed to be present, members of the German army, Gestapo agents and even what appeared to be one or two Dutch collaborators.

The General joined Eva, who was sitting on a stool over at the bar.

'I've got a bad feeling about this whole operation,' he told her while leaning his elbow on the bar.

'Well, there's only one way to find out,' Eva replied, the General looked over in the direction that Eva was looking, and he saw Heidi and Von Braun enter.

'Thought she would've made some effort dress-wise,'

Eva said sarcastically; the General smirked at her.

Heidi and Von Braun began to greet the people they passed.

'Well, here goes nothing,' said Eva as she took the glass and made her way over to Heidi.

The General lit a cigar while he watched the interaction between Heidi and Eva. Eva handed Heidi the glass of wine with a convincing smile. Heidi willingly took the glass and simply held it while they exchanged a few words. He then noticed that Heidi appeared to excuse herself while passing the glass to Von Braun to hold, and while Eva was left talking with Von Braun, Heidi made her way over to the bar; she leaned on the bar near to where the General was standing.

'Congratulations,' said the General as he blew out a puff of smoke.

'Thank you,' she replied without eye contact, she simply stared at the barman at the other end of the bar and beckoned him over.

'Yes Fraulein?' he asked as he approached her.

'A schnapps for the groom, please,' she ordered. The barman prepared the drink at once.

'I informed Eva that you adore any type of white wine, so that is what she ordered you, that is what your husband is holding for you,' the General felt the need to clarify.

The barman came over and placed the drink on the bar in front of Heidi.

'I suppose I should thank you for that then, Klaus,' she said as she looked down fiddling in her bag.

'I wouldn't go that far,' he puffed out more smoke as he noticed her discreetly drop a small pill in the glass.

'Your loss,' she replied as she took the glass and walked off in the direction from which she'd come.

The General observed, intrigued, as he saw Heidi hand Von Braun his glass, and he handed her hers. Eva said goodbye to them both and made her way back over to the General. She stood beside him with her back to the bar, and leaned back on her elbows, as they both observed Heidi and Von Braun.

'I suppose now would be a very good time for me to tell you that you're not the only one who has a thing for poisoning drinks,' said the General puffing on his cigar.

'What do you mean?' she asked.

'While she was over here getting his drink, I saw her slip a pill in,' the General explained.

Eva was shocked as she looked over at them mingling with the guests. 'So tonight could be the end for both of them,' she said thoughtfully.

About half an hour later, the General put his glass down on the bar, then turned to Eva and said, 'I think it's about time I went to get that car we discussed, I'll bring it round the front,' he said and slipped away. Eva nodded in acknowledgement and walked on over to Heidi and Von Braun, both of whom were now complaining of headaches and dizziness.

'Are you feeling all right, Ludwig? You're looking quite pale,' said Eva with a convincing concern.

'As a matter of fact, I'm not feeling well at all, neither is Heidi,' he replied. Heidi agreed.

'Well, why don't you both come outside with me, the fresh air will do you good,' Eva suggested.

Heidi and Von Braun stood up out of their seats,

shook hands with a select few people, apologised for their premature departure, and then followed Eva out to the front door of the German headquarters.

Once outside the night air hit them hard and they both collapsed on the pavement. Eva managed to catch Heidi on the way down, so she didn't hit the ground as hard as Von Braun, who was now sporting a slight cut on his temple. A black Gestapo staff car approached at speed with a screech, and out got the General.

'Eva, drop her and help me get him in the back seat, will you?' the General told her. While he picked up Von Braun under the arms, Eva grabbed a hold of his legs and together they bundled him in the back of the car. The General propped him up so that he looked like he was simply sitting still; they then did the same with Heidi while keeping an eye on the surrounding area, hoping not to draw attention, and then casually closed the back doors.

'Get in the front, Eva,' he told her as he got back in the driver's seat.

'Right,' said the General, closing his door, 'we'll take them to the hospital.'

'The hospital?' asked Eva utterly confused.

'Yes, the hospital,' he replied starting the engine, 'we have to make everything look genuine so as not to arouse suspicion,' he explained and he pulled away, slowly, hoping to keep Heidi and Von Braun propped up in the back.

•

Angelina was fast asleep in the silent ward, Jakob sitting by her side holding his daughter, Carice in his arms, wrapped in her soft pink blanket, and Otto on the other side of the bed engrossed in his newspaper, *De Waarheid*.

'Anything interesting?' asked Jakob.

'Only one thing really,' Otto replied as he folded the newspaper and dropped it down by his side. 'Looks like the German battleship *Gneisenau* was hit in an RAF raid on Brest; other than that, not much,' he replied. 'And how is she doing?' Otto asked, referring to baby Carice.

'Fast asleep at the moment, which is good, Angie could do with a rest.'

'Well after giving birth to a nine-pound baby, I can't blame her,' Otto chuckled. Jakob smiled and looked down at his daughter, his face so proud.

'No news on the radio lately then? Jakob asked.

'Not *on* the radio no, *about* the radio however…'

'How do you mean?' Jakob asked.

'Oh, it's probably nothing, but there's talk that the Germans could be listening into our radios, there's this particular buzzing sound, you see, apparently it happens when someone is trying to listen in,' Otto explained.

'But that's no problem, is it? I mean we have the codes, don't we?' Jakob said, feeling hopeful.

'Well, yes, but it's important that we keep changing the codes. You remember that one we used back when Anton was with us? The one where a number represented each letter of the alphabet? They cracked that in minutes of discovering what code we were using. We used it again a few weeks later, but we got lucky somehow.'

Jakob's jaw dropped.

'So you see, we have to be on our guard, but the most important thing is that they don't find out where we are transmitting from; as long as we can keep that secret, we're safe,' Otto explained reassuringly.

'OK, so any ideas as to who exactly it may be?' asked Jakob.

'Well, there's one or two who…' Otto broke off and stared at the door behind Jakob.

'Otto? What is it?'

'I could've sworn I just saw Eva walk by with the General,' Otto got to his feet and walked over to the door; he opened it and peered outside. He saw nobody but two doctors and three nurses.

'No, must've been mistaken,' he said, and he simply walked back to his chair.

Angelina began to wake.

'All right, sweetheart?' Jakob said smiling.

'Jakob, how's little Carice?' she asked sleepily as she struggled to sit up.

'Here, let me help you.' Otto assisted her to sit up in the bed.

'She's fast asleep at the moment, do you want to hold her?' said Jakob leaning forward in his seat.

'No, not if she's sleeping, I don't want to disturb her.'

•

The General was at Heidi's bedside; she was awake but drowsy.

'How are you feeling?' he asked standing over her.

'He poisoned me, didn't he?' she said in a certain voice.

'It would seem so, yes, I think you're probably best having your marriage annulled and going back to Berlin,' he told her.

'You mean leave Holland?' she exclaimed.

'Yes Heidi, I think that would be best for everyone.'

•

Eva was at the bedside of Ludwig Von Braun; he too was awake but looking drowsy.

'How are you, Ludwig?' she asked standing over him.

'What happened exactly?' he asked a little confused.

'Heidi poisoned your drink,' Eva replied simply.

'No, I don't believe that. I won't believe it,' Von Braun replied stubbornly.

'It's true, just ask Klaus, he's next door with her now.'

Von Braun lay silent for a moment processing this information.

'No, why would she do that?' he asked, still struggling with cognitive dissonance.

'Because that's what she's like, Ludwig; she planned to marry you, kill you and then take all your money.'

Von Braun looked at Eva with a mixture of shock and confusion etched on his face. Just then, the General entered through the curtain.

'Is it true?' Von Braun asked desperately. 'Did she poison my drink?'

'Yes, I'm afraid it is true, Herr Von Braun,' the General replied, 'and she now thinks that because she poisoned you that you poisoned her; it was of course Eva who poisoned her after she found out that she poisoned you.' The General gave Eva a slight smile. Eva looked straight to Von Braun, hoping he'd take this well; to her relief, Von Braun gave her an appraising and grateful look.

'And so,' the General continued, 'she has agreed to annul the marriage, and tomorrow morning I shall be personally escorting her back to Berlin by train.'

'So I'll be all right then? I'll survive the poison?' Von Braun asked desperately.

'Oh most definitely, we got you to the hospital straight away,' the General said with his chest puffed out.

'But how did you know I'd been poisoned?' Von Braun asked.

'It was I who saw Heidi slip the pill in; of course I couldn't be sure it was poison, so when Heidi wasn't looking, I slipped my hand in her bag, and emptied one of her pills in her own drink; turns out it was poison after all,' Eva cleverly invented.

'But of course, we knew you'd be fine as long as we got you to a hospital in time,' the General added.

'So what happens now?' asked Von Braun.

'Now we are going home, and in the morning, when you and Heidi are free to go, I shall escort Heidi on the train bound for Berlin,' the General explained.

'But what about the annulment? Klaus, they're going to have to go to court,' said Eva.

'Oh there's plenty of time for that; right then, I'm off home, coming Eva?'

'No, you go ahead, I have a friend just down the corridor whom I want to see,' Eva explained.

'Very well, goodnight, Eva, Herr Von Braun,' he nodded to him and left.

'Right then, Ludwig, I'm off now, you get well soon,' Eva said as she turned to leave, but as she did so Von Braun gently took hold of her wrist. Eva looked back in surprise.

'Thank you,' he said most sincerely.

Their eyes locked for what seemed to Eva to be too long; she smiled politely and exited through the curtain.

TWENTY-ONE

GARY'S SECRET

April 11, 1941. 10:00

The sunshine was beaming down beautifully on the platform as the train began to depart. The steam that filled the platform as the train pulled away slowly began to disburse to reveal Heidi and the General sitting on a bench outside the public convenience on the platform.

'So this is how it all ends,' Heidi said, gazing at the ground.

'You know he'd kill you if you stayed,' explained the General, 'and besides, there's nothing here for you now.'

'And to think we actually got engaged,' she looked to the General.

'Well, I've had worse days,' he said sarcastically as he lit a cigar.

'You can't tell me you didn't enjoy parts of it,' she smirked.

'Yes, well I'm sure Ludwig, Gary and many others

enjoyed that part too,' the General took another puff of his cigar.

'Gary? Who's Gary?'

The General paused for thought; he'd forgotten that Heidi wouldn't have known his name.

'Nobody,' he replied simply.

'Anyway, can I help if I'm irresistible?' She made a point of pulling up her tight black dress over her knees to reveal her silk stockings and crossed her legs.

'Do you want me one last time, Klaus?' she said with a slight smirk.

The General looked at her for a second, then faced ahead. 'Now why would I want to do a thing like that?' he said, still facing the front.

'Because I know something about Gary that would destroy Eva's reputation if I ever let it slip in Berlin… and I know you have a soft spot for her, and I'll let it be known that I found out from you, and she'll never want to have anything to do with you again.'

'Heidi, what the hell are you talking about?' the General asked convincingly.

Heidi pulled out a piece of paper from the inside of her fur coat and handed it to the General.

'What's this?' he asked, unfolding it. In front of him was a list of words he did not recognise. 'Well, what does it say?' he asked perplexed.

'It's a shopping list… in English,' she replied slowly. 'Yes, Klaus, your Eva, your beloved Eva, is in a relationship with a British spy.'

Klaus was speechless as he stared in disbelief at the piece of paper.

'So how did you get hold of this?' he asked finally.

'While he had his trousers off,' she said with a smug face.

Suddenly, a train could be heard in the distance; the General stuffed the piece of paper in his inside pocket and got to his feet. Heidi too got to her feet; she shimmied her black dress straight and picked up her suitcase.

The long black steam train entered the station accompanied by a thick layer of steam, which smelled surprisingly pleasant. They walked over to the train through the thick carpet of steam and were greeted by passengers stepping out of the carriages. Once there was a free gap, the General ushered Heidi onto the train before following her closely.

•

Otto was having problems with the radio down in the cellar.

'Hello? Hello? I only got half your message, hello?' He gave up and switched off the crackling radio. 'Bloody thing,' he muttered, and leaned back in his wooden chair just staring at the radio, his features dancing in the flickering dim light of the candle.

•

Upstairs in Eva's and Gary's room, Eva was getting dressed, the sunlight beaming through the drawn curtains onto her soft glowing skin. As she turned to pick up her blouse on the bed, she realised Gary was awake watching her.

'I didn't know you were awake.' She smiled as she put on her white blouse.

Gary smiled and said, 'I have something for you.' As he reached under his pillow, Eva frowned with uncertainty as she buttoned up her blouse.

Gary pulled something out from under his pillow, got out of bed dressed only in his striped pyjama bottoms, and got down on one knee.

'Oh, my goodness.' Eva paused in the middle of tucking her blouse into her black skirt, her eyes staring unblinking at the diamond ring in Gary's hands.

'Eva, I know this isn't really the time or the place, but I love you more than you will ever know. Eva, will you do me the great honour of becoming my wife?'

Eva's blue eyes began to sparkle with tears, but a smile appeared on her face and she nodded and managed to whisper a clear 'Yes.'

Gary got to his feet, and slowly slipped the diamond ring on Eva's left ring finger. It sparkled beautifully in the sunlight blazing through the drawn curtains.

'Oh Gary,' she sniffed, 'it's stunning.'

•

Meanwhile, on the train, Heidi and the General were kissing passionately in the bathroom. He pulled rather roughly at her hair-tie to release her long golden locks, causing her to wince in slight pain, but she seemed to enjoy it as she began to unbutton his shirt. While pulling his shirt off he told her to remove her fur coat. As her coat slipped to the floor, the General turned her around, and forcefully hunched her over the basin.

•

As Otto was slowly stepping out of the cellar, he realised someone was pulling the long red carpet off the opened door for him.

'Oh, Gary, thank you,' he replied. He closed the door up, then pulled the carpet back across. He looked back at Gary who was wearing a broad grin on his face.

'What is it?' Otto asked.

Gary nodded over to Eva who was coming down the stairs; she held out her hand to show off her new engagement ring with a smile. Otto saw it and looked back at Gary with an open mouth.

'Yes, we're engaged to be married,' Gary clarified for him.

'Oh Gary, congratulations my friend.' He shook Gary's hand. 'Eva, congratulations.' He kissed her on each cheek. 'Well, I suppose you'll both be waiting until the war is over? After all, it would be a little tricky marrying a German woman to an Englishman,' he joked. Gary and Eva laughed.

'True, true,' said Gary, as he turned to walk into the kitchen followed by Otto and Eva. 'On the other hand, you never know which day will be your last in a war like this,' Gary continued as he reached for the orange juice in the fridge.

'Well, there is that, I suppose,' said Otto as he took out a breakfast bowl from the cupboard, 'but where are you going to find a vicar or a priest who'll marry a German woman and an Englishman?'

'He's right, Gary, we're going to have to wait until the end of the war, whenever that will be, and whichever side wins will depend on where we get married,' Eva explained, spreading jam on her bread.

'Perhaps, and I suppose that way we won't have all that drama that Jakob and Angelina had at their wedding,' Gary added, pouring milk over his cereal.

'Oh yes, I remember that like it was yesterday,' said Otto, 'Jakob's ex-wife Rini turning up at the wedding with that spy.'

'Yes, and all those gunshots going off, and then you got into that little predicament,' Eva smiled, winding Otto up.

'What do you mean?' he smiled back. 'I was the hero that day, I remember,' and he stood up to re-enact the scene. 'I crept up behind the German spy, held my gun up against his back, I went to take his gun when he raised his hands in the air, but then he knocked me down,' Otto went down on the kitchen floor with dramatic effect. 'I then kicked the gun out of his hand—'

'And that's when I became the real hero and shot him,' Eva added to a big laugh from Gary.

'Well, yes all right,' Otto smiled as he got up off the kitchen floor and sat back in his seat.

'But you did get back inside the church in time to give Jakob the ring,' said Gary fairly.

'There you are,' Otto smiled at Eva.

'But this time around it's going to be a peaceful wedding, whether it's a wartime wedding or not,' Gary added.

•

Back in the bathroom of the Berlin Express, Heidi and the General were re-clothing themselves, the General buttoning up his shirt while Heidi was brushing her hair. Heidi noticed the General's jacket lying on the floor. Hoping that he wasn't looking, she bent down on the pretext of adjusting her shoe, and she discreetly took out the shopping list from the inside pocket. When she stood back up, a large hand had seized her tiny wrist.

'I'll take that,' said the General as he snatched it out her hand.

'You really do love her, don't you?' she said as she tied up her hair. 'It's a shame really, you two would have made a lovely couple, but I suppose it's just not meant to be, not with her seeing a British spy,' she added in an appalled tone.

'You're trying to wind me up, it's not going to work, I care only for Eva's happiness.'

'Then you're a fool; you could have her all to yourself if only you would let me tell them in Berlin,' said Heidi, almost on the point of pleading.

The General suddenly made a grab for her throat with one hand; she froze as her eyes bulged in fright.

'Now you listen to me and listen good,' he began, his face inches from hers. 'If you so much as talk in your sleep about Eva or Gary, I will personally hunt you down, and I will shoot you like the dog that you are, do you understand me?'

She glared into his angry eyes; for a second, she looked a little defiant, but she soon nodded her head quickly and the General released her.

•

Otto, Gary and Eva were still sitting at the kitchen table.

'Are you sure we shouldn't open up the shop?' asked Gary.

'Well, how can we, none of us can be seen behind the counter, can we?' Otto explained.

'Yeah, I know, but he's losing money, isn't he?' Gary said, concerned.

'Look don't worry, Jakob will be back tomorrow,' Eva explained.

'Oh, OK, fair enough,' said Gary.

'Right, well now that's cleared up, I'm going to try and fix this radio,' said Otto as he stood up and made his way in the direction of the hallway.

'Why, it's not broken is it?' asked Gary.

'No, it's not broken,' Otto stopped at the doorway and looked back, 'it's just that we're getting a lot of interference lately.'

'Interference? But doesn't that usually happen when somebody else is trying to listen in?' said Eva.

'Well, yes, but we're not too worried; the code we're currently using is unbreakable,' he smiled and walked on towards the cellar door.

Gary and Eva exchanged looks of mild concern.

•

Four hours had passed. Heidi and the General were sitting next to each other in their own compartment. The General was sitting on the outside and looking intently at the shopping list. Heidi was staring absent-mindedly out of the window, until familiar surroundings brought her back to reality. The familiar architecture, SS men going about their business, two Hitler Youth boys selling flags.

The General put the shopping list away as he felt the train begin to slow down. As they approached the station, he looked around at all the fascinating propaganda posters on the walls of the platform. One was of a blonde Hitler Youth boy, with the writing 'DER DEUTSCHE STUDENT' at the top. Another was of a German soldier standing in front of a Swastika flag, the writing at the bottom read, 'DER SIEG WIRD UNSER SEIN'. The General looked over to his other side, and saw a Poster of a mother, a father and three children. This poster read, 'NSDAP SICHERT DIE VOLKS GEMEINSCHAFT'.

'Here we are,' said the General as he stood up and opened the compartment door to let Heidi out. He took her suitcase off the top rack and handed it to her; she went to take it, but he didn't let go; she turned to look at his deadly serious face.

'If you so much as whisper what you know to an old lady, or a passing Hitler Youth member, I will hunt you down and I will dispose of you myself, that's a promise.'

Heidi snatched her case and spun on her heel before marching down the train corridor.

As she stepped onto the platform, the General watched as she walked over to the nearest bench, she sat down and placed her suitcase by her side, she then looked up at the train and saw the General looking back at her out the window.

The last of the people were now boarding the train. The whistle blew and the train began to move. As it did so, Heidi took out a piece of paper from the inside of her fur coat with a slight smirk and held it up for the General to see. The General looked confused. He quickly looked down at the shopping list in his hand; he then looked back at Heidi, who obviously had something else in her hand, but what?

TWENTY-TWO

INTERCEPTED

May 15, 1941. 06:00

The sun was beginning to rise over the beautiful city of Amsterdam.

The shop was deadly quiet, curtains drawn, not a soul awake, until… knock, knock, knock! at the back door. Eva began to stir. She was lying on her side facing away from Gary; she yawned and slowly rolled onto her back.

Knock, knock, knock!

Eva opened her eyes. 'Did you hear that?' She looked to her side to see Gary facing her still fast asleep.

'Gary, wake up.' She nudged him; he slowly began to wake.

Knock, knock, knock, knock!

'What was that?' he asked, rubbing his eyes.

'There's someone at the door,' Eva replied earnestly. She pulled back the blankets, revealing her luscious slim body in her black, shimmering silk nightdress.

'You're not going down, are you?' asked Gary.

'No, you can, I'm going to call Jakob,' Eva replied as she put on her red silk dressing gown.

'All right, fine,' he climbed out of bed in his red striped pyjamas.

Knock, knock, knock! This time a little louder.

'All right! All right! I'm coming!' Gary called out as he descended the stairs.

Gary could see the silhouette of a man in a hat through the net curtain of the back door. He opened the door to a rather short, stout man in his fifties, in a black hat and spectacles.

'Mr Jansen?' he asked while lifting his hat to reveal a balding head.

'Er, no, but he is on his way, please come inside,' Gary said kindly. He gratefully walked inside and removed his hat at the sight of Eva.

'What's going on? Who is this?' Jakob asked, coming into the kitchen dressed in his soft white dressing gown.

'Er, are we among friends?' asked the man tentatively.

'Yes, we are all on the same side,' Jakob replied cleverly.

'Please could everybody sit down,' said the man as he took a chair himself. 'I have extremely important news for you all.'

Everyone sat around the table in their usual fashion.

'Wait a moment, what about Otto?' asked Eva.

'Would you mind going to get him, Eva?' asked Jakob.

Eva walked out into the hallway, pulled back the carpet and knocked on the cellar door. 'Otto! Otto! Come up here quick, there is someone who wants to speak to us!' she called and walked back into the kitchen. They heard the cellar door open, and moments later Otto emerged in the kitchen in his blue pyjamas.

'Oh, hello,' Otto said cautiously while rubbing his eyes.

'Otto, is it? Please take a seat, my friend, I have important news,' said the stranger. Otto pulled up a chair, and everybody leaned into each other, elbows resting on the table.

'My name is James Wilson,' he began, 'and I work for British intelligence. I was brought here at great risk to give you some very bad news. The radio in your cellar is being tapped into; the person responsible is none other than Heidi Eichmann, the German spy, and she's been listening in for a very long time.'

The faces around the table dropped in horror.

'But I'm afraid I have other bad news,' James continued. 'Your old friend Anton, I used to work with him back in England, but he is no longer in England, for the past two weeks he's been in a Prisoner of War camp in Germany.'

'No!' Jakob responded; they all looked round at each other in complete shock.

'Obviously, we couldn't tell you any of this over the radio, so I was sent here to tell you all in person, and while I am here, I thought I should assist you in rescuing him.'

'Rescue him? You mean go to Germany?' asked Otto.

'Precisely,' James replied enthusiastically. 'Now, the name of the camp is Altengrabow; it is situated on the outskirts of west Berlin, and my plan is as follows...'

•

Two hours later, James Wilson, Otto and Gary were all standing in the main shop, each dressed as a German officer, all of a different rank, including one of an SS officer, which gave the shop a very ominous atmosphere. James was dressed as an SS Sturmbannfuhrer, Otto as a Captain, and Gary as a Private.

'Good, there is a car outside waiting for us,' said James looking out through the blinds of the front door. Otto looked through the blinds too.

'Who left that car there?' he asked.

'I'm afraid I'm not a liberty to say,' James replied.

'But we're all on the same side,' Gary queried.

'Young Gary, you'll soon learn that even those who are our allies, are better left in ignorance concerning certain matters, now come on,' said James as he stepped outside with a jingle of the bell, followed by Otto and Gary.

'No, no, no, Gary,' said James as Gary went to sit in the back seat of the black open top car, 'you're in the front.'

'What, I'm driving, am I?' asked Gary.

'Well, we outrank you, son, you're a Private, you would drive us,' James explained as he and Otto got into the back, while Gary sat in the driver's seat.

'I'm glad you came prepared with papers,' said Otto getting himself comfy in the back seat, 'there's no way I would've been able to get papers for you for at least another week.'

'Never underestimate British intelligence,' James smiled at him.

The sun had now made an appearance in the form of a scarlet sky, as Gary pulled away.

•

Jakob, Eva, Angelina and little Carice were sitting at the kitchen table now fully dressed.

'I've got a bad feeling about this,' said Jakob biting his nails.

'What do you mean?' asked Angelina sitting next to him holding their daughter.

'I mean, I know what it's like when travelling long distances; they're bound to come upon roadblocks between here and Berlin; I just hope their papers are good enough.'

'Yes, he's right,' Eva agreed, 'I mean that's just going from here to Berlin, never mind coming back again, and that's not to mention what might happen at the camp.'

'Well, to look on the bright side,' said Angelina, 'at least it's all for a good cause, to get Anton out of the camp and out of Berlin.'

'True,' said Eva, looking down at her engagement ring, 'I just hope Gary will be OK.'

•

James, Gary and Otto were travelling at top speed through the winding countryside. The sun shone beautifully on all the greenery, the fields and trees shining a lighter shade of green, the smell of freshly cut grass filled their noses.

'Slow down, Gary, we want to get there alive!' James called to Gary in the front, holding his hat on his lap for fear of it blowing off.

'I want today to be over with a soon as possible!' Gary called back, the wind rushing past his ears.

'Well, just take it easy on the bends then!' Otto called out.

'Oh no! Roadblock up ahead!' called Gary.

'Well, we had to expect them, just let me do all the talking!' James explained.

Gary pulled up inches from the barrier. Two soldiers came over brandishing their machine guns.

'Papers,' said the soldier nearest to Gary, who slipped his hand inside his jacket and revealed his pristine identification papers. The soldier studied them for a moment then handed them back to Gary.

'Where are you heading to?'

'We've been invited to an urgent meeting with all the top officers,' James interrupted with authority.

The soldier looked at James suspiciously.

'Forgive me Herr Sturmbannfuhrer, but I have not heard of such a meeting being mentioned, where is this supposed to be taking place?' asked the young soldier.

BANG!!! Suddenly a gunshot went off not too far in the distance; everyone jumped and looked around for the source.

'What was that?!' asked the second soldier, looking around utterly bewildered.

The soldier questioning them turned and headed for one of the fields, ducking low as he entered, his machine gun poised.

'OK, let them pass!' he called back to the other soldier as he continued cautiously on through the field surveying the entire area.

'What the hell was that?!' asked Gary as they drove on.

'Or where?!' said James.

'Or who?!' added Otto.

The rest of the road was a clear run through beautifully sunlit hills, over-reaching trees, and neatly cut hedgerows.

•

Jakob walked over to the front door and turned the closed sign around to say 'Open'. As he walked back around the counter, he heard the little bell jingle as the door opened.

'Morning, Jakob,' called a fellow Dutch customer, a short stocky man of about sixty years of age.

'Ah, Peter, nice to see you,' smiled Jakob.

Peter came casually walking over to the counter with his hands in his pockets.

'You heard the latest then?' Peter asked.

'Well, that all depends,' Jakob chuckled, 'I hear a lot of things, but whether they're the latest or not is a different story.'

'Well, I've heard through the grapevine that we have another General in town,' said Peter matter-of-factly.

'Well, that can't be right, General Schneider won't stand for that.'

'Well, unless Schneider is leaving?' Peter suggested.

'No, I wouldn't have thought so, General Schneider loves it here, plus he has a thing for Eva, the beautiful blonde,' Jakob clarified.

'Well, maybe we're getting two Generals then,' Peter guffawed as he went across to pick up a loaf of bread.

'Well, only time will tell,' said Jakob as Peter placed the loaf on the counter.

'I suppose it will,' Peter handed Jakob some change,' see you again Jakob,' he said and left with his loaf of bread.

•

Some hours later, James, Otto and Gary had arrived at Altengrabow Prisoner of War Camp. The camp was vast, situated right in the middle of the German countryside on the outskirts of Berlin. There was an eight-foot-high perimeter fence, finished off with a barbed-wire topping. Soldiers and German Shepherd dogs guarded the camp. Gary stayed in the driver's seat as James and Otto climbed out and went straight up to peer through the wire mesh.

'Oh my God, it's Anton!' said Otto, shocked.

'What? Where?' asked James, his eyes darting all over the camp.

'Over there, third barracks from the left,' Otto explained.

'Oh, my goodness, so it is, quick, get his attention.'

Otto started waving his hands trying to attract his attention.

'It's no good, he's not looking this way at all,' said Otto, disheartened.

'Oh hell!' James whispered loudly.

'What is it?' asked Otto.

'Here comes a bloody camp guard, just let me do all the talking.'

One of the guards came walking over to them from the other side of the fence with a sceptical face, MP40 poised.

'What are you doing?' he said rather sternly.

'Haven't you been taught to salute a senior officer? Pull yourself together!' James barked.

'I'm sorry, Herr Sturmbannfuhrer,' said the young soldier, who rapidly dropped his gun, clicked his heels and saluted all in succession.

'That's more like it,' James continued, 'now listen to me, I want—'

BANG!!!

A random shot rang out, and the camp guard on the other side of the fence slumped heavily to the ground. The alarm rang out.

'What the hell?!' Otto exclaimed.

The guards up in the watchtowers shouted out, 'Halt!' and pointed their MP40s at James and Otto, who automatically threw their hands into the air.

'Where the hell did that come from?!' James said, looking hopelessly around. He looked over to Gary in the car who looked just as bewildered as they did.

'Well, they can't blame us, they'll see we're unarmed,' said Otto shouting over the alarm.

Several soldiers came bustling over, brandishing their machine guns. The one at the front stopped right in front of James and Otto, but on the camp-side of the fence. It looked as if he was about to bellow in anger, but the sight of James' uniform seemed to stop him in his tracks.

'Herr Sturmbannfuhrer.' He clicked his heels together and gestured to the guards up in the watchtowers to lower their weapons, and then said tentatively, 'May I ask what is going on here?' he said, looking down at the lifeless soldier with a hole in his head.

'We were in mid conversation when a shot rang out of nowhere, but as you can see, we are unarmed, it is a most perplexing mystery. I suggest you search the grounds now!' James ordered authoritatively, and convincingly.

'Right, everybody out searching the grounds now,' he told his men and they left to search the surrounding areas, all except the one who appeared to be in charge, who remained rooted to the spot.

Both James and Otto noticed that Anton had disappeared.

'So, Herr Sturmbannfuhrer, may I ask what your business is here?'

'Er, we've come to take one of your prisoners, Anton Ackerman; we need to take him directly to Berlin for interrogation,' James explained.

Otto had the distinct feeling that this would not persuade the guard.

'I'm afraid we can't do that, Herr Sturmbannfuhrer, we have received no information about this.'

'Well, this is why I am here, what do you think I am? A British spy who just so happens to be dressed as an SS Officer?' There was a brief moment of anticipation in the air. When, thankfully, the guard cracked a smile and began to laugh, James and Otto joined in until they were all laughing heartily, but the reminder of the dead German soldier by their feet brought them all back to their senses.

'Even so, Herr Sturmbannfuhrer, I cannot allow anyone to collect our prisoners without proper authorisation. I'm sure a man of your seniority can appreciate that?' The guard smiled curtly.

James and Otto looked at each other, they both knew it was hopeless, nothing short of a good shoot-out would break Anton out of this camp, and that would lead to all kinds of unnecessary complications.

'Very well,' James said, defeated. 'Come on,' he told Otto, and they made their way back to the car.

'What the hell just happened?' asked Gary exasperated.

'Just get us back to Amsterdam, I'll explain on the way,' explained James.

'I was just about to step out and stretch my legs, when that gunshot rang out,' said Gary pulling away. It wasn't until they were well away from the camp that Gary finally asked, 'So what's happening with Anton?'

'Well, we both saw him outside the barracks,' explained James, 'but after that shot rang out, he disappeared; obviously wondered what the hell was going on and ran back inside like everyone else.'

'Yeah, and to top it all, our uniforms were no good at all in getting Anton out,' Otto added disappointedly.

'So, this has all been a wasted journey then?' asked Gary.

'Basically, yes it has,' James replied with a sigh.

•

Jakob was busy stacking tins on a high shelf when Angelina came into the shop from the kitchen, with little Carice in her arms.

'Who's this then?' she said to Carice showing her to Jakob. 'It's Daddy.'

'Hello ladies,' Jakob replied as he stepped down off his stepladder. He kissed Angelina on the cheek, then nudged his daughter's rosy cheek with the knuckle of his index finger.

'Aw, how is she?'

'She's fine, she's just been fed.'

'And where's Eva?'

'She's upstairs getting ready to come out with us,' Angelina replied.

'But we're only going clothes shopping for Carice, she has to get ready for that?' Jakob asked with a grin.

'Well, you know Eva, she even has to look good when she's putting out the rubbish,' Angelina chuckled.

'I heard that,' Eva said as she came into the shop from the back.

Jakob and Angelina both broke into laughter.

'Do you usually dress up to go shopping?' asked Jakob still laughing.

'When I was a little girl, I dressed up just to put the cat out.'

Angelina smiled at Eva's answer.

'And besides,' Eva continued, 'I have to try and keep my mind off of Gary, I am worried about him.'

'Eva, I'm sure he's fine, they've probably picked up Anton by now and are on their way back to Amsterdam,' Angelina consoled her.

•

James, Otto and Gary were just coming up to the same roadblock they'd encountered on the way out of Holland. Gary slowed the car down.

'Don't worry, men,' said James confidently, 'they let us go one way, they're bound to let us go the other.'

'Ah, Herr Sturmbannfuhrer, how was the meeting?' said the guard as he approached.

'What? Oh yes, it went well thank you.'

'I seem to remember we got interrupted last time, and I didn't get to see your papers, could I see them now please?'

'Oh, er, yes I've got them here somewhere,' James said caught unaware, and fumbling in his pockets.

Suddenly a speeding car came hurtling up behind

them. The guard quickly turned around and aimed his gun straight ahead.

'Halt! Slow down!' the guard shouted, but the green military-looking car appeared to have no intentions of slowing down, it just came straight at them, overtook them, smashed through the roadblock, and continued on at tremendous speed.

'Quick! After them now!' the guard called out to the other soldier, and they ran straight for the motorcycle and side car, started it up and rumbled on past James, Otto and Gary.

'There have been some really strange occurrences today,' said Gary as they pulled away.

'Well, I'm not complaining about them,' smiled Otto.

'Yes, but it's confused me,' said James. 'I mean, things have happened that I expected not to happen, and the one thing I expected to happen didn't happen, and that was getting Anton out of Berlin.'

•

Jakob was driving his car, Angelina in the front, and Eva in the back with baby Carice on her lap. He pulled over and parked on the side of the busy street. The street lights were on as the last few minutes of daylight slowly evaporated.

'We won't be able to spend too long; we have to be back before curfew,' explained Jakob.

The streets were relatively busy with cyclists, Germans and shoppers alike.

Jakob got out and went round the other side to open the door for Angelina; she stepped out while clutching her black purse with a gold chain. He then opened the back door to let Eva out and offered to take Carice.

One particular shop they entered was a very large and posh clothes shop. The ceiling was about twenty feet high, and the whole place had a variety of clothes on display, including a little boys' section and the little girls' section, into which they headed.

'Oh look,' said Angelina, picking up a little white dress and holding it out for them to see.

'She's a bit small for that at the moment,' said Jakob.

'Yeah, but in time,' she replied, admiring it.

'Ah, here we are,' said Eva, picking up the exact same dress but in a smaller size, 'this is for newborns.'

'Oh Jakob, can't you just see her in that?' Angelina said as she put the bigger one back and took the smaller one from Eva.

'Well, it is nice, but what's the price?' asked Jakob sceptically.

Angelina looked inside for the price tag and her face said it all; she showed Jakob.

'How much? That is ridiculous,' he exclaimed.

'Please let me get it for you,' Eva intercepted.

'What?' they said in unison.

'I said let me get it for you.'

'No, we couldn't allow that, not at that price,' said Jakob adamantly.

'No please, I really want to, it's a thank you for… well, for everything,' Eva smiled at them as she took the dress over to the counter. Angelina smiled back shaking her head.

•

'What a day that was, I'm fit for bed,' said Gary as he switched off the engine outside Jakob Jansen's Food Shop. It was now a pitch-black moonless night.

'Well, it looks like the others are still up,' Otto nodded to what appeared to be the kitchen light reaching out subtly through the blind of the front door. James got out of the car and walked up to the front door; he went to push open the door when he noticed it was slightly ajar.

'I see he's not exactly security-conscious,' said James turning back to Otto and Gary.

'That's very unlike Jakob,' Otto said suspiciously as he followed James into the shop. Gary tagged along behind. As they walked through the dark shop, they heard voices coming from the kitchen where the light was streaking through the hallway. The kitchen door was wide open, and as they neared the kitchen, they all had the shock of their lives. Sitting at the kitchen table facing them was none other than Anton, and even more surprising was the man sitting beside him; none other than General Klaus Schneider.

TWENTY-THREE

THE GENERAL'S SECRET

Otto, Gary and James stood frozen as they stared into the eyes of the General sitting at their kitchen table, fully aware that they themselves were dressed as German officers, not to mention their old friend whom they hadn't seen for many months. Was this the end of the line? Had they finally been rumbled?

'Please, take a seat, gentlemen,' the General smiled pleasantly.

Otto and Gary, in particular, were surprised at his unusually friendly manner towards them as they took their seats opposite.

Suddenly the back door opened to reveal the sound of chatter, as Jakob, Angelina and Eva returned home with bags full of shopping. The chatter soon died out, however, as they realised that the General was sitting at their kitchen table beside their old friend, Anton.

'Anton,' Jakob gasped with shock.

'Klaus, what's going on?' asked Eva, concerned for her friends.

'Please listen to what I have to say; the time has come that I must tell you all something of great importance,' the General explained.

Jakob and Eva placed their bags on the floor and stayed where they were, waiting with anticipation.

'I'll just go and put Carice down,' Angelina said as she made her way out into the hallway.

The General leaned forward and rested his forearms on the table, clasping his hands together before addressing them all.

'I am not who you think I am,' he began; the focus of attention on the General was razor sharp.

'Since the outbreak of war, I have been nothing more than a cleverly orchestrated product of propaganda. You remember the infamous story of the Jews I had massacred in Poland? It never happened.'

Jaws around the silent kitchen dropped. Klaus then looked from Jakob to Otto.

'Do you two recall my first day here in Amsterdam? It was about a year ago, you both looked through the blinds of the front door when you heard those shots fired, and you saw two Jews being loaded into the back of the truck. I can tell you now that it wasn't me who shot them, but it was one of my men, I had to give the impression that I was responsible, or that I was at least in agreement.'

Jakob and Otto exchanged awestruck looks.

'Jakob, do you remember when I short-changed you for that bottle of water? It was because I had Captain Fritz Muller with me at the time; I had to keep up appearances.'

Jakob had to pull up a chair before he fainted and proceeded to stare in disbelief with everyone else as Klaus continued.

'I had a funny feeling that you had borrowed my armoured car to destroy the train that night. I decided to turn a blind eye, and I must congratulate you, Eva. I thought you played your role well that night, even if I did already know,' he smiled at her, a sheepish grin spread on her surprised face.

'Of course, you're all aware that it was me who helped Jakob when he got into a sticky patch with the Gestapo after being caught near the train. I made a special recommendation about this shop when the Gestapo were searching for that money. Unfortunately, of course, Reich Commissioner Seyss-Inquart thwarted me on that occasion. I covered for you, Eva, when you were on the phone to Hitler.'

Eva nodded with recognition.

'I helped out with Jakob's ex-wife, when you had her tied up in this very kitchen, despite the fact that I already knew she had nothing to do with those cases, or with the shooting of that spy.'

Eva and Otto exchanged astonished looks.

'And who do you think enabled you three to pass that roadblock today with the gunshot creating a distraction? Who do you think shot that prison guard who was becoming suspicious of you? And who do you think blitzed past you in a speeding car, creating yet another diversion?'

Shocked looks were exchanged around the room.

'My other reason for that, of course, was so that they would not recognise Anton here.'

The room was silent as this almighty bombshell sunk in.

'Er, Klaus,' said Eva tentatively, 'are you saying that… that you're a… double agent?'

'I am a German General, Eva, but let's just say I've always had a mind of my own,' he smiled.

'Well, I would be lying if I said I wasn't in shock,' said Jakob staring down at the table but not really seeing it.

'So where does Anton come into all this?' asked Otto.

Klaus looked sideways at Anton. 'Would you like to tell this one?'

'Well, I'm just as surprised as all of you,' he said, looking round at them all. 'I was in my barracks minding my own business, when Klaus here burst in, accompanied by a camp guard, and he shouted at the top of his lungs, "That's the one who tried to assassinate me," and they dragged me outside the camp and into a car. I was of course petrified thinking that this was it, that my time was up, when Klaus explained everything to me on the way here, and I've got to say, it's really good to see you all, and to be back here again.'

'It's good to see you too, my friend,' said Otto, shaking Anton's hand rather vigorously.

'Yes, it's great to see you,' said Jakob, also shaking his hand.

'Glad you're well,' Gary nodded.

'So, this is the General you tried to poison?' asked James.

'I'm afraid so, yes,' Otto replied, a little embarrassed.

'But didn't he shoot you?' James asked Anton.

'Yes, that's a point?' Anton looked at Klaus.

'Anton, you didn't think I shot you in the leg because I missed your head, did you? I never miss, young man, again

I had to make things look genuine, convincing,' explained Klaus.

'You are full of surprises, Klaus,' Eva smiled.

'But why are you telling us all this now?' asked Jakob.

'Because I'm leaving,' he replied simply.

'What?' Eva said in a tone of surprise.

'I'm to go to Berlin, where they feel I will be of better use, so I will no longer be around to help you,' replied Klaus regretfully.

'I… I don't know what to say,' said Eva, evidently confused and upset.

'Here,' said Jakob as he stood up and offered Eva his seat.

'Well, I would just like to say thank you, General, for all you've done, seemingly from the shadows,' Jakob smiled as he offered his outstretched hand. Klaus shook it gladly.

'You're most welcome, Jakob, you're all welcome,' he said as he let go of Jakob's hand. 'But please, don't say your goodbyes now, you're all invited to my farewell leaving party tomorrow night at the German headquarters. But right now, I have a little business to attend to,' he said as he stood up to reveal his intimidating six-foot-four-inch frame. 'I have a little surprise in the back of my car,' he added, and he made his way around the table and out to the shop.

They all watched as the hat on his head just missed the door frame as he exited the kitchen. They all then turned their attention to Anton. Otto stood up and held his arms open. Anton got to his feet, and they had a manly embrace, clapping each other hard on the back. Next, Eva wrapped her arms around Anton's neck. 'It's nice to see you,' she told him.

'Likewise,' he blushed.

Gary then extended his hand. 'Good to see you again.'

'And you.'

The happy reunion was cut short as the front door burst open, with the sound of muffled screaming. Klaus, to everyone's surprise, was dragging in a kicking and screaming Heidi, who appeared to have just been to a very posh gathering, as she was wearing a red silk gown with a split up one leg, long black satin gloves just past her elbows, and her long golden locks tied up high with loose hanging ringlets.

Klaus placed her in one of the kitchen chairs; her hands were already tied behind her back, he just placed her arms over the back of the chair as she sat down, and she had some grey tape over her mouth muffling her angry screams of protest. She gave those around her a filthy look. Klaus removed the tape across her mouth.

'You bastard! You pig!' she shouted, attempting to break free.

'Now, now, settle down,' said Klaus calmly as he took a chair from the small stack to his right, and placed it in front of her and sat down. He leaned forward, her bony knees inches from his locked hands as he leaned his elbows on his knees. Everyone looked on in silence.

'All I want is some answers, and they'd better be the truth,' he told her.

'I'm telling you nothing,' she replied defiantly.

'You'd better start talking,' Otto piped up, 'you've been infiltrating messages on my radio.'

Klaus raised his hand up to Otto to signify that he had everything under control.

'Heidi, let's face it, you're not exactly a lady, are you?

You attempted to kill Von Braun, you attempted to sleep with Gary, you've attempted many things but never quite succeeded,' the General said as he leaned back and folded his arms. Heidi just looked back at him with pure hatred in her eyes.

'Although that's not entirely true, is it?' he continued. 'You managed to listen in on conversations over Otto's radio,' he leaned forward again. 'Tell me what you know,' he said darkly.

'Never!' she spat.

Klaus nodded, shrugged, and then reached into his pocket pulling out several photographs; he placed them on the table where everybody looked at them in complete shock, especially Heidi.

'Heidi, if you don't start talking, I am going to take these photographs of you sleeping with this Jewish man, and I'm going to take them with me to Berlin, where I shall have you shot for such a crime.'

Heidi looked at the photographs with shock and confusion on her face, much like the others around the table.

'I will tell you what you want to know on one condition,' Heidi finally spoke. 'All these people leave the room.'

'No way, I want to know what you heard on my radio,' Otto said defiantly.

Heidi looked sideways at Otto. 'You're such a complainer, you weren't complaining when you were in bed with me,' she said in a cruel seductive voice. Otto looked livid.

Klaus leaned back in his seat to have a quick think.

'OK, everyone, if you wouldn't mind,' he looked to Jakob.

'Right, come on everyone, let's give them a few minutes,' said Jakob, leading everyone out of the kitchen and into the hallway; they closed the kitchen door behind them.

Heidi's expression went from angry to seductive. She uncrossed her legs and crossed them over again to the other side, revealing one long firm thigh through the split of her red silk dress. Klaus tilted his head to the side to see right the way up her thigh.

'Come on, Klaus, you were the only man I ever loved, why don't we just run away together, to Switzerland or somewhere, just you and me?' she said hopefully, trying to hide her eagerness.

Klaus took a deep breath and sighed as he thought about this.

'If I agree to run away with you to Switzerland, do you promise to tell me everything I want to know?' he asked, his head raised looking down at her.

'Yes, I'll tell you everything, but kiss me first,' she said leaning back and looking submissive.

Klaus got to his feet; she looked up at him almost childlike. He leaned over her and placed his hands on her chair either side of her thighs, he leaned in to look at her closely. The scent of her perfume, face cream and shampoo, all met his nose, it was heaven. He closed his eyes and moved in; their lips touched.

Jakob, Otto, Gary, James, Eva, and now Angelina, were all listening on the other side of the door.

'Can you hear anything?' asked Jakob.

'Nothing, it's gone all quiet,' said Otto with his ear up against the door.

Suddenly, to their surprise, the door opened up, causing

them all to jump back as if they hadn't been eavesdropping at all.

'Nope,' said Klaus, 'she never heard anything of any importance over the radio,' he told them.

'Phew, thank goodness for that,' Otto breathed a sigh of relief.

'So what happens now?' asked Jakob.

'Now, I take this filth back to my car.' He turned to look back at Heidi who now had the tape back over her mouth.

'What will you do after that?' asked Eva.

'Perhaps I could get her a room and put a guard outside it?' Klaus replied. 'And in the morning, I will escort her once again to Berlin.'

Heidi gave Klaus a seductive wink.

TWENTY-FOUR

FAREWELL

May 16, 1941. 18:03

The Great Hall at the German headquarters was teeming with life. All attention was on the humble-looking Klaus, who was conversing with other military men and women. Three main scents filled the air: smoke, alcohol and the exotic aroma of perfume and cologne.

Klaus finished his conversation with a curt nod and a smile, then went over to the bar to put down his glass. He then made his way over to Eva, Jakob, Otto and Gary, all standing in a huddle, all with a drink in hand, and all dressed to impress.

'You are very popular tonight, Klaus,' smiled Jakob.

'It's just the uniform and rank,' Klaus shrugged modestly.

'If only they knew,' Eva smiled over the top of her glass. Klaus returned the smile.

'So what's the plan now?' Otto asked him.

'Well,' Klaus looked around to make sure everyone

was distracted by their own conversations, 'I've got Heidi upstairs in my room at the moment.'

'Is that a good idea?' asked Gary tentatively.

'Oh, don't worry, she's locked in, and I've got the key,' Klaus replied, 'and her only means of contact up there is the telephone,' he grinned.

'We'll miss you, Klaus,' Eva said randomly with almost puppy-dog eyes.

'Eva, save it for later, right now I have to get upstairs to Heidi. Don't worry, I'll be back,' he said reassuringly with his hand placed gently on her shoulder. He smiled then turned around and made for the stairs in the centre of the hall.

•

Heidi was standing in front of the long mirror in Klaus's luxurious bedroom. Still dressed in the same silk red dress from the night before, she made her way around to her old side of the bed. Sitting down, she took a look through the top drawer, still full of her lingerie.

Suddenly, Heidi heard the lock turn and the bedroom door open; she turned around and to her surprise saw Anton standing in the doorway.

Heidi stood up and saw the hairpin in his hand he'd used to unlock the door.

'What do you want?' she asked sceptically.

'Answers,' Anton replied simply as he entered.

'What's going on here?' came Klaus's voice.

Anton turned around, 'Klaus, I overheard her speaking on the phone so I—'

CRACK!

Heidi had hit Anton over the head with her hand-held mirror; he collapsed in a heap on the floor.

'What was all that about?' asked Klaus confused.

'Isn't it obvious? He wanted to question me,' explained Heidi, walking back around her side of the bed. Klaus, still looking confused, grabbed Anton under the arms and dragged him over to the wardrobe.

'I'll have to hide him in here before anyone asks questions,' he grunted as he placed Anton's body into the large oak wardrobe and closed the doors. He turned to face Heidi; she was sitting on her side of the bed with her back to him. He looked hungrily at her long slender back in her backless dress, her shoulder blades protruding as she continued looking through her lingerie in the top drawer. He walked slowly over to the bed, not taking his eyes off her. He knelt on the bed and crawled over to her. He began to gently kiss her soft smooth neck, her hair tickling his nose while breathing in her sweet perfume.

'What are you doing?' she whispered with a smile.

'What do you think?' he whispered in her shell-like ear.

'No,' she replied and got to her feet, much to Klaus's surprise.

'What's wrong?' he asked looking up at her.

'I'm just not in the mood right now,' she said in a businesslike manner, as she stuffed the clothes from the top drawer into her open suitcase on the floor.

'Perhaps you're right,' he said as he climbed of his side of the bed. He then began pulling all the sheets off the bed.

'What are you doing?' she asked frowning at him.

'We're leaving by the window to avoid awkward

questions,' he replied as he began to tie the ends together.

'What about my suitcase?' she asked.

Klaus walked around her side of the bed, closed her suitcase, picked it up and threw it out the window. Heidi's mouth dropped as her eyes followed him back around his side of the bed.

'Don't worry,' he replied as he continued to tie the sheets, 'your suitcase has merely landed in the small bush under the bottom window, you can pick it up once we're down there.'

Klaus then walked over to the open window, tied one end of the sheets to the metal bed frame, and threw the other end out the window. He checked where the sheets came down to, 'Yeah, that's long enough, right, climb on to my back,' he told her.

'What?'

'Come on, just hold on tight around my neck, you'll be fine, honestly,' he assured her as he knelt on the windowsill. She climbed on his back and held on around his neck, while he took each of her long legs and wrapped them around his waist.

'Are you ready?' he asked.

'Ready as I'll ever be,' she replied.

Klaus grabbed a tight hold of the sheets, turned to face the room, and he began to descend. Klaus didn't have to do all the work, as the bed slowly made its way closer to the window with the weight of them. Before long, he felt the ground under his feet and Heidi hopped off his back; she straightened her dress then picked up her suitcase.

'Here, I'll take it,' he offered, and taking the suitcase he led the way down the street, closely followed by Heidi.

'We have to be quick, your plane is due to land soon,' he told her.

'I still don't understand why I can't go on the train with you?' she asked.

'I told you, it's too risky, we don't want people talking, just trust me, it'll be a lot easier for both of us if you fly to Berlin, and I take the train and meet you there,' Klaus explained. They continued on down the road into the darkness of the night.

•

'So, what do you think Klaus's plan is then?' asked Jakob, sipping on his wine.

'I haven't a clue,' said Otto.

'Well, I know one thing,' Eva interjected, 'if I know Klaus as well as I think I do, he's going to take Heidi to Berlin, and take her straight to the Fuhrer himself.'

'He'll have to tape her mouth up first in case she tells Hitler everything she knows about him,' explained Gary.

Otto took a sip of his drink with a concentrated expression. 'I have it,' he said, 'he's going to leave Heidi behind in his room for us to deal with.' The others looked at him incredulously.

'Oh, come on, think about it,' Otto explained, 'how is he going to take Heidi with him all the way back to Berlin against her will?'

They all exchanged looks of enlightenment.

'Hang on,' said Jakob, 'he put her in the back of his car and drove her all the way here against her will.'

'Well, instead of speculating, why don't we go upstairs

and find out for ourselves,' Eva suggested. They all agreed and made their way through the people and over to the stairs.

'Halt! Where are you going?' A guard blocked their entrance to the stairs.

'Oh, we er…' Jakob stumbled out of fright.

'The General has invited us to his room,' Eva smiled.

'All of you?' the guard questioned.

'Yes, he er, wants to talk to us about Operation Barbarossa,' she said convincingly.

The others looked at her completely nonplussed. The guard however looked impressed and stepped aside.

'What the hell is Operation Barbarossa?' asked Gary as they climbed the stairs.

'I don't tell you everything,' she smirked at him.

•

Heidi and Klaus could hear the noise of the 1920s Dutch biplane waiting in an open field just past the next hedgerow.

'Stop,' said Klaus, and he pulled out a long black piece of material from the inside of his sleeve; it was a blindfold.

'Turn around,' he told her.

Tutting and rolling her eyes she turned around and said, 'Is this really necessary?'

'Yes, it is. You know I don't like emotional goodbyes, this way when you get to the plane you won't feel compelled to turn and look at me,' he told her as he tied it at the back of her head.

'But it's not really goodbye though, is it?'

'Yes, I know, now then, let's get you on that plane, the

gentleman will help you climb aboard,' he told her as he prompted her forward.

'I'll see you there,' she said as he guided her through the open gate and across the field.

•

'This is Klaus's room,' Eva announced as she turned the handle and opened the door quietly.

'Klaus, are you there?' she asked as she opened the door wide; the room was completely deserted; the others followed her inside.

'Well, they're clearly not here, we may as well go,' said Jakob, sounding disappointed.

Suddenly they all heard groaning coming from the wardrobe. Otto looked at Gary.

'It wasn't me,' Gary said defensively, 'it came from that wardrobe.'

More groaning commenced, and they all walked cautiously over to the wardrobe. Jakob opened the wardrobe door and to their surprise saw Anton on the floor slowly waking up.

'Oh my God,' Eva clapped her hands to her mouth.

'Anton, are you OK? What happened?' asked Otto, as he and Jakob helped him out of the wardrobe and to his feet. They helped him over to the bed where they sat him down, then all stood around him impatiently anticipating his explanation.

'I overheard Heidi on the phone to Von Braun,' he began while rubbing his sore head. 'She was orchestrating a plot to kill Klaus.'

'What?! Are you sure?' Eva asked completely in shock.

'Certain. Right now, they're on their way to catch a plane, well Heidi is anyway, you see, Heidi thinks she's going to Berlin to meet Klaus there so they can live happily ever after, but she knows they won't as she's arranged for his assassination. Likewise, Klaus has organised for Heidi to be taken to England in a Dutch civilian plane, where she will most likely be put in the Tower of London,' Anton explained.

The room went deadly silent as they attempted to process this new and shocking information.

'How do you know all this?' asked Jakob sounding impressed.

'Klaus told me of course.'

'Of course,' Jakob shrugged.

'So just to recap,' said Otto trying to clarify, 'the good news is that Heidi is not going to Berlin, she is going to London, and the bad news is, Von Braun is now out to kill Klaus?'

'But this doesn't explain how you ended up knocked out in the wardrobe?' Gary added.

'I undid the lock with a hairpin, came in to confront Heidi, Klaus came in, I turned to face him, that's when I felt a blow to the back of my head from Heidi, they then must've put me in the wardrobe out of sight.'

'And climbed out of the window, judging by these,' said Jakob as he pulled all the tied sheets back up through the window.

•

'Right, I'll see you in Berlin!' Klaus called over the top of the engine of the plane to Heidi, as he passed her suitcase to her.

'I'll meet you there,' she smiled and went to take off her blindfold.

'No!' Klaus called. 'Don't remove the blindfold, in fact as you're not a fan of heights, I'd suggest not removing it until you land.'

'What?'

'Promise me.'

'Oh OK, fine.'

The plane began to pull away; Klaus watched until it was eventually airborne in the night sky.

•

'Gary, can you carry that case downstairs please? It belongs to Klaus, he'll be taking it with him to Berlin,' asked Eva, Gary picked up the suitcase on the bed.

'What time is the train?' Jakob asked Anton.

Anton looked at his watch. 'About half an hours' time,' he replied.

'Right, let's get downstairs, everyone, Klaus will be back soon,' Otto suggested as he opened the bedroom door for them all to pass.

•

Klaus entered through the front door and into the Great Hall. Everybody turned to look at him and the orchestra over in the corner stopped playing, as he walked into the centre by the stairs with the long Swastika flags and raised his hand to speak. Jakob, Otto, Gary and Eva looked on intrigued from their seats right beside the stairs.

'Ladies and gentlemen, friends and colleagues,' he began. 'I would like to thank you all for attending my leaving party this evening. I've spent a little over a year in Amsterdam now, I've made some good friends,' he gave a subtle look over at Jakob's table.

'And I've had a very eventful year. But now the time has come for me to move on to pastures new. You've all no doubt heard that I'm leaving for Berlin, I'm going to be working inside the Reich's Chancellery itself.'

A round of applause and cheers erupted around the hall.

'I bid you all farewell, enjoy the rest of the evening,' he finished off to another round of applause. Klaus made his way over to Jakob's table.

'Anton, I apologise, my friend, but I had to keep up the pretence in front of Heidi, you understand,' he told him most sincerely.

'Don't worry, you weren't the one who gave me a headache,' Anton smiled rubbing his head.

Klaus smiled, and then noticed his suitcase over on the floor by Gary. 'Ah, I notice you've already got my case for me, thank you so much,' he said as he picked up his case. Gary got to his feet and extended his hand to Klaus.

'It was a pleasure meeting you, Herr General.'

'The pleasure was mine.' Klaus shook his hand.

Everybody stood up to say their goodbyes, and finally Eva was face to face with him.

'Klaus, I'm really going to miss you,' her blue eyes began

to well up, 'you've helped me out in so many situations.'

'It was my absolute pleasure, Eva,' he replied, and leaned in for a hug; she wrapped her arms around his neck.

'You have a good man in Gary,' he said in her ear.

'I know,' Eva agreed as she pulled away, 'now you take care of yourself, Klaus.'

'I'll be fine, Eva, I hear that British Intelligence treat their workers very well.' He smiled; they all gave each other looks of astonishment around the table and applauded as he turned to leave.

•

Sometime later, Heidi had removed her blindfold, replaced it with goggles, and was questioning the pilot, a slim middle-aged Dutchman, about their location, about the large area of water they passed looking uncannily like the North Sea.

'I keep telling you, Fraulein, that was the Rhine, just trust me,' he called back to her as he began to descend.

They eventually landed in a field in the middle of the countryside.

'Just stay here a moment, Fraulein, I will give you a hand down once I am out,' he said and as he climbed down from the plane and landed on the ground with a thud.

'Where are we exactly?' Heidi asked removing her goggles and looking around with a puzzled look on her face.

'The outskirts of Berlin,' he told her while holding out his hand to help her down.

'But we're out in the middle of nowhere,' she exclaimed looking round at the surrounding hills and fields, and as she did so, she noticed four men coming towards her in the distance. 'Who're they?' she asked, squinting in the sunset.

'Oh, they're just here for your protection,' the pilot told her as he climbed back into the cockpit.

'Well, where are you going?' she asked him.

'I have to get this plane back to Holland, I only did this as a favour to the General, and besides, I can let him know you landed safely.' He started up the plane. 'And don't worry,' he shouted over the top of the engine, 'these men will see you're all right.'

Heidi turned to face the four men approaching her, and noticed that three of them were carrying handguns, and as the fourth shorter one came into view, she was sure she recognised him, but she couldn't think where from. She turned to mention about the guns to the pilot, but realised he was already pulling away. She felt helpless; she didn't know whether to call after the pilot or trust what he had told her.

The short stout man at the front was marching up to her with determination, puffing on a cigar. Heidi, still squinting at the men, suddenly realised who the short stout man was. Her eyes widened in terror as the seriousness of the situation dawned on her. General Klaus Schneider had double-crossed her. She was not safe in Berlin; she was in big trouble on the outskirts of London. Her heart skipped a beat as she was approached by none other than the British Prime Minister, Winston Churchill, and three armed guards.

•

Klaus was strolling along the canal carrying his suitcase. He walked halfway along the bridge, put his suitcase up on the wall, and leaned his forearms on it to admire the dazzling sunset reflecting off the water. Everything was so tranquil, the birds were singing their last tunes for the day, the wind was gentle, and only the trickle of water could be heard. He noticed an elderly lady across the street open her upstairs window and begin watering her flowers up on the balcony. He then heard a click echoing somewhere behind him; he turned to see the figure of a man in a hat on the adjacent bridge brandishing a handgun. Klaus tried to squint to see who it was under the hat.

BANG!!!

Klaus was launched backwards over the wall, followed by a heavy splash.

TWENTY-FIVE

AUF WIEDERSEHEN

The old lady at her window watering her plants gasped in shock, but not loud enough for the man with the gun to hear. She dashed out of sight. The man hastily put his gun away in the inside pocket of his long coat and ran over to the other bridge to look down over at the lifeless body floating in the dark waters. It resembled the shell of a turtle as if it had risen to the surface. He then ran around the side of the bridge and stepped cautiously down the bank to the riverside. He leaned over the body as it drifted closer to the bank; he reached out to grab the suitcase that had also gone in the water when he was suddenly grabbed by the wrist and pulled under the water.

The old lady was persuading her husband to put his newspaper down and go and look out of the window.

'What do you mean, someone's been shot?' asked the old man looking up as he lowered his paper.

'I'm telling you, a man was shot and landed in the canal,' she told him.

'Rubbish, I didn't hear a thing, I think you're imagining things, woman,' he said and opened up his newspaper again.

'Well, come to the window then and see, I'll prove it,' she pleaded.

'Oh, all right, fine, let's get this fantasy of yours over with,' he agreed reluctantly as he got up, walked over to the window and looked down over the newly watered flowers, and he too gasped in shock as he saw a body floating in the canal.

•

Angelina was sitting at the kitchen table cradling Carice in her arms as she fed on her bottle.

'... and your daddy will be a hero of the Dutch Resistance, yes, he will,' she smiled at her daughter. The bottle she was feeding on made a slight squirting sound of air escaping as Carice gave a big toothless grin.

'Aw, was that a smile?' Angelina screeched; she stood the bottle on the table, picked up Carice under the arms and stood her on her lap.

'Come on then, give Mummy another smile.' Carice just stared at her intently as drool dripped from her chin.

Suddenly there was a knock at the kitchen door.

'Oh, I wonder who that can be?' she said to Carice, and she scooped her up and lay her in her pink Moses basket to her side, then went to answer the door. She pulled back the lock and opened it.

'Thanks,' said Jakob as he entered, followed by the others, 'not one of us took our keys,' he rolled his eyes.

'You had a good time then?' Angelina asked as she closed the door back up.

'Yeah, sad but good,' Jakob said as he leaned over little Carice.

'So, Klaus has really gone then?' Angelina asked.

'Yeah, safe and sound, luckily,' said Otto taking a seat.

'I am going to miss him, though,' Eva said sullenly as she too sat at the table.

There was a second knock at the door, only this knock was more urgent, more prominent than Jakob's knock.

'Who can that be at this time?' asked Angelina still standing by the door. She opened the door, and to everyone's complete surprise there stood Klaus, leaning against the door frame dressed in a long dark coat and hat, his right hand clutching his left shoulder, blood seeping through his fingers and running down his hand.

'Please,' he gasped struggling for breath, 'help me, I've been shot.'

'Oh God!' Eva cried out as she sprang up out of her seat and made a beeline for Klaus.

'For God's sake come in here,' Jakob exclaimed.

'What the hell happened?' asked Otto utterly bewildered.

'We expected you to be on the train to Berlin by now,' Gary added, staring in shock at the state of Klaus, as he and Otto helped him inside.

Eva took out a sponge from the cupboard under the sink, while Angelina filled a bowl of hot water. Jakob gave up the chair he'd not long sat down in to Klaus.

'I was walking to the train station when I decided to stop on a bridge, and just look across the canal and take in the beautiful sunset one last time, when I heard a noise behind me. I turned around and saw a man on the bridge opposite pointing a gun at me. Moments before he fired the gun, I recognised who it was, that Gestapo scum, Ludwig Von Braun.'

'That explains Heidi's phone call,' said Anton darkly from the corner. Everyone turned to face him.

'What phone call?' asked Klaus, wincing as Eva and Angelina attended to his injured shoulder.

'When I was outside your room, I heard her making a phone call to Von Braun. I couldn't hear it all; I could just make out bits and pieces. I was trying to tell you when she clobbered me on the back of the head, and I didn't tell you afterwards when you came back from taking Heidi to the plane, because I assumed that if anything bad was going to happen, it would've happened by then,' Anton explained.

Klaus winced with pain as he was distracted by Anton's story.

'Sorry,' said Eva as she mopped his wound with the sponge. The water was now a dark red.

'So where is your uniform?' Angelina asked as she pulled his shirt further over his shoulder.

'I was playing dead in the water when the shadow of a man fell over me. I knew it was him, so I made a grab at him and pulled him under. I choked him out, and when I was absolutely certain he was dead, I beat his face in until he was unrecognisable, then I switched clothes. When somebody finds him, they'll assume it is me.'

The whole kitchen had fallen silent.

'So, you managed to drown him, beat him, and switch clothes without anybody seeing you?' asked Eva sceptically.

'It was getting dark, and besides, it's shadowed by that bridge.'

'What about your suitcase?' asked Otto.

'I left it in the canal, there's nothing important in there really, just clothes, I have my wallet and identity papers on me.'

'But why would you want people to think you're dead?' asked Gary.

'Honestly, I was too panicky to think, I certainly wasn't thinking straight at the time, I just knew that nobody could know it's Von Braun. To be honest, I'm regretting putting my uniform on him now.'

'Thankfully the bullet went straight through,' said Eva, as she pulled his arm out of the shirt sleeve with great difficulty, and to Klaus's painful protests, to reveal the exit wound at the back.

'So, what now?' asked Jakob as he winked at little Carice in her basket.

'Well, I have the perfect plan in mind,' said Eva as she began dabbing at the exit wound.

Everyone, including Klaus was all ears.

'As I recall,' she began, 'your handwriting is very similar to Von Braun's, almost identical. So if you were to write a suicide note, and put it on a pile of his clothes, the clothes you're wearing, someone will find what they think is your body, beaten up badly, then they'll find his clothes with a suicide note on top, saying something along the lines of how he felt bad after what he did to you, that he couldn't live with himself any more, and that he decided to end his life, and how he's already organised the burning of his body so that it can't be found.'

'Eva, that is genius,' said Klaus in utter shock.

'You scare me sometimes,' Gary smirked at her.

'Ah Gary,' Eva replied, 'you're around the same build as

Klaus, and you're only a couple inches shorter, think you could take Klaus upstairs and find some clothes to fit him?'

'Well yeah, but shouldn't we get him some treatment for his wound first?' asked Gary.

'It's a clean wound, all it needs is a few stitches.' Eva looked to Jakob. 'I think that's your department, Jakob.'

'Well, if you'll just come with me then, Klaus, we'll get you stitched up, and Gary will get you some clothes,' said Jakob as he led him out of the kitchen.

•

May 17, 1941. 02:17

Klaus struggled to get comfy as he wrestled with his blankets on Jakob's kitchen floor. He decided to sit himself up as best he could, using his right arm, and shuffled himself back against the wall. He leaned his head back on the wall and took a deep breath. With his left arm now up in a sling, he used his right hand to hoist himself around onto his knees and got to his feet. He then put his right hand on his lower back and leaned backwards as if to relieve tight muscles.

The moonlight was shining beautifully through the kitchen window, and not a mouse was stirring.

Klaus pulled up a chair and sat down at the table. He noticed a pen in the centre of the table beside a notepad. He took the pad, flipped the page and picked up the pen with the same hand. He paused and thought for a moment before putting the pen to paper.

•

03:00

Klaus, while wearing Gary's long beige overcoat, one sleeve hanging down at his side, and a hat pulled down over his face, was walking alongside the canal with a pile of clothes in his good arm.

Amsterdam was nothing more than a ghost town. Not a soul in sight.

He came to the same spot at the canal and scanned the area, double-checking he was alone. The only sound was the hoot of an owl in the distance. He squatted down on the bank and placed the clothes of Ludwig Von Braun on the grass. He then reached inside Gary's coat pocket and pulled out the note he'd written, then placed the note on the clothes, and weighed it down with a small rock on the bank. He then stood up and took another look around the vicinity; it was completely dead.

•

07:06

Jakob came strolling into the kitchen in his white fluffy dressing gown.

'Mmm… morning Klaus,' he said through a yawn, 'hope you slept… well,' he was surprised to see nothing but a pile of blankets on the kitchen floor.

'Eva! Come quick!' he called.

'I'm coming, I'm coming, what is it?' she called back, entering the kitchen in her red silk dressing gown. She too stopped and stared in disbelief at the pile of blankets.

‘Look,’ Jakob said pointing to the table, ‘he’s left a note.’

Eva went over and sat down at the table to read aloud. Jakob was all ears looking over her shoulder.

“Dear Eva, I took your advice, I’ve taken the pile of clothes to the canal, and left a suicide note signed by Ludwig Von Braun. I’m sorry to have to leave you like this, but you know how I can’t stand emotional goodbyes. Please thank Jakob for his hospitality, and thank you Eva, thank you for everything, love always, Klaus.”

Gary then came strolling into the kitchen in his red striped pyjamas.

‘I thought I heard voices,’ he said and planted a kiss on Eva’s cheek, ‘what’s that?’

‘It’s a note from Klaus,’ she replied.

Otto, Anton and Angelina came in, all in their night clothes.

‘Morning all,’ smiled Anton.

‘Where’s Klaus?’ asked Otto.

‘What’s that, Eva?’ Angelina asked while rocking Carice in her arms.

‘Klaus, he’s gone,’ she replied as she turned to face them all. ‘He’s taken my advice about the suicide note, so when they find Von Braun’s body, they’ll assume it’s Klaus, and when they see the suicide note from Von Braun, they’ll assume he killed Klaus and couldn’t live with what he had done, and committed suicide…’

‘… and had his body burned on his orders so they won’t think it strange that they can’t find it,’ added Gary with a smile.

‘You remembered,’ Eva smiled back.

‘So where is Klaus now?’ asked Jakob.

'My guess, probably in England by now courtesy of his friend's plane, the same plane that took Heidi to England,' Eva explained.

Jakob nodded and looked round at everyone; they all looked back at him curious about what he was about to say.

'Well, everyone, I'm sure the war is far from over, but this here marks the end of an era. General Klaus Schneider is gone. And we Dutch… and the British,' he looked at Gary, 'and even the odd German,' he smiled at Eva, 'are now on our own. But we will not give in, we will not surrender, we will fight on, because that, my friends, that is Dutch courage.' Jakob received a round of applause from everyone. Angelina hugged Jakob while cradling baby Carice in one arm, Gary and Eva embraced, Otto looked at Anton and then back to the room.

'Well, we may as well join in.' Otto held his arms open while shaking with laughter; Anton chuckled and clapped Otto on the back.